THE
BOYFRIEND
LAUNCHER

ALSO BY RAECHELL GARRETT

Promposal

THE
BOYFRIEND LAUNCHER

RAECHELL GARRETT

LITTLE, BROWN AND COMPANY
New York Boston

Copyright © 2026 by RaeChell Garrett

Heart border © LovedDesign/Shutterstock.com
Flower chapter opener © hmorena/Shutterstock.com

Cover art copyright © 2026 by Erick Dávila. Cover design by Gabrielle Chang. Cover copyright © 2026 by Hachette Book Group, Inc.
Interior design by Gabrielle Chang.

Little, Brown and Company
Hachette Book Group
1290 Avenue of the Americas, New York, NY 10104
LBYR.com

First Edition: February 2026

Little, Brown and Company is a division of Hachette Book Group, Inc. The Little, Brown name and logo are registered trademarks of Hachette Book Group, Inc.

The publisher is not responsible for websites (or their content) that are not owned by the publisher.

Little, Brown and Company books may be purchased in bulk for business, educational, or promotional use. For information, please contact your local bookseller or the Hachette Book Group Special Markets Department at special.markets@hbgusa.com.

Library of Congress Cataloging-in-Publication Data
Names: Garrett, RaeChell author
Title: The boyfriend launcher / RaeChell Garrett.
Description: First edition. | New York : Little, Brown and Company, 2026. | Audience: Ages 12 and up | Summary: Seventeen-year-old Dru makes a surprising discovery when she fake dates her best friend to uncover why her exes always become someone else's perfect boyfriend.
Identifiers: LCCN 2025007509 | ISBN 9780316372640 trade paperback | ISBN 9780316372817 ebook
Subjects: CYAC: Dating—Fiction | Best friends—Fiction | Friendship—Fiction | Soccer—Fiction | African Americans—Fiction | LCGFT: Romance fiction | Novels
Classification: LCC PZ7.1.G3763 Bo 2026
LC record available at https://lccn.loc.gov/2025007509

ISBNs: 978-0-316-37264-0 (trade paperback), 978-0-316-37281-7 (ebook)

Printed in Indiana, USA

LSC-C

Printing 2, 2026

Go ahead. Launch.

THE FIRST OF 24 DAYS

I n my car, I Febreze my practice shorts and tank top with a heavy hand.

Satisfied I won't offend anyone, I pop out of the car. The gust of wind that whips up my shorts and clings to my still-damp sweat chills me to the bone. It's spring in name only.

Shivering, I trot up the driveway to the garage and knock on the door that leads to the house. Nobody answers. Loud laughter I recognize comes from the other side, telling me someone's home. Not to mention, I'm expected—pretty aggressively if I go by the voicemails. I knock harder. Still nothing. I send a text.

> **Dru:** How are you going to explain me
> freezing to death in your garage???

About ten seconds later, Winston Portis flings the door open in a way that tells me he slid into it on his socked feet. Winston and I, along with his fraternal twin, Jake, met in the womb at a mom support group. Now he's my soon-to-be sort-of brother-in-law with an emphasis on *brother*. Moriah, the younger of my two older sisters, is engaged to the eldest of the three Portis boys.

Winston's hand shoots up to stop the door from slamming into the wall behind it. Two red rubber bracelets with messages in languages I bet even he doesn't recognize tumble into place on his wrist. "I thought you were going to be late."

I slip past his tall, lanky frame and inside to warmth. "You said your career was done if you didn't go live on time tonight. It sounded like you might cry."

He smiles, ever-present dimples deepening. "That worked?"

I press my lips together and raise an eyebrow. "The last time I saw you cry, when I accidentally destroyed your village in *Minecraft*, I ended up on punishment for staying up all night trying to rebuild it for you. You *knew* the sound of tears in your voice would work. But it won't again."

Especially when I'm starting to feel like the need to do this interview today has less to do with timing and more to do with his taper fade looking super crisp and his twists perfectly shiny.

"Accidentally?" He crosses his arms high up on his chest and looks down at me. "Your memory is strong in that villain POV."

I put both hands up, pleading my innocence. "How long are you going to blame me for that?"

He puts a hand over his heart and gives me sad eyes. "Until the pain ends."

I smack my lips at his dramatics.

He laughs, but it fades quickly as he sniffs the air suspiciously. "How many times do I have to tell you, your funk is too potent for Febreze."

"I didn't have time to go home. Remember. The crying." I pull my small knotless braids from their thrice-wrapped bun on top of my head and sigh from the relief. "I need a face towel, moisturizer, and does anybody here use edge control?"

He nods, but instead of going to get what I need, he leads me to his kitchen. He takes an apple and a jar of peanut butter out of the refrigerator, and a slicer out of the pantry.

My mouth waters. "Please say that's for me. I'm so hungry."

"Figured you would be." He holds the apple under the faucet and wipes it dry. Then he gets a bowl and spoon for the peanut butter. "Is Meegan still tripping?"

Meegan is a two-time all-state senior striker on my high school soccer team. We're co-captains. It's her last year, so she's been really focused all season. But these last few days, she's been a monster. Her intensity has been playoff level not just at practice but even in our group chats.

I do get it. I'm only a junior and still everything feels like a chance I won't get again. It makes sense that she wants to see everyone giving as much as she is on the field every game. That's why I try to back Meegan up when I can. Even when more and more of my teammates seem to want her to take it down some.

While Winston slices the apple, I spoon three heaps of peanut butter into the bowl. The apple isn't that big, but I've been known to eat peanut butter like it's ice cream. "It wasn't Meegan this time. It was Coach. He said an undefeated season is just an undefeated season. If we plan to win a championship, we all need to look ourselves in the mirror and ask if we're giving all we have to the team."

He shrugs a shoulder. "Just regular coach motivational stuff, then?"

"I guess," I say around a big chunk of apple. "But his eyes are always on me when he says stuff like that. Like if we don't do what everyone expects us to, it's going to be on me."

He tilts his head. "I'm sure he's looking at the whole team. Everybody knows how hard you work."

I get what he's saying, but there *are* holes in my game. I can admit that.

The doorbell rings, and Winston turns toward the front of the house, where real guests come in instead of through the garage like me.

I'm smacking on a slice of apple that I didn't bother to bite in half, covered with the biggest smear of peanut butter, when I hear HIM and Winston greet each other. I freeze when I should actually keep chewing, because by the time Kai Waller's standing on the threshold to the kitchen my mouth is still too full to close.

His tight, spiral curls bounce as he steps into the kitchen. I stiffen, and the urge to run in the opposite direction is strong. Winston has already told me the air freshener is doing no good, and I must look like some type of animal with all this food in my mouth.

But Kai doesn't laugh, raise an eyebrow, or lean away from the potential of my stench. He tilts his head and smiles as he gives me this slow-motion finger flutter of a wave that makes me question whether he invented the gesture.

Somehow, I end up attempting the same thing, but I know it's not having the same effect. There's no way I look flirty or cute like he did. I try to play it off as a self-soothing rub along the back of my neck.

I want to tell him the royal-blue sweatshirt he's wearing makes his bark-colored skin glow, and he should wear it every single day all the time. Instead, all I can do is put a hand over my mouth and chew enough to get out, "You're here?"

He smiles then, and I know I've said those two words as if his presence is the best thing that has happened to me in my whole life. "I am."

Winston narrows his eyes at me. "Of course he's here. I wouldn't be able to kick off the series if I didn't have you both."

Still a bit speechless, I turn and shoot Winston a look. At the same time, I catch another whiff of myself. This is really bad.

This isn't school, when Kai walks me to class or when he sends me soccer articles or pops up in my notifications when he openly stalks my social media. I'm prepared for all those things. My hair is right. My breath is nice. I've used my time in my car on the way to school wisely by coming up with conversation starters.

On this evening, I am wholly unready to receive the boy I like but absolutely will not have.

"I thought I told you. I want to interview the best female and male athlete in each sport in the area." When I still don't move, Winston brushes by me and starts cleaning up. "And for soccer, that's you two, of course."

Like me, Kai plays center mid. And, for lack of a better way of putting it, he's a superstar. He's taken a different route to his dreams than I have. He plays academy soccer all year round with the same club as me instead of bothering with high school for half the year like I do. He plays all around the country with the upper echelon of players in front of a lot more college coaches on a regular basis. But for a few months, I get to play in my backyard, with girls I sit next to in class, in front of people who love me.

I admit, it's a really big trade-off, but when there's a crowd to celebrate when I make a great pass, I don't regret anything.

I heard he got invited to play for a professional academy team on the East Coast. I haven't confirmed it for fear of looking like the fan that I am. But I believe it.

I may or may not have watched some or all his games on our club's site. He's that good.

I fold what's left of my apple slices into a paper towel and put them in the refrigerator. I should be saying something. Something... smart? Flirty? Inspirational? "Oh. You're interviewing the best male and female athlete in each sport, and for soccer that's me and Kai."

Okay, so, parroting Winston doesn't fall into any of the categories I was considering, but it's out there now and I feel like a complete clown. If I could ask for a do-over, I would.

Kai just keeps smiling like my inability to form an original thought doesn't faze him. "Do you think he should've picked someone other than me?"

I blink and shake my head hard enough that if my braids were still up they would've started falling out of the bun all on their own. "Who? You're definitely the best."

I duck my head so fast I can't see his response. My first guess is secondhand embarrassment. Obviously, he was just messing with me, and here I am professing my admiration like a rabid groupie.

But I don't need to see him to feel the certainty of his words. "You're definitely the best too."

"Huh? ... I don't... No... You mean..." I shake my head and huff out a breath. "I think... See... I always..." I look up at him through my lashes. He's staring down at me like he's actually curious about what I have to say. There seem to be fewer choices for responses than there were seconds ago.

I bite my bottom lip. "Thank you. Kai."

"Now that we all understand each other," Winston pipes up, sounding like a teacher getting control of a class that has gone rogue, "it'll be a minute on your demands, Dru. I'll be right back."

Determined not to be left alone with Kai, I awkwardly wave at him and head to the bathroom, where I silent scream and chastise my reflection. I am maybe, potentially, unwell. I need to regroup.

While I wait for the tools that will help make me look mildly presentable, I message my best friend, Aubrey.

Dru: HE's at Winston's.

She's at an SAT study session so I'm not expecting a response right away. It just feels good to let somebody in on my anxiety. But seeing my situation as the emergency it is, she responds right away.

Aubrey: Whoa. Out of context Kai? Did you survive or are you contacting me from the afterlife?

Dru: No and I believe so.

Aubrey: Don't let your demise be meaningless.
Talk to him. Find out whether he's
actually on you or not.

In any other circumstance I would agree with Aubrey, and at least attempt to follow her advice. But I already know the answer to the question. Kai is interested in me. It's obvious in the small things. Like the way he waved when he came in.

Kai's not the problem. It's me. And if Aubrey had analyzed my love life to its pulp the way I have, my faults would be obvious to her too. I can't set me or Kai up for what I know will happen if we act on feelings. I will ruin it. I always do somehow.

When Winston comes back with everything I asked for plus some lip balm I take as a hint, I set my phone on the counter. The notifications keep coming as if Aubrey can figure out my life without me.

After I finish freshening up, I tiptoe out of the bathroom, peeking around corners trying not to be surprised by a person I already know is here. The coast clear, I head to the basement where Winston and I graduated from having tummy time to conducting lengthy foosball tournaments while our moms talked.

The space he uses to record his shows is a repurposed closet in the back of the basement. By the time I get there he has everything set up, with me and Kai seated across from him and two cameras. Winston's standing next to his chair wearing a forced smile while Kai talks.

8

"Did you just happen to have clothes for a pig cadaver lying around or did you go buy them?" Kai raises his eyebrows. "How premeditated was this?"

Kai's asking about freshman year, when Winston dressed a pig cadaver during biology. Before any teachers caught on, people were having photo shoots with it. School administration did not appreciate his creative expression.

Maybe it's because no one in our junior class has topped his ingenuity yet, but this . . . incident still gets brought up all the time. Unlike half the people who shake their heads at Winston's delinquency, Kai is fascinated, curious, and genuinely interested in what was going through Winston's head back then. Which is fair. I was curious too.

But I don't think the answer he gave me with a shrug back then—"I felt like it"—is the answer he'd give now. I'd ask the same questions myself if not for the look on his face every time it's brought up.

Only I, and maybe his twin, would know Winston's super embarrassed. His smile is probably the most easy and open thing about him. If his smile is off, there's a problem.

"I'm ready," I screech, and practically dive into the room. I sound a little overexcited, but I've done what I meant to do. The conversation about Winston's infamous past is over and his smile looks real again.

Winston makes a show of pulling out my chair for me and patting its back. After that, I try to keep my eyes on him. It's difficult when he asks questions that force me to interact with Kai. Then I look at Kai. He focuses on my words in a way that convinces me my points are so interesting that I should keep going and going.

Eventually I feel like I'm rambling, and I just let myself trail off until he or Winston rescues me.

In the past, this kind of attention from a guy I've liked for months would be all I'd need to give myself permission to flirt a little. But mostly I just want his eyelashes to stop being super long and him to stop agreeing with me about being prouder of assists than goals and encouraging me with nods. What girl doesn't like this treatment?

After thirty minutes, Winston wraps us up with a joke that makes me laugh so hard I snort. Sometimes when I'm watching him, I just know he's doing the thing he's supposed to be doing. A national sports show with his name on it will be a thing someday.

Kai stands, head up, shoulders back in a posture that I know intimidates the competition on a regular basis. Honestly, it intimidates *me*. "That was fun. I didn't talk too much, did I?"

Winston and I stand too. He's all bones, but he towers over both of us. Not because we're short, but because he's unnecessarily tall. "Nah, you were good. You sounded like a guy who knows his stuff about the thing he loves."

Winston's eyes shift to me then, and he gives me a quizzical look as if to say *you on the other hand were the exact opposite*. I give him the same look right back. Neither of us backs down for a full five seconds.

Kai clears his throat, and finally Winston nods toward the door, signaling the end of the night. Kai motions for me to lead what I assume is all three of us out of the studio. But once we're in the main living area, the energy suddenly feels a little less populated. I stop in my tracks and turn around. Winston is nowhere to be found.

Kai looks back toward the closet studio. "You forget something?"

"Um…" I avoid his eyes altogether and look at the carpeted floor. "I was just looking for Winston."

Kai delivers an "Oh" that suggests either my words came out wrong or he took them wrong.

I consider letting him think whatever he's thinking about me and Winston, but I don't want him to think I'm into somebody else, no matter how helpful that might be in making sure whatever this is never escalates. "Winston's kind of my brother-in-law. My sister and his brother are getting married in a few months."

I say that part about being my brother-in-law to draw Winston out of wherever he's hiding so he can turn this duo back into a trio. But for some unknown reason his persistent need to correct my understanding of familial relations is noticeably absent.

"Oh," Kai says again, but this time there's an entirely different spin on it. I don't want to call it relief but that's what it sounds like. "Makes sense why you guys seem close."

It *is* the wedding, but also kind of just me and Winston. Even as we got older, started making our own friends outside our families, and didn't have to go everywhere with our parents, we never drifted from each other. If my parents said they were doing something with the Portises, I was there and vice versa. And I know it could have turned out different. Jake has been here the whole time too, but I have no clue how he feels about condiments. Winston hates them all.

"Okay, well…" Kai's pause has weight. I can't help but focus on him. The eye contact is searing, which is crazy considering his eyes are hooded enough that you can barely see the whites when he smiles. "I just wanted to ask when we're going to see each other outside of school."

Every part of me goes hot. Not like when I'm on the field. This heat is coming from the inside out. I lace my fingers behind my back and fill my mouth with air. There's this part of me fighting to say I'm free on Friday. But the other part of me that knows this won't end well is keeping a steady hand clamped over my mouth.

"Um..." I look over my shoulder toward Winston's studio, but there's no rescue coming. What I need to say is I'm not dating. That's not a lie. I'm not dating, but if he's an option, I'd like to be. I'd like to not be afraid of my own history. But I can't tell him any of this. Especially not without the words being the end of any possibility between us.

What I need is just a little bit of time to figure out how not to make all my normal relationship mistakes... whatever they are.

"Our team made a pact for playoffs. No dating." The lie slips out before I realize I'll need to get the whole team to agree to it. That could be impossible. But with a pact making so much sense, it all comes together without me having to think too hard. "We have a real chance at a championship. We all just want to stay sharp."

He tilts his head back and admiration fills his face. "That's cool. The most any team I've ever been on can agree to is not shaving or not getting a haircut. Anything that might make them uncomfortable, somebody's saying no. And if they do agree to anything, they don't actually stick to it." He nods approvingly. "But you are?"

I swing my hands from behind my back twice before I register the tell my sisters called out when I was little. They discovered it after finding clues that I had been in their room or touching their things without permission. Feeling caught, I cross my arms securely over my chest. "Yep. I am. No dating. Just soccer."

"I would do the same." He tilts his head to one side. "Just to be clear. You *do* want to hang out? I haven't been building something up in my head that's not—"

I shake my head to stop him, the part of me that just wants to like him winning out for long enough to finish what it's started. "I do want to hang out. Yes. After seven games...or twenty-four days."

I hold back from giving him the to-the-second countdown found on our team page. That might sound a little desperate.

He smiles. "Twenty-four days?"

I nod and try to suppress a smile, but it just won't be contained. Neither will his. On his way up the stairs, I lose count of how many times he turns around to see if I'm still watching. I am. At one point, we both laugh a little. I'm the first one to look away, but only for a second.

But when he's gone and I'm out of the haze of being alone with him, all the potential endings to this situation start to populate my mind. The most logical one is the loudest.

Twenty-four days could be an undershot for how long it will take to figure out what happens after I make a boyfriend an ex. As it is now, I'll go out with Kai, we'll end as quickly as we start, and before I can even digest it, he'll be off being the best boyfriend to some other girl, as if dating me was the prerequisite to his success. Because I am the indisputable, wildly successful boyfriend launcher.

STILL 24 DAYS TO GO

I stomp back into the studio and find Winston chilling in his cushy host chair with his feet pulled up so he can use the table to propel himself into a spin.

I point sharply at him. "What are you doing? You just left me alone with him to do nothing?"

He grabs the table and stops his rotation. "He asked if I could give you guys some alone time. All those hearts dancing in your eyes when he came in made it hard for me to say no."

HE asked to be alone with me? Heat pushes up my chest, but keeping a straight face with Winston is way easier than it is with Kai.

Winston makes a clicking noise with his cheek and back teeth. "Yep, that's the look."

Well, keeping a straight face with Winston is easy unless I'm talking about Kai, apparently.

I focus on my phone. I'm not just going to stand here and let him analyze my face. "There's no look."

He chuckles. "And during the interview, you didn't stumble over your words or sound like you aren't really sure how to play soccer either." He spins in the chair again. "Kai had no effect on you."

I decide not to respond. I know Winston. He'll patiently wait until I say too much because he's good at that.

"Can I borrow some jogging pants? You know how long it takes for my car to warm up."

He raises both eyebrows at the obvious subject change. But, in true friend fashion, he also goes with it. "You'll trip on the stairs."

"I'll roll the waistband."

He starts pulling his pants down. I shriek and squeeze my eyes shut. We're close, but there are boundaries.

"I have on shorts underneath. Settle down." He chuckles as he tosses the pants. They land on my head. "Before you complain, they're cleaner than you."

They don't smell fresh out of the dryer, but they don't stink either. I pull them on. "I'll bring them back to you tomorrow."

Even after rolling them at the waist, I have to gather the crotch of the pants in one fist. The potential danger of this doesn't stop me from taking the steps two at a time on my way back upstairs.

Jake sits at the table in the eat-in kitchen with his laptop popped open. He glances up, eyes more mysterious than curious and sparkling like Winston's.

Immediately, I cover my mouth and whisper behind my hand. "Oh my God. Are you writing? Am I interrupting your genius flow or something? Should I be quiet?"

Jake, the blatantly overachieving twin, has an actual book coming out. Like to be sold in stores. It's going to be more than a year before anybody can hold the book in their hands, but the streets have gone crazy for his story of how AI has taken over. It even has a love triangle.

He shakes his head and runs his hands over his deep waves. "I was just watching the show."

Winston slips past me, gets the snack I didn't finish earlier out of the fridge, and hands it to me. I thank him like he's just saved my life. And he might have. With no Kai to keep my adrenaline up, I'm starving again. The slices are a little brown now, but I don't care. I bite one in half.

Jake waits for me to finish chewing before he asks, "Why'd you lie about that pact? You seemed pretty into him in the interview."

I slap my palm to my forehead. Okay. They've both said it now. I have to face the fact that I looked starry-eyed toward HIM on camera. "You were listening?"

He runs two fingers along the trackpad of his laptop. "No, I just overheard. The basement is the worst place to have a private conversation in this house."

"Wait." Winston jerks his head back, surprise in his eyes. "You lied to him about that?"

Trapped, I look from Winston to Jake.

They look like more than brothers and less than twins. They have the same clear chestnut-brown skin, perfect rainbow-arched eyebrows, and round nose. But Winston has teardrop-shaped eyes, dimples that leave indentations no matter what his face is doing, a smile made for the camera he aims to be in front of, and way more hair. But because people love to compare two like things, Jake has been called the better-looking one for as long as I've known them.

In my opinion, Winston's looks are taken lightly because he's not soft-spoken like his brother. His personality doesn't leave room for the viewer to focus on his features, nor is he trying to win anybody over with his face. Winston's winning you over with himself, without trying. And this isn't a best-friend rose-colored glasses thing. These are the things girls say around me, hoping it gets back to him. I always make sure it gets back to him, but it's never turned into anything on his part.

The space between Jake's brows crinkles. "I just assumed you made it up, because girls on your team are in actual relationships... which would make that a lie with a lot of holes."

I frown. But, I mean, that's a minor hole, right?

I finish the rest of the apple slice, then another whole one as I think. "You can't tell people in relationships to break up. And like anything else it's the honor system. I can't help that I choose to honor what some people don't. He gets that."

"So, there *is* a pact?" Winston says, drawing my eyes back up to his. And that's all it takes for him to figure me out. "Oooh. You lied. I'm telling."

I growl at him.

He eyes me for a second. "Why'd you lie? You obviously like him."

I shrug. "That's not the point."

Winston laces his fingers behind his head and leans back against the stainless-steel refrigerator with his eyes closed. "Yes, it is."

I shake my head. "Uh-uh."

Winston opens his eyes and looks at me as if the intensity of his stare alone can change my opinion. "Okay. One point for The Twins. Zero for Dru."

Clearly, I'm not seven anymore, but this points system still gets to me. Not just because it's two versus one. But because I hate hearing "The Twins" as a collective. It reminds me of "The Girls"—a label that can exist without me but not without either of my sisters. I like to think it's because the two of them were an entire entity for eight years before I came about. Even in their twenties LeArra and Moriah are still flattered when people call them that.

Jake presses his laptop shut and leaves the room. He's obviously not as invested in my point or Winston's. I stuff the last apple slice in my mouth, throw away my paper towel, and turn to the door to make my own exit. I don't want to get into this. What good would it do to spill all my feelings about my relationship failures to Winston? How would that get me closer to resolution? All I've given myself time for is fact-finding.

"Dru. No jokes. Seriously." He speaks louder, as if volume will stop me from leaving. I keep walking. "When you guys were talking alone, I thought the nervous, shook thing was because you like him. But you lied, which I don't know you to do all that much. I just want to make sure you're good."

That makes me pause and turn around. There isn't a sign of mischief anywhere. He really is just checking in, and it's valid. I *did* lie. Even if I can get my entire team to agree to the pact, I'm starting a relationship with a lie. That's a new one, even for me. I don't need a millisecond, let alone twenty-four days, to tell me that's not the right way to do things.

On one hand it *could* be a compliment to Kai that I want to make sure he can be *my* great boyfriend instead of someone else's. On the other, no one wants to be lied to, even for a *good* reason. And let's say I manage to get my team to go along with it. What exactly do I expect to do in twenty-four days that will make the lie and the time I've bought myself worth it? How do I expect to come to any conclusions on my own? I'm obviously not objective about myself.

Winston's eyes are unwavering, as if he can stare my truth out of me. Could *he* help? Definitely. He's objective. He has never and will not ever have any feelings for me. I've mostly only given him the broader points of my relationships—cute boy, nice boy, we're together, we broke up—so he's yet to reach eye-roll status from too much sharing.

I could give him a rundown of the boys I've launched, show him exactly how I've done it, and he could help me figure out where I've gone wrong.

Would he help? Of course he would. He wouldn't have wanted to make sure I was good if he wasn't at least open. And if roles were reversed, I would help him, without even questioning it.

The only thing standing in my way is getting over the embarrassment of explaining my issues to Winston. I shift my eyes upstairs toward the bedrooms. I'm only ready to tell one Portis my secrets.

His eyes follow mine. We pick up the faint sound of music and a running shower. "We're good. That's where his ideas come to him. He takes forever in there."

I gather the sweatpants in a fist to avoid tripping on them, go back over to the counter, and bounce my hip against it trying to figure out where to start.

"The point is, me and Kai will date. It won't work. I'll break up with him for being a subpar boyfriend and he'll follow me up...

in likely less than twenty-four hours…with a meaningful or long-lasting or some otherwise monumental relationship."

There it is. Nice and simple.

He reaches behind me and flicks on the kitchen light. The effects of daylight savings time haven't fully taken hold. We were about to be in the dark. "Did this all come to you in a dream or something?"

"That would be a nightmare and it's my life." There's no emotion in my voice. This is a matter of scientific fact. "Michael and Michaela. They've been together a year and a half. So perfect together they have the same name. Jayden M. and Malia. They're in my sixth period and I swear I've witnessed Jayden sigh while watching Malia speak. Trinity, Justin W., Black Cole, Erik with a *k*, Big Donny, Santoro… They all dated me right before they found someone they wanted to be best boyfriend ever to."

He plays with one of the drawstrings of his hoodie and turns his lips up as he mimics my posture against the counter. "When did you date Santoro? I don't remember that."

"Sixth grade."

"Okay." He shakes his head and blinks wildly. "How do you go on to have a meaningful relationship at twelve?"

"The very next day after I ended things with him, he met up with Lauryn W. at Freedom Festival. Rode all the rides with her and bought her treats. I haven't been on a date that satisfying still to this day." I pull my braids over one shoulder and shake my head. "That's why no matter how I feel about Kai, things just need to stay exactly how they are. He can go cut his teeth on however many other girls it takes to gather the level of knowledge and experience I can provide all in one go."

He scratches at the roots of his springy twists, a true look of concentration on his face. "What if you've just dated the wrong guys?"

I smack my lips. "I just named eight legitimate examples throughout my short life and your response is it's not you, it's them?"

"What is it about you, then? What makes guys go from you to relationship goals?" he challenges, in a way that makes me feel like maybe he doesn't get it.

"That's the problem. I have no idea, and if I don't figure it out, I'm just going to keep doing it to myself." I sigh. "And I really don't want to do that with Kai."

"Because you really like him. Just like I thought." He says this somberly, as if he finally gets what I'm dealing with.

I focus my attention on my hands again. I don't love saying any of this out loud, and eye contact makes me feel like he opened the door while I was getting out of the shower or something. "I do like him. And this isn't the first time. Just the first time he's acted interested. I didn't want to lie, but it was either reject him or buy myself some time."

He cranes his neck toward me and narrows his eyes. "But Dru... how do you know he's worth all this? He's asking for one date. It could be a horrible date."

"Orrrr"—I drag out the word—"it could be a great date and I just have to wait and watch it fall apart afterward." I look at the floor. The more I try to convince Winston of my problem, the more dire it feels to me. "And I just have a feeling, when we're around each other, you know. Like, did you see how he waved at me when—"

"Yep. Saw that. Got it." He goes back to his spot by the fridge with his eyes closed. "Maybe you could just ask some of your exes. Not Santoro or anybody from middle school. People more recent who things kind of lasted with, like Jayden."

Jayden Mitchell was my longest relationship. He was also my last boyfriend. My introduction to something more than just disappointment that things didn't work out. The trajectory of the relationship from great to WTF kind of broke my heart. Being the person to do the breaking up didn't protect me from the hurt of it. I really, honestly tried with him. I tried to be a good girlfriend. And *he* knows I tried. In the end it didn't matter.

But there are some things I can't even tell Winston, no matter how much he pokes at me.

"I can't ask Jayden. I don't want him to think I still care or that I'm still interested. I don't want Malia mad at me or have it be weird in class for the rest of the year. Same with Trinity and Michael."

I round the counter and sit on a stool. He stays on the other side but comes to the counter and rests his elbows on the hard surface. He leans toward me like we're really a team solving a problem. And I know for sure then, he's the perfect person for this. "I need *you*."

His eyebrows go up. "What? What'd you say?"

I nod and bite the corner of my bottom lip. "I need somebody to let me demonstrate my girlfriend skills to them for honest, objective critique. You're the best choice."

He stands up straight and swipes his hands through the air. "Nope. Can't be me."

I jerk my head back. This is the opposite of the response I'm expecting. "Why not?"

He shakes his head wildly enough that he has to be getting dizzy. "Because it's not a job for me."

I bite my bottom lip again. How can I make him understand enough how much I need *his* help? It's not like I can go around pleading my case to guys until someone accepts my invitation.

"Which one of the qualifications don't you meet?"

He keeps quiet. Everything about him is saying no. The way his lips are pressed together as if he's done with the conversation. The way he's backed as far away from me as he can get and is resting against the refrigerator again. The way he's looking at the ceiling as if my request will disappear if he can't see me. The way he won't stop shaking his head. But I've just spilled all my embarrassing secrets. It can't be for no reason.

"I'm not asking for something for nothing, if that's the problem. Do you need an assistant for your show? I would be a great assistant."

He nods. "You would." But then he shakes his head. "I can't."

"Do you think I'm going to get mad at you or something, shoot-the-messenger kind of thing?" I shake my head. "I promise I won't. I know there's no reason for you to lie or be afraid to tell me the whole truth. I can trust what you tell me."

Instead of a wild shake, he begins to move his head slowly from side to side, as if in the middle of praying for a miracle.

I give him a questioning look. "Do you like somebody? Because I promise not to get in the way of it. We'll be so covert. It's not like we aren't together a lot anyway. It's just going to be a different tone."

He hasn't even mentioned a girl to me in that way in…a really long time. For sure not this year or last. He does have options, though. Like Kai, girls ask me for clarification on my relationship with Winston too. It would make sense if somebody had finally caught his eye.

But still, he's not giving me anything more than a headshake.

I rest my chin on my palm in thought. How can he go so quickly from making sure I'm good to this rejection? Make it make sense.

"Oh." I frown at myself for not thinking of it sooner. "Does imagining me saying girlfriend stuff to you give you the ick?"

He pushes his hands into his pockets and puts one socked foot up on the fridge. More importantly, his head shaking stops. It's not a yes, but I'm onto something.

"Oh. Wait." I perk up even more. "You're worried about playing the boyfriend part? *That's* what's giving you the ick."

He looks at me then, the tension in his face fading into something closer to pity. He obviously thinks he's hurt my feelings.

"I'm not offended. I get that you don't think you could even fake it with me." I sigh heavily. "I guess I hadn't thought that far ahead yet, but obviously in order for a real critique you're going to have to give boyfriend sometimes in order to inspire my girlfriend. You wouldn't be able to get the full picture otherwise. I don't know a way around that."

"Yeah, me inspiring you to be girlfriendly... That would definitely be different." He says it so pensively that I actually start to feel bad about asking for his help.

I put my head down on the cold counter and laugh humorlessly. "Sorry. I should've thought it all through before I said anything. It would be too weird."

It's quiet for a minute before he calls my name.

"What?" I whine into the counter.

He says my name a second time. The same soft tone of his voice that made me stay and tell him my secret is back. I look up.

He leans onto the counter again. His eyes flit around my face as if he's trying to get an answer to a question without asking it. But eventually he gives up. "If I thought I could actually help, I would. You know that, right?"

I sit up straight and try to give him the most convincing nod I can. "Being my friend doesn't mean you have to do something you don't want to. I get it. I'm not mad at you about it." I squeeze my eyes shut. "I'm mad at myself. I shouldn't have lied. I shouldn't like him. I shouldn't like *anybody*. Ever. I'm doomed. The more I like somebody, the worse it's going to be."

"Dru." This time when he says my name it's kind of stern. He shakes his head. "You're not doomed. You've just got something you need to figure out. Everybody does."

I let my shoulders droop. "It doesn't feel like it."

"Yeah, I hear you." He looks down at the counter and nods slowly as if he really gets it. I wonder what he thinks he needs to figure out. Before I can ask, the music coming from the bathroom stops and

25

Winston takes a step back from the counter. The question feels out of place after that.

I slide off the barstool. "I'mma get out of here. I still have homework."

Winston walks with me to the back door. He rubs his hands together in front of his face like he's contemplating a plan. "What are you going to do?"

"I guess I'm talking to the exes." Once the words are out in the air I feel committed to them, which makes me feel kind of sick.

I do not want to ask any ex anything about our relationship.

He stops rubbing his hands together and sighs. "I don't know if I'd be able to do it if I were you, but they're the ones with the answers."

I hate that he could possibly be right, but as usual Winston is giving me advice that makes sense. It's why he's one of my best friends. And if he's not going to help me directly, taking his advice might be the next best thing.

WINDING DOWN THE 24TH DAY

When I get home, Dad calls out to me from the basement, where the hum of the treadmill and the clink of metal on metal tell me my parents are doing their usual evening workout routine. They train like active athletes though neither of them has been one since college, when Dad played football and Mom played volleyball.

I head downstairs and see them for the first time all day. When I left this morning, Dad was already in a meeting in his office with the door closed and Mom was in the shower. I keep on my sweatshirt and Winston's sweatpants. Our basement is finished, but less family room, more home gym. We keep it cool down here.

"Practice?" Dad pants, using the fewest words to get his message across.

I stretch, groaning as my body pops in several different places. I take a seat on the weight bench next to where Mom is in the middle of a set of dumbbell dead lifts. "Practice was practice. Coach has been saying the same things for three years."

"Man has to repeat himself that many times means somebody's not listening." His words are broken up by heavy breathing. Dad is not on a leisure walk.

Mom grunts her agreement.

I deep sigh and lean back on my palms. "I'm listening to him, Dad."

"I know. I know." His voice goes high as if to say, *don't blame me, I'm just doing my job.* "Just remember the goals you made for the season. Ask yourself if you're executing where you should be in order to get your team there."

"I know. I know," I repeat, mimicking his tone. Goals are something everyone living in this house is required to set twice a year and/or anytime we start something new. Based on my sisters' level of success, I'd have to guess they've continued this practice since moving out.

The treadmill beeps in quick succession. Its hum is less strained as Dad enters his cooldown. He towels sweat from the cattail-reddish-brown skin he gifted to me and my oldest sister, LeArra.

"I was able to register you for the summer ID camps you were interested in. No waitlists. You should be getting emails."

I perk up at this. "Oh. Thanks, Dad."

This will be my last summer to try to catch the eye of coaches I'm interested in playing for in college. I can always play at Midwestern, where my dad is the athletic director. I'd get to go tuition-free, but sometimes that feels like such a cheat code. No matter what I do, I won't have earned it to *some* people.

My sisters both got enough money from other schools that it covered more than just tuition. LeArra got athletic and academic money and Moriah was all academic. I don't want to be the one who chooses Midwestern because she has no other options. And what if I get to Midwestern and my teammates assume the only reason I got recruited was because of my dad. People get these things in their head about you and it's hard to change it.

Set over, Mom drops both weights and adjusts her tightly tied scarf over her silk press before going into dumbbell snatches. All of this is why my mom still looks like she can spike a ball into any opposing court.

"Did you vote in Moriah's poll?"

Mom's referring to the poll Moriah posted earlier about her dress that has been on order for two months now. The dress that we spent four weekends straight finding. She's "having second thoughts." If the dress she ordered was really "THE dress" would she have been torn between two? Isn't she supposed to "just know"?

I shake my head. "I don't have the right answer."

"There is no right answer, Dru." She grunts. Her recovery time is up. She's moving on to the next set of reps. "If you don't vote, there will be a moment, and we can't have a moment every day up until the wedding. I don't have the energy for refereeing. It's exhausting."

And by "moment" she means another argument with one or both of my sisters about me being allowed to do whatever I want because I'm spoiled, and my parents are too tired to parent me correctly. Too bad me voting in the poll won't stop that "moment" from happening. Anytime we're together for more than five minutes it's bound to come up.

"Isn't she already locked in?" Every conversation we had about the dress included having it selected by the eight-month mark. The wedding is now four months away.

"We'll figure it out. Just vote so she can decide what to do."

I pull out my phone and look at my poll response options:

❏ Keep looking for dresses. You haven't found the one.

❏ You made a mistake. Get the dress you left behind.

❏ Stick with the dress you ordered. It's the one.

I frown down at the phone. How am I supposed to know what Moriah wants?

"What was your vote?" I can't be wrong if I vote with the person who's paying for a portion of this.

Mom pauses, twenty-five-pound weight above her head. "Your sister wants your opinion. Just give it to her. Please."

As if summoned by the word *sister*, my eldest, LeArra, sends my phone into vibration with a video call. If this were anyone else, I would consider myself saved. But in the case of LeArra, I know better.

I lie back on the bench and click answer. "Hey, LeArra."

"Just getting home on a school night, huh?" LeArra pulls her lips to one side in distaste. "How times have changed."

Dad tuts a chuckle, openly unfazed by the shots fired in judgment of his parenting skills. Mom's grunt reads *girl, please* as opposed to *strength training is tough*. I scratch my head, dumbfounded. Why has she been allowed to keep access to everyone else's whereabouts when she stopped sharing hers years ago? And we're ten years apart, not fifty.

She wraps her thick, bone-straight hair around her fist and lets it fall past her shoulder as she stares at me. "Sister."

The way she makes a really nice word sound so disgusting is a thing only she can do.

I take a deep breath. "Yeah?"

"You do know that you should be recording RSVPs for the shower every day? If you get careless, we'll forget somebody and it will be embarrassing."

I clear my throat. "I record them on the spreadsheet as I receive them."

"Well, that's really weird, Dru." She leans back. Looking off camera and then at me again. "Only guests who received night invites have been recorded."

"Because that's all who's responded." I say this very slowly, questioning myself as I go. But, yeah, I've recorded RSVPs even in class just to avoid conversations like this. "If you were worried, you could've taken the RSVPs. I could've done something else."

"I don't have time to get texts all day, any time of day, Dru. This program requires everything."

She says that last part so often I'm tempted to say it with her. I don't because she isn't exaggerating. She's becoming a physicist. That's something I could never do, so I let her have it. I won't mention that the Eason-Portis wedding shower theme was all her idea and makes everything about ten times more complicated.

Although my parents are paying for the shower, as maids of honor, LeArra and I are the planners and hosts. LeArra came up with the idea to have the guests bring gifts specifically for morning, noon, or night, with invitations to match. For example, a third of the roughly sixty guests were asked to bring gifts that they think Moriah and

Rashid would use after dark and the invites are black card stock with a smattering of silver stars. And the party favors will be gifts those particular guests can use after dark. In this case, candles with a calming lavender scent. I swallow my thoughts. "I'm not being careless."

She hmmms a hmmm that should really be reserved for her PhD program. "We'll see. Hopefully it'll be in time to prevent disaster. And can you please vote in the poll. I know you've viewed it. We're waiting on you."

She yells goodbye to my parents before ending the call.

Dad grabs my hand to lead me off the bench and out of the way of the rest of his routine. When I'm standing, he teasingly says, "I guess you better vote in the poll."

I roll my eyes at him, head upstairs to the kitchen, and screenshot the poll to send to Winston. I've told him about every single piece of petty I've gotten from my sisters for my whole life. He knows how a simple wrong response to this question could turn into a problem I can't see coming. Sometimes, people who haven't been here from the beginning, like Aubrey, who I love and I know loves me, don't get why it all stresses me out so much.

Dru: This feels like a setup

Winston: It definitely does

Dru: What should I vote???

Winston: Do you have to vote?

              Dru: It's a mandate

Winston: Say what you think

              Dru: You answered way too fast
                   and that's what you always say.
                   Don't you want to think
                   about it?

Winston: If all the answers are wrong
         you might as well give the one
         you want

              Dru: I want to give the one that means
                   we don't have to go dress shopping
                   again

Winston: Do you really?

              Dru: Yes
              Dru: No
              Dru: I want Moriah to be happy

Winston: Say that

I groan. It's never that easy, but Mom says I have to respond, so I guess I have to respond.

I reopen the poll. My opinion isn't an option. I select "other" and comment instead. "Whatever you're feeling is the right answer."

In return I get the poll results from me, LeArra, my mom, and Rashid's mom, Ms. Teddy:

❑ Other = 40%
❑ Keep looking for dresses. You haven't found the one. = 20%
❑ You made a mistake. Get the dress you left behind. = 20%
❑ Stick with the dress you ordered. It is the one. = 20%

The fifth "other" comment is unexpected and unsolicited according to the private chat members. "In case you forgot, I'll marry you in that holey T-shirt and shorts you clean in."

I've voted with the groom. That can't be bad.

And also, I can't help but wonder if some random girl from high school launched Rashid, and if every day she's watching Moriah and Rashid's wedding social media pages wondering what she did to miss out.

23 DAYS AND OFFICIALLY COUNTING

Standing in front of my mirror before school, I can only think about two things. One of them is how I'm going to ask my exes about our relationships. The other thing is how to convince my teammates that not only do we need a team pact, but we all need to be romance-free.

The more I think about it, the more I'm convinced that a pact could really help our team stick together. Of course it doesn't have to be this exact pact—a pact that could potentially help me—but I do love that it could be.

My phone buzzes on the counter. When I see who the text is from, I realize I'm in denial. I'm actually thinking about three things. Kai Waller is one of those things, but he's definitely not number three.

Kai: 23 days and officially counting

I smile as if he's standing right in front of me saying those words. Damn. Kai Waller is counting down the days until we can hang out. I love that.

Of course, I can't *say* I love that. That would be weird. But what *should* I say? What would make him smile the way he just made me smile? I groan. How am I thumb-tied? How did he do that?

It feels like I'm not even meeting the low bar, but I just send the blushing smiling emoji. But then he sends the blush back, like I'm doing something to *him* and not the other way around. Then I send another back. Then he sends the blushing face with the hand covering its smile emoji. And I don't know why but that kind of sends me. All I can do is react with a heart.

As soon as I get out of my car at school, Aubrey is stomping toward me from the school building at an unusual pace. There's little to no difference between us in height—five foot six—or weight—even though I'm deceptively heavier than I look, being that I'm mostly lean muscle, but anybody watching this scene from a distance might think I need protection.

I look over her shoulder. "Why are you coming from that way? You have school already?"

She waves toward the building. "SAT study group."

"I thought you had a study group last night?"

Aubrey is the one who we were sure wouldn't be compelled to take the test more than once. Her PSAT scores and grades have always been the best and she completed an entire workbook. Somehow, when we got the results back, she had scored way below the projection for people with her grades. And while I got the better score, it was in line with my grades and pretty much every standardized test I've ever taken. Ten percent of my peers are and have always been better at them than me.

"Last night was a one-on-one SAT tutoring session. This morning was an SAT study group."

"And I'm still doing the vocab with you on Saturday?"

"Yes, why wouldn't you be?" She thwarts any other questions I might have with a headshake. "Don't try and change the subject."

I side-eye her. "We have a subject?"

She tilts her head and smirks like a movie mean-girl imitation. "Where your man at?"

I side-eye her more. "Excuse me?"

She rolls her eyes and comes at me with a lowered voice. "You really thought you could text me about seeing Kai, be completely incapable of formulating anything coherent in that interview, eye flirt and invent verbal displays of affection, and then just leave me hanging? Either you got a man or you forgot your words or did some other weird thing you tend to do when Kai comes around."

I scratch my head. "Was the interview *that* bad?"

"I mean..." She tilts her head, and the purple tips of her two thick French braids brush her shoulders. I can tell she wants to walk back her honesty. Do the supportive best-friend thing. But she's having a hard time figuring out how.

I bail her out. "He asked when we could hang out."

"It wasn't all bad, then. Something good came out of your performance." She nods and smiles. "When is this finally happening?"

I shrug. "We didn't make a specific plan."

"You said he said 'when.' How did you guys not make a when?"

I did say he said *when*, didn't I? How did she not get a perfect SAT score? How?

I feel my forehead wrinkle under the scrutiny. I don't really want to get into this again, less than twenty-four hours after spilling everything to Winston. It's not like the conversation feels good. Plus, Aubrey will rip my theory apart. That's not what I need when I'm trying to get up the courage to talk to my exes. Instead of hyping me up, she's going to try to talk me down. And when she finds out I made up a pact, she's going to maybe call me out of my name.

"He said 'when' and I said it can't be until after the season is over because of my team's no-dating-until-the-end-of-the-season pact."

Aubrey gives me a questioning look, her barely brown cheeks glowing with the morning chill. "You guys have a no-dating pact? Why have I never heard of it?"

I duck my head and my shoulders drop. I *could* say she's never heard of the pact because it was irrelevant since I wasn't trying to date anyone. But a lie under duress to save myself is one thing. A lie to my best friend just to avoid being embarrassed isn't a snowball I want to start rolling downhill. "Because I made it up after he asked me out."

"Made it up? When? Why? You lied to him?" She purses her lips in disbelief. "Girl. What is wrong with you?"

That's the real question, right. What *is* wrong with me?

But I can't say that. I can give all the examples I gave Winston last night and she won't see the correlation. If she hasn't picked up on it while we've lived through my relationships together, then she'll never see what I see.

She calls me out on my faults all the time. Her not seeing this one is something I don't understand. The only thing I can come up with is that this particular fault doesn't have an easy solution, so she pretends it doesn't exist.

I would never have even told Winston, a person I've told a lot of things to, if he hadn't caught me in a moment of weakness and I didn't need help.

Aubrey looks me in the eye and nods, encouraging me to speak. "Dru. What are you thinking? Just tell me so I can tell you you're wrong and you can go get your man."

She's right. I'm thinking a lot of things, and they won't make sense to my friend. All I know is, the common denominator in my interactions with guys is me. That can't be explained away with perception or coincidence. That is fact, viewable from every angle.

I meet her eyes and try to sound confident but also nonchalant. "I'm not thinking anything. It just felt like the right thing for right now. I'm busy."

She squints at me as if that will make things clearer. "A boy you've liked on and off for the past year asked you out and you made up a whole lie to get out of it and you expect me to believe you aren't thinking anything? You're just busy? And so you made up a whole thing?"

"I—"

"Did you think he was joking and you got embarrassed and decided you needed to make a joke too?"

I shrug one shoulder noncommittally.

She eyes me with her lips in a thin line. "Was it awkward because Winston was there?"

I frown. "Why would it be awkward because of Winston?"

She pulls her head back as if questioning my seriousness. I'm not sure why. Then, without explanation, she puts both of her palms up in exasperation. "I don't know. Did Kai's breath stink? Did *he* stink?"

"Actually"—I tilt my head and balance on the sides of both feet—"I was the funky one. I'd just come from practice."

"Dru, this is bananas," Aubrey says sternly. "And I hope you realize I'm never going to stop asking you why you lied. Never. Like if you say, *hey Aubrey, how's your day going.* I'm going to say *why are you making up stuff.* You say, *tacos or burgers* and I'm going to say, *why are you weaving tales.* You say—"

I put my hand up to stop her. "Okay. I think I get the sequence now."

She nods slightly as if offering some sort of grace or patience.

I swallow hard and bite my bottom lip. "The only reason I wasn't in a hurry to tell you is because I know you'll have my back like only a real friend can. You'll try to talk me out of what is obviously a recurring issue in my life. You'll say I need to stop being scared."

"Tell me what's going on first. Provide the reasoning I won't agree with second. There's no excuse for your best friend to be on the edge of her seat about your life."

I put my hands up, asking for patience. "I told him we have a team no-dating pact until the end of the season because I need time to figure out why every guy I've dated since the sixth grade gets disinterested really quick, which leads to me breaking up with him and then him becoming the best boyfriend ever to some other girl."

She nods slowly and runs her tongue along her bottom lip in thought. "Technically that's exactly what happened with Michael and Jayden."

"And Trinity," I add, not bothering to go into the relationships before high school, when I didn't know Aubrey. "And what other way is there to look at it than technically?"

To my surprise, she shrugs a reluctant agreement. There's no fight here. Facts are facts. I am the common denominator in the boyfriend launcher mission. That hurts even though I've been thinking it for months.

Validation is not the relief people claim it to be.

"I don't want that scenario to happen again, especially not with Kai. So basically, I asked Winston to let me pretend... sort of narrate or act out a relationship with him when necessary and he could let me know where I'm going wrong." I sigh. "But he said no because it would be too weird because we're such good friends."

"Mmm," she says, as if she's just received the most intriguing information. "*Such* good friends, yeah."

"He told me I should ask my exes instead. I'm starting that today if I don't pass away from embarrassment first."

Aubrey nods slowly, as if it's all coming together. "It could be worth it, though. I like this for you."

I jerk my head back. "You do?"

Aubrey puts her hand on her chest passionately. "You're trying to figure out how you can keep a good guy for yourself instead of sending him out into the world fully formed. The last thing I'm going to do is shame you for trying to resolve what could be a you problem."

I scratch my head. I'm not sure if Aubrey supporting this is better than her being against it after all.

"The afterglow up of your ex-men could be a coincidence. Even if it isn't, no one says you have to change. But there's something to be said for knowing your issues and just saying, *whatever, I am what I am.*"

I turn toward school, leading her away from the doors we normally go in because that's where I always run into Kai. Any other day, I look forward to seeing him, but I don't want to get into a situation where I have to lie again.

"Now I just have to get the team on board." I let my shoulders drop. "How am I going to do that?"

"How?" she squeaks. "You're co-captain. Just talk about sisterhood and team bonding. Tell them how it's going to be. You're not asking."

The closer we get to the doors, the more people we're near. She takes her voice even lower. "Your real problem is, what if you guys don't even make it all the way to the championship? This could be twenty-something days, or it could be one. You could lose tomorrow. The season would be over, and you'd be out of excuses."

I stop dead in my tracks and stare at her. "Why are you even putting that in the air?"

She shrugs again but doesn't stop walking. "It's something to consider."

I absolutely will not let myself consider it. Not just because twenty-three days may be barely enough to determine and resolve my issues. Mainly because my team not making it to the championship game would be soul crushing. We were two games away last year. This year, we're so much better. It will be hard, but we'll do it.

I'm locked in and committed to figuring this out, but I'm not planning for the worst.

Michael Rose was my second-longest relationship, but mainly because I didn't know when to say when. He tuned out in a few weeks. I thought I could get him tuned back in—just by being myself and being around more. But I think I might have over-exposed myself and it came across as a little clingy. That's the only thing I've been able to come up with.

Then again, nine times out of ten when I see him, he's with Michaela or talking about being with her. They definitely look clung.

After I put my things in my locker I start to make my way to where I think his locker is. I take my time walking down the hall and eventually up the stairs to the second floor. Not only am I not looking forward to asking Michael about our relationship, but I also don't know how to. How do I ask without seeming interested or still stuck? How do I not embarrass myself?

All I know is, if Michaela is with him, this mission will be aborted. There is absolutely no way I'm having this conversation in front of her.

When I get up to the second floor and come out of the stairwell, I spot him coming toward me. He's alone. He seems to be approaching me with intention. I know what that's probably about.

Slowly, he struts up to me. This kid has the most confident walk, like he thinks the whole world has been waiting for him. Not going to pretend that didn't draw my eye initially. It's a little annoying now, though. Just saying.

"Dru. Hey. You saved me a trip." He gives me a pound. "I need another favor."

I hold out my hand, palm up.

He squints one eye at me. "You sure you don't mind?"

I roll my eyes. "I've been delivering your love letters most of the year. Why would I suddenly mind now?"

He places a neatly folded letter in my hand. "Make sure—"

"She's not looking when I put it on her desk. I remember," I finish for him, even though I'm pretty sure Michaela knows I'm her mail person.

He smiles his crooked smile. "Thank you, friend."

He always ends our interactions with *friend*, like I'm somehow going to get the nature of our relationship twisted. Even though, for me, *friend* is a pretty strong word in our situation. He turns to walk away. In an effort to stop myself from chickening out, I blurt his name a little too loud. I say it again, quieter and hopefully with a little less urgency.

"Can I ask you a question?"

He scratches his chin, immediately suspicious. "Okay."

I bite my bottom lip, thinking of how to ask the question. Then I realize if I think too hard I won't ask at all. I just go for it. "Not being weird or anything. I'm not interested. Just curious. Remember when we were together?"

He tilts his head toward me as if he didn't hear me right. "Together?"

I give him the same head tilt in return, but mine is confusion. Do people actually forget relationships? Is it a superpower? Sign me up.

"Yeah. We went to homecoming together sophomore year."

He nods slowly. "Oh, yeah, that."

I scrunch up my face and let out an embarrassed chuckle. "That?"

"I mean…" He raises the corner of his lip. "I don't really consider us a real relationship."

Okay, so, I don't in any way want Michael Rose. But I can't lie. His words sting. Not just in that figurative way. In a physical way. Like he's taken a tiny piece of my skin and is holding it as tight as he can between two fingernails. It didn't work out. I failed at it, obviously, but it was real.

I cross my arms over my chest. "Well, that's funny. I remember you asking me to be your girlfriend and me saying yes."

I also remember a whole lot of anxiety trying to figure out how to end it. But with the way he's telling the story, admitting that would be way too pitiful. Even though he's only a few inches taller than me, I'm feeling very small.

"Yeah, I remember all that too." He validates me with a few deep nods. "I just mean, you didn't really give a girlfriend vibe."

I frown. I didn't expect any particular answer. Obviously, if I had any idea of what happened in my relationships I wouldn't be here, but not giving girlfriend vibes would never be my guess.

I look down at my hands and run my thumb along a chipped spot on the nail of my pointer finger. I need a breath before I can look at him and ask the next question. "Okaaay. What wasn't girlfriend about me?"

He puts his arms over his chest and looks up at the ceiling as if really putting thought into his answer. Great. That's what I want. I want a real, honest answer that leads to some sort of epiphany that solves all my problems. But, also, not great. The possibility of his answer scares me.

I didn't "give a girlfriend vibe"????

Where do we even go from there? He keeps looking up at the ceiling, making me more impatient. I need to get my answers and leave. Avoid ever seeing him again.

"If I wasn't your girlfriend and we had a *that* instead of a relationship, then what were we doing?"

"You were my girlfriend." He shifts a little on his feet, as if this conversation is making him as uncomfortable as it's making me. "That's what I called you. Before we became official I thought we would be good together, but everything kind of stayed the same." He lowers his head and shakes it. "I don't know. I don't think I realized what a girlfriend actually is until I got with Michaela. I just knew it wasn't me and you."

"But you knew it was you and Michaela because she gave girlfriend vibes?" I don't know why I feel the need to clarify this. That's obviously what he's saying. He launched because I showed him what a girlfriend isn't, making it easier for him to spot the real thing when he found it. Could it have been that way with all of them? Is that possible?

He nods. We're quiet for a few uncomfortable seconds.

He looks behind him like somebody's called. "I gotta go. Don't forget to—"

I hold up the perfectly folded square and try to sound like what he just said didn't hurt my feelings. I push down this feeling of nausea that's creeping up from the center of my chest to my throat. "I won't forget."

I turn away first, nearly running into Winston.

"I'll do it," he blurts.

23 DAYS, PART 2

I shake my head to clear it and try to figure out what Winston might be talking about.

"What you asked me last night. I'll do it."

I lean back on my heels, everything registering. Embarrassment that I don't normally feel with Winston slinks up my body. "You heard all that?"

"Not everything." He runs his palm along his chest and shoulder uncomfortably. His eyes reflect what I feel. "Enough to know I gave you bad advice. He wasn't helpful. He was mean."

"I asked. He was just telling the truth." I bite my bottom lip. "You don't have to be uncomfortable because you feel bad for me. He could have a point, I guess."

"A point? Dru—"

"Hey, Winston," multiple voices coo at once. I look up to find three girls I know of but not well gliding past us, wearing big, flirty smiles. I school my face into something friendly.

He acknowledges them all by name, giving a lazy smile in return. It's more polite than flirty, but it doesn't stop the dimples from popping all the way out. One of the girls, the only white one in the group, makes a noise and pulls her shoulders up to her ears as if he's just snuggled her in a cozy blanket.

I'm thinking this might be a good opportunity to leave. Normally, when girls flirt with him, I do. But I would rather just wait it out to have this conversation Winston wants to have now and be done with it. I don't want to relive Michael's critique at any time after this one.

The same girl twirls her fine, brown ponytail around her finger. "We watched your show last night."

"You were so good," the tallest of the three says as she pulls her box braids over one shoulder.

"Oh." His smile is more than polite this time. It's warm and genuine. "Thank you."

They slow down, all three of them giggling again. The one who hasn't had the courage to say anything yet makes direct eye contact with him and speaks up. "We were wondering if we could get a tour of your studio."

I don't know if it's because this particular girl seems a bit shy or because of the eye contact, but Winston looks at his shoes. "Mmm. I'll have to think about that."

The shy one looks at her shoes too. "Let us know what you decide."

They giggle and walk away as if they've accomplished their mission to get Winston's attention. But the way his face goes right back to the concerned look he was wearing before they showed up tells me their tactics weren't all that effective.

The bell rings. He waves his hands between us as if to say *forget what's just happened* and pulls me into a stairwell. We huddle together to avoid being heard by stragglers.

He watches my eyes as if he's afraid I might cry or something.

"Anyway, ever since you left last night, I've been thinking about changing my mind about what you asked me. Even before I heard what Michael said."

"Why?"

He presses his hands into the pocket of his sweatshirt, his dark eyes focused on some point above my head. "Last night you said you trusted me."

"You didn't know that already?"

He looks at me then, answering quickly. "I did, yeah. Generally. But nobody has ever trusted me with anything as important as this is to you."

"Except Jake."

He looks down at his hands in his pocket. I can tell they're in fists now. "He worked on his book a long time and he never told me anything about it. Never even asked me to read it."

"Oh."

He shrugs lightly. "It's fine. I'm just saying."

It's not fine. If it was fine he'd be looking me in the eye.

"Maybe just ask him if you can read it. I don't ever say so, but I'd like it if one of my sisters ever asked me how a game went."

His eyes dart up to mine as if he had never thought of that. "Maybe."

This makes me laugh a little. So does he.

I eye him, trying to figure out if he's telling me everything. Yesterday his decision seemed final. "This isn't about you feeling guilty or thinking I'm mad at you, is it?"

He shakes his head. "I don't think you're mad at me."

This seemed like a much better idea last night, when I didn't know digging into my launching issue could be a punch in the face. As much as I trust Winston, it doesn't mean I want him to see whatever this not-girlfriend thing is I have. But it's either accept his help or move on to my next ex. After the conversation I just had with Michael, twenty-three days isn't enough time to build up the courage to have another one.

"If it makes you feel better, I have something you can help me out with."

"Okay." I sigh as I think. I don't want this chance at real help to get away from me. And if Winston needs me for something, I want to make it easy for him to say so. "But first let's make sure I can make it less ick for you."

I let my backpack drop to the floor and lean back against the wall. "We should always let each other know when we're in a boyfriend/girlfriend scenario. That would give you a chance to get in the right headspace and, like, brace yourself."

He taps his temple. "That's smart."

My eyes snap to his. This next point is probably the most important. "We'll narrate anything physical. I'll just say *kiss kiss*...or you can say it if you feel like it's a kiss situation or a situation that Girlfriend Dru would be kissable in or whatever."

He tilts away from me and laughs a little like *he's* embarrassed.

It makes me laugh too. Even though it's my life we're talking about, it's weird making guidelines for how to be a girlfriend to my guy friend.

"Do you think we should call it something else?"

He straightens his face and swallows. "Kiss kiss when Girlfriend Dru is kissable. We can go with that."

"And the one thing we have to be careful about is my teammates." I sigh. "*If* I can get them to agree to the pact, seeing me in any type of girlfriend/boyfriend situation is going to be a big problem. Most people know we're close as friends, but sometimes they still have questions."

"That all sounds doable." He looks at me thoughtfully. "I know I asked you last night, but I just want to make sure. You really like him that much? You want to go through all this? Maybe risk your teammates seeing us and getting the wrong idea?"

"I want to figure me out. If at the end something happens between me and Kai, that would be the cherry on top." I don't try to suppress the smile that comes with the idea. But Winston's stern face brings me back to this moment and the situation I'm in now. The one where I might be stretching the bounds of friendship. "Now. What do you need my help with?"

"Hold on." He goes completely still and listens. Then he looks up the stairs and down before peering into the main hallway. Even though he's verified privacy, when he starts talking he keeps his voice low. "Every year I apply for this broadcasting camp at Midwestern. They have some of the best, most well-known podcasters from everywhere come in. People I would never get to talk to otherwise."

I can see the passion in his eyes as he talks. Obviously this means a lot to him.

"That sounds cool, but I don't ever remember you going. How come you never told me about it?"

He licks his lips. "I never get accepted. Three times they've rejected me. Three."

I tilt my head and look at him questioningly. "Why didn't you just ask my dad? I'm sure he could help. At least put in a good word or something."

"I didn't think he would. And . . . I didn't want him to," he admits.

My look doesn't change. I think I know where he's going with this, and I don't like it. "Why wouldn't he? And why didn't you?"

He frowns, letting me know he doesn't appreciate my attempt at ignorance, or isn't falling for it, or both.

I give him a long, high shoulder shrug. "Okay, you made a few bad choices."

He looks around again and lowers his voice even more, as if what he's about to say is the most scandalous thing ever uttered. "I was expelled. I spent second semester of freshman year online."

"And you think my dad is holding that against you?"

"Maybe." His eyes go big and it only exaggerates how irrational he's being. "People still talk about it. Make jokes about it. And the two times a year we have to meet with our counselors I can tell she's checking in on my ability to deal with my impulses."

I lift my chin and shake my head as if I refuse to hear any more. "He's not holding it against you. Period. Why wouldn't you want him to help you?"

He mumbles something. All I can make out is the first word. *Jake.*

I lean down as if to get in his line of vision, even though it's impossible with the way he's focused on the ground.

"I want to be able to show up and tell everyone something good I've done"—he meets my eyes—"on my own."

Like Jake. Jake who never even told anyone he was writing a book or sending it to publishing people until he had to talk to their parents about signing a contract. No one even suspected he'd been writing. Even though their grades are pretty similar, Jake's considered the studious one. Being attached to his laptop was never questioned.

Now Jake's book is all anyone talks about. Even I talk about it a lot. I *know* that feeling.

"You don't have to do things the way he does to make people proud of you."

He lets out a long breath and focuses his eyes somewhere past me.

Recognizing that maybe that wasn't the right thing to say— especially after I was just gushing over Jake's genius last night and Kai was shaking his head at Winston's questionable choices—I change direction. "What do you need me to do?"

"The application deadline is coming up and I wasn't even going to apply, but since you're offering…" He licks his lips. "I don't want your dad to pull any strings or anything like that, if he even knows anyone in the School of Communications. I just want to know why I keep getting rejected, and what kind of person they're looking for. Maybe if I know, I can submit a better application."

"That's it?" I pull my phone out of my back pocket. "We can just ask my dad now."

He grabs my phone and holds it out of my reach. "And your mom can't know. Because if your mom knows, my mom knows, and then everyone finds out about my life of rejection."

Okay. Not so easy. My parents are tell-each-other-about-their-day people. My father would just mention helping Winston as a bullet point. Never tell Keith anything you don't want Angela to know and vice versa, because if pillow talk was people, they would be my parents. And Winston would feel like an even bigger failure when my mom inevitably mentioned it to her best friend.

The last thing I want is to embarrass him, especially about something this sensitive. And I get it. I'm not exactly the standout sister.

"I will swear my dad to secrecy. It'll stay between us three and he'll never make you feel any kind of way about anything he finds out." I wait for a disagreement before I continue. One never comes. "My dad will tell only me whatever he finds out and I'll tell only you. Does that sound okay?"

He nods in agreement and hands my phone back.

"Good." I run my fingers through the braids at the nape of my neck. "All I need to do now is convince my teammates. Or else everything comes tumbling down."

He tilts his head and pins his eyes to mine. I'm expecting some commiserating or good advice, but instead he says in a small, hesitant voice, "Kiss kiss."

I blink and start a ramble that rivals the eloquence of last night's interview. "What? Oh. Kiss kiss like *kiss kiss*." I crinkle my nose. "You didn't warn me. And this isn't a kissable moment. There's nothing kissable about me right now."

"It would be weird if you thought there was." His eyes are still pinned to mine and his voice is still so small. This try at Boyfriend

Winston might even be weirder for him than it is for me. If it is, one or both of us might quit this plan before we get anywhere.

"You know what I mean."

"I don't." He scratches his head, leaving a bit of a dent in his dense twists. "All I know is Boyfriend Winston decided his girlfriend is kissable and she second-guessed him. I have notes already."

"No. You don't have notes. You can't have notes yet." I roll my eyes at myself and pick up my backpack off the ground. "I just ... This is going to be hard, right? When we think of a boyfriend or a girlfriend we don't think of each other. Or we don't think of girlfriendly or boyfriendly things. We think of a friend."

"Hmmm." He bites his bottom lip and finds something else to look at on the ground.

I nod as I look for the words to talk us both out of the ick. I don't want either of us to get too discouraged already. "But we're going to work on it. The rest of the day I'm going to be Girlfriend Dru and you're going to be Boyfriend Winston. It's going to be just like when we used to play *Among Us*. We had roles. Remember?"

He sniffs a laugh. The ick seems to melt away. "I do remember. That used to be fun."

"Right?"

"Right."

"Okay?

"Okay."

Without waiting for anything more from the other we turn our backs to each other and walk in opposite directions.

23 DAYS, PART 3

On game days, the team always sits together at lunch. It's not a mandate and hasn't really been an entire-team sort of thing until this year, when Meegan became captain. Even if I wasn't co-captain I'd do it. Lunch with my team used to be one of my favorite parts of the week. Then, about midseason, it became clear how good we are and that we could actually make a real run. After that, joking, poking fun at each other, and complaining about classes turned into game and player critiques provided mostly by Meegan. Not that I don't think we need to talk about the way we play and how each of us can get better, but between practice and games we have twelve hours a week for that.

I have really high hopes for today, for my own reasons, but as a team, we need something. It seems to me the less fun we have off the field, the less we have on it, and the worse we play.

Even though I'm sitting with them, in the true girlfriend spirit I've committed myself to, I split from Aubrey at the salad bar and head for Boyfriend first. He obviously has his Girlfriend radar on. As soon as I make the decision his eyes are up and on me. I know I'm not doing anything worthy of the intense look he's giving me, but I appreciate his dedication to making me feel like I am. After the weird *kiss kiss* episode from this morning, I was worried he'd tell me he couldn't go through with this. The look lets me know he's still trying.

I say hey to Jake and bend down to whisper in Winston's ear. He startles, but I don't create any more distance. The last thing I need is this going anywhere beyond his ears. "Girlfriend would get closer, but that would raise a lot of questions."

He takes a deep breath as if I have already overstepped the closeness boundary even for our fact-finding mission.

I lean away. "My bad."

He glances quickly over at me and then rubs the side of his face. This is obviously super uncomfortable for him. Me asking my dad to help him doesn't feel like a fair trade right now.

"Sorry."

"It's fine. You're good." His light tone doesn't match the look he just gave me at all.

I raise an eyebrow. "Girlfriend can't sit by you. She has to sit with her team today."

He nods and turns to me. Our faces are definitely invading each other's personal space again. I don't shift away. I can tell he's braced himself for the girlfriend/boyfriend interaction now. "We're going to see each other at some point today, right? Like, just-me-and-you time?"

I scratch my head. I'm not really sure what he means by "just-me-and-you time" specifically. It sounds like something for only Boyfriend Winston and Girlfriend Dru to know. In a real situation, I'm sure I'd be clear on what's what.

I also don't have time to clarify now. "Yeah. Of course."

He gives me a Winston smile that would make most girls reconsider walking away. Mostly the whole thing just makes me wonder if he's make-out king or something. If so, I'm not sure I want to know that about him.

I catch up to Aubrey in the salad bar line.

She eyes me. "What was that all about?"

I tense. "Why? What did we look like it was about?"

"*You* looked normal, but W—"

I let out an exaggerated breath. "Okay. Good. Don't scare me like that."

"What's going on?"

I lean into her. "Winston changed his mind about my investigation. We're going to boyfriend/girlfriend each other."

She presses her lips together. "Why would he change his mind?"

"He overheard me talking to Michael. I think it made him embarrassed for me."

"Why? What did Michael say?"

I roll my eyes to the sky. I've spent the last few hours going over what Michael said. I really don't think I'm ready to repeat it all yet. "I'm still processing."

She nods slowly. "You know I'm all for this investigation. I already told you. But you really think Winston's the right person for it?"

I side-eye her. "Are you doubting him because of the stink bomb and the whole dressing-the-pig-cadaver freshman year? He doesn't really do stuff like that anymore."

"Nope. He got me two extra days to study for a geometry exam and the pig was already dead. I never understood why people were suddenly upset about the way it was being treated. I'm asking because…" She squints at me, unexpectedly serious. "Has he never hinted to you about anybody he's interested in or, like, given you a clue as to why he never looks in the direction of anybody who's interested in him? I mean, he could have a lot of girls. He's fine."

I nod, as this is a matter of fact. I mean, he could've had his pick this morning.

Aubrey turns her head toward Winston's table and admires him for a second. My eyes follow hers. Both he and Jake are looking at us. I cross my eyes and stick my tongue out at them before I get me and Aubrey back on subject.

"I'm not really worried about his lack of experience. I asked for his help because he's my friend and I trust him. We always look out for each other. You know that."

Aubrey eyes me for a minute, taking me in from head to toe, then shrugs. "Winston for president, then, I guess."

It's my turn in line. This is another time I'm guaranteed to see Kai. He sits at a table diagonal from the bar. If I look up while I'm dumping ranch on my salad I'll have a perfect view of his entire face. I shouldn't look, but it's not like locking eyes with him will make my lie any bigger than it already is. So I peek.

Ugh. He isn't even looking in my direction. My disappointment is a secret I plan to take to my grave.

But as soon as I look away, I feel eyes on me. HIS eyes. I look up just as he's looking away. He must feel me the same way I felt him, because he glances back. We both smile. Neither of us wants to be the first to lose the eye contact. I hold on until Aubrey elbows me. I've missed my salad and poured a ladleful of ranch all over the compartment of bacon bits. Aubrey is cackling next to me. The girl behind her groans.

I frown and mumble a "sorry." This makes Aubrey laugh even harder. I'm embarrassed, but I can't move along without taking one last look at HIM. He's still watching me. His smile tells me he's a little proud of the way he stole my undivided attention.

We reach the soccer table before the council or STEM tables where Aubrey and I would normally sit together if it wasn't a game day.

"You got this," she whispers before we separate and I sit down.

As usual, the team is split into a few groups. Some watching TikTok. Others catching up on Snaps. A few talking about classes or guys or girls.

And then there's Meegan. Riley is next to her. She's another senior standout. *I* would've picked her as co-captain over me. I even told Coach that. He saw things differently. He said the team needed balance and a leader who didn't think exactly like Meegan. A leader who earns respect a different way.

It's not panning out the way he thought, though. When Meegan or Riley speaks up, everyone snaps to action even if they don't like what's being asked of them. I don't think that would happen in my case.

Meegan and Riley are talking soccer and that's it. The conversation is passionate and focused. I'm two seats away from them. I have to lean in to hear.

"Switching the field is going to be key, especially tomorrow." Meegan turns her occasionally brown, occasionally green eyes toward me. It makes sense, since this tactic would fall under my responsibilities as central midfielder. It's also a little intimidating to walk right into being told how important your own play will be for the team. Not that I don't already know and feel this during every game.

I nod. "If people are showing, I'm passing it that way."

Riley rests one elbow on the table and turns her full, spray-tanned body to me. "Or dribble into it. Find your shot. Ask for the ball. Make sure everything goes through you, and if you see something take it."

I remind myself of what Aubrey said earlier about sisterhood and bonding. I can't let myself get defensive. This me-taking-my-shot thing has become a top-three conversation piece on the team. I know it's the weakest part of my game, but I have to pick my spots, and being the assist leader in the district for two seasons straight is the biggest possible flex for me as a midfielder. I don't mind leaving the shooting to the forwards. But nobody likes when I say that.

So I press my lips together and nod. This isn't the time to start debating playing styles. I'm going to give the team my best always. We all know that. I can't let the critique of my game get me off task.

"And what are you eating?" Meegan scoffs as she leans over the table, getting a better look at my tray. "Salad? On a game day? You're supposed to be carb loading. What is this?"

Meegan looks away from me and starts addressing the entire table about their eating habits.

Capri, another junior and the only other Black girl on varsity, scrunches her face. Ninety percent of the time we find ourselves sneaking looks across the huddle and laughing at jokes only we would get. I'm not sure if we would've found each other off the field, but on the field we feed off each other's energy. We both think about what makes the next person look good before we think of ourselves. She's been my favorite person to play with ever.

"I can't believe you let them talk to you like that," she whispers as she separates her signature low, straight ponytail into two and pulls to tighten it. "You're the best player on the team and a captain. We can win without Riley. She's just Meegan's muscle. But we can't win without you. And Meegan is doing too much. She isn't the coach."

"*Meegan* is the best player on the team." I push my salad away from me and eye the line for pasta. Meegan is right. I'll get more carbs. "She might be a little extra right now, but it's good to have a voice other than Coach's keeping everybody focused."

Capri scrunches her face even more, creating worry lines everywhere. "Good for who? I don't need her to motivate me. I have my own goals, like I know you do."

There's a hum of agreement somewhere around us, but when I look away from Capri, I can't tell who gave it. She has at least one cosigner. That's one too many. This isn't the time for us to unravel.

We need something a little less hardcore to think about as a team. A pact is perfect.

I don't even try for the perfect segue. I put both elbows on the table, leaning toward Meegan and Riley to regain their attention. "Remember my freshman year when the seniors made us all eat from the same bag of chips on the bus to away games?"

I'm surprised to see Meegan smile big as if she appreciates the memory. "How can I forget having a better away record than home?"

"We need something like that this year, but bigger." I shake my head. "Not a superstition. But something that shows we're serious and committed to actually being as good as everyone says we can be."

This catches the attention of Lauren, another senior. "What? Like, we don't shave our legs or armpits or something?"

I shake my head. "No. Something that would help keep us all focused."

"Winning keeps us focused," Riley says. "That's what we need to be thinking about. All the rah-rah stuff is just noise."

Capri shifts next to me. "I disagree. I'm interested in whatever your idea is, Dru."

That backup is greatly appreciated. It's unexpected without first hearing my suggestion. I'm not sure it would've happened if someone different had tried to shut me down. Half the table is looking at me now like *spit it out*. They must assume I have an idea. Otherwise, I wouldn't have brought this up. I take the assumption as a good sign. People are at least open to some team bonding.

I lick my lips and let out a big breath. "You'll probably think it's too out there but…what about no dating until we win the championship?"

Meegan narrows her eyes. "I don't date."

And by that she means she doesn't take anyone seriously or allow anyone to call her girlfriend. She's more like anti-dating but pro any of the benefits. I hadn't really thought about that. And I don't have a chance to before Capri chimes in.

"Should be easy for you, then."

Lauren frowns. "I have a boyfriend. Am I supposed to break up with him?"

Thanks to the conversation with Winston and Jake, I *did* think about that. I raise my voice over the mumbling at the table. "Um... how about no contact starting after the practice before game days?"

Lauren's blonde ponytail swings behind her as she shakes her head in disbelief. "So I should've stopped talking to Mason last night?"

I cross one foot over the other and nod nervously. "And everyone not in a relationship can't start one. No making out, hooking up, hanging out."

There are mixed reviews around the table. And I hear more of what's been building for weeks. Team Meegan and Team Dru.

I hate that my idea is today's fuel for our team division, but I can't take it back now. I can't tell what the split is. I *can* tell those in favor of a dating pause are quick to agree because it's not Meegan's suggestion. There are under-the-breath comments like *Meegan can't decide everything* and *Dru's a captain too.* By my new count, Capri has seven cosigners. Not half the team, but enough.

Meegan pipes up, looking thoughtful and unfazed even though I know she has to hear the tone around her as clearly as I do. "I think it's a good idea."

Lauren scoffs. "You're just saying that because you don't have anybody."

Meegan scoffs right back but keeps all emotion out of her voice. "Just because I don't tie myself down to one specific person doesn't mean I don't have any *bodies.* I'm saying I'll go along with this because it's obvious, based on your play, some of you have too many other things on your mind. Dru's come up with a way to eliminate at least one."

"And if you can't go twenty-four hours without your man, or anybody else"—Capri eyes Meegan and a few other girls at the table—"or can't go a few days without taking your clothes off for the sake of the team, you really need to do some self-evaluation."

"No idea why you're looking at me. I'm agreeing. We're doing it," Meegan yells over any objections, and starts stuffing sandwich bags and empty wrappers back in her paper bag. "Put it in the group chat."

Most of the rest of the team starts cleaning up too, even though we're only halfway through lunch.

"Why is the conversation over just because she says so?" That comment comes from Charlotte, all the way across the table. I'm not sure whose team she's on.

Meegan doesn't pretend not to hear this. "Because one captain suggested it"—she points at me—"and the other captain agreed." She points at her temple. "What else needs to be said?"

This pronouncement doesn't feel like a win. Even if it does mean I can get the Girlfriend Dru/Boyfriend Winston thing rolling… stealthily, of course. The sooner I do that, the sooner we can get to the bottom of my romantic-life-threatening issues.

I remember that feeling I had a few minutes ago when I spotted Kai at the salad bar and channel all of that into a cute text to Boyfriend Winston.

> **Dru:** Girlfriend Dru: I miss you. Can
> me-and-you time be now?

20 MINUTES OF ME-AND-YOU TIME WITH 23 DAYS TO GO

Winston tells me to meet him by the stairwell that dead-ends at the textbook room. It's only open during the first half of the day, and probably one of the few places to attempt being completely alone with someone at LeBeau High.

My suspicions about what he means by *just-me-and-you time* might not be too off base. He's leaning back on the stairs, looping the pointer finger of one hand around the bracelets on the other wrist.

As hard as it is, I match his smile, as any good girlfriend would. I'm not going to work against myself and let the fact that I know there's a pin holding together a huge hole in the underarm of this boy's sweatshirt stop me from uncovering my boyfriend-launcher problems. "You got here fast."

"Why didn't you get here faster?" He turns his phone face up in his hand, checking the time. "We only have, like, twenty minutes."

I snicker as I sit down on a higher step so I don't spend the whole time looking up at him. "Only twenty minutes," I mock.

"Yes, only twenty minutes." He imitates me imitating him. He's still smiling but looking at me with serious confusion in his eyes. "What's funny about Boyfriend Winston wanting to maximize time with Girlfriend Dru? If he could've gotten twenty-one minutes, then he would be feeling cheated right now."

First of all, he is really good at this. If I liked him, I would love hearing him say that. It's weird to hear something so perfectly flirty and sweet coming from my best friend. If he were Kai, I still would've laughed, but for different reasons.

"You embarrassed me." Admitting being embarrassed about a boy having zero problems telling me he wants to be around me embarrasses me even more. I can barely look at Winston now.

"Why would you be embarrassed? I'm the one who said it." He leans forward with his chin in the palm of his hands and looks back at me. His smile has disappeared. "And if you're not used to hearing stuff like that, then you must have a really bad boyfriend."

"It would make Girlfriend giggle no matter how much she hears it. She'd never just assume Boyfriend wants to see me." I blink at him. "So . . . kiss kiss or whatever."

"Kiss kiss or whatever back." Somehow he manages not to laugh or crack a smile or even look away. We're making progress. We're both trying. "But why would you have to assume? Why wouldn't you know?"

I sit on my hands and lean back so it's impossible for him to maintain eye contact with me without standing up. "Is that a boyfriend question or a friend question?"

"Does your answer depend on who's asking?"

I'm refusing to look at him, but he sounds like he's wearing that same confused face from earlier.

"Yes." I don't even have to think about it.

In my peripheral, I see him turn away and rest his chin on his fist again. "Okay, then. Your boyfriend is asking why you don't just know he wants to see you. What would you say?"

I sit up straight. "Something flirty or kiss him maybe. Whatever it took to avoid answering."

I watch the back of his head as he nods slowly. "What would your friend answer be?"

"Um..." I sit for a second deciding if there are possibly three answers instead of just two. The boyfriend answer. The friend answer. The truth. "I'd say, just because you tell me something today, it doesn't mean it stands tomorrow. Maybe you see something in me tomorrow that you don't like."

He turns his whole body toward me. "And then I don't want to see you? Feelings change just like that?"

I nod with a shrug. "Or maybe they were never there."

"Possibly." Winston tilts his head like he just doesn't get me or something. "Are the boyfriend and the friend answers always different? Because I think I would want to know if my girlfriend thought my feelings could change that easy."

"I don't think you would."

"I'm telling you I would." He blinks. "I think Kai would."

That's nice to hear, but Winston can't actually know that. Kai might not even know that about himself. He might think he's that guy who wants to know everything about one particular girl, but then he realizes once it's too late that he doesn't. That happens.

"I think it depends," I tell him.

"On what?"

"The information or the person or both."

He tilts his head and sighs a lot before he decides on what to say. "This is going to have to be one of those situations where you trust me because we're friends and I want to help you. If something comes up with Kai and you have more than one answer in your head, give him the most complete one. The Dru answers."

"It's not like I haven't done that before."

"How many times?"

I swallow hard, thinking about the time I decided to give a boyfriend a complete answer. All it led to was getting my feelings hurt even more than if I'd kept my mouth closed.

"Enough times to know lack of sharing isn't my problem. But either way, you haven't seen me girlfriend enough to really come to any conclusions." I shrug. "I'm sure this isn't your idea of me-and-you time."

He looks around the empty space. "Actually, this is a perfect example of me-and-you time. Me and you—me and my girl—are the only requirements."

"Yeah, but I'm sure there has to be some fun or happy feeling type of element attached to it. Not"—I wave my hand around in the space between us—"this. Nobody makes time for this."

Winston looks at me quizzically. "I guess we see things differently, then, because the happy feeling would be *us* being here together. Whatever happens after that is just what happens."

I rest my forearms on my knees and try to imagine what he's

saying. "I've been happy to spend time with my boyfriends, obviously. But I've never had a feeling like our *existence* was the happiness."

I laugh a little at the sound of what Winston has described. It isn't funny. It's just an involuntary reaction to hearing something that sounds so unlikely. What would I have to go through with another person to even realize that kind of happiness? It feels like a lot of uncomfortable pressure where someone's expecting you to be something you probably aren't.

Winston seems to get it. He doesn't look offended by my reaction. "What kind of feelings have you had?"

I take a minute to seriously think about that question. This is probably a better place to start to figure out my problem. What kind of feelings have I had and where did they go? I decide to go in order through my three high school boyfriends.

"I don't know if you've ever had Trinity in a class or anything, but that boy"—I shake my head in wonder—"outside of being really, really fine, is crafty with the words. He will have you thinking you're the smartest, kindest, most beautiful thing in the world and he's the smartest, kindest, most beautiful guy."

I press my fingers to my lips and remember.

He leans back against the wall, head resting on the stairwell. "And?"

I roll my eyes toward the ceiling. "I guess I didn't believe what he was saying. He sounded like he had a database of the perfect things to say stored in his head, and they just come out all smooth and at the perfect time. It would feel rehearsed.

"I'm not saying it was. I feel bad even making it sound like that, but *you look so good today* shouldn't just flow out of his mouth like nothing."

Winston's eyes flit around my face. "Would you have believed him if he was sweating while he said it?"

"You're not funny."

"It's a valid question, though. What could he have done to make you believe he really thought you looked good?"

I shrug. "I don't know."

"Anything?"

"Winston." I'm kind of irritated and I don't know why. "He just didn't need to say it so much."

"If someone says good things about you too often, you don't think they mean it."

I side-eye him. "Winston."

He shrugs and turns his palms up. "What? That's what I heard."

"That's not what I said." I inhale deeply and let it out before I speak again. "He didn't need to say it at all. That's all I'm saying."

"You didn't want him to talk about how he felt."

He doesn't make it sound like a question, so I don't confirm or deny. Also, his interpretation doesn't sound wrong, and I don't want to examine it right now. There's nothing wrong with sharing feelings.

I click my tongue against my teeth. Just because I signed up to be analyzed doesn't mean I have to like it.

"Anyway, I came up with a nice breakup speech. Said it. He said 'cool'...like it was nothing. Eleven days later, he's standing at a locker across from mine with some girl I don't even know. Rarely saw him without her from that day on, and every time I did, it was like they were having their own private party."

Winston scrunches up his face. "They're not together anymore, though, right?"

"Because she moved!" I shout, and then look around for anyone who might've heard. I lower my voice. "Yes, this had happened to me five times before, but I hadn't really put it together yet that the common denominator was me. That didn't happen until Michael.

"He's just fun. We had fun. I know it didn't look like it today, but he always had jokes and just wanted to do fun things. I really liked being around him. He made me smile a lot.

"But after a while it just became this thing where each of us would see who could outlast the other's pettiness. Like, *he took three hours to message me back, I'm going to take three hours to message him back* kind of thing. It just got super childish. But the *didn't see me as a girlfriend* thing." I sigh with a big shrug. "Why were we being petty if there was nothing there?"

Winston laughs a little.

"Two days after we broke up, I was deleted from all his social media, and Michaela was there like they had spent every minute since we broke up trying to tell their relationship in pictures. At first I thought it was just a rebound thing and then they became an institution."

"That's wild." He looks at me, waiting. "Jayden?"

"By Jayden, I had accepted what was happening and had been happening since middle school." I find it hard to look at Winston when I say the next part. I brush imaginary fuzz off my jeans. "It's not really about the relationships ending. I know not everything lasts, obviously. So, it's not about *why* things ended. I knew why they were ending. I'm the one who ended them every time, except once in middle school. It's more about what people aren't seeing in me that would make them want to be *that* guy. They obviously have potential. It only takes the next girl a few days to bring it out."

I look up. Winston's looking at me like he's really trying to understand. Like he really wants to help me. It's really the only reason I find it possible to say this last part.

"With Jayden, I actually saw it. We *had* it." I shrug. "At least *I* thought we had it. He was so sweet, and honest. He always walked me to class, texted to see how my day was going. And he always remembered things like when I had a test or a hard practice and would check in about it. It made me feel like he was interested in me and wanted to know me. And we laughed too. We had a string of iMessage games we used to play all the time. He hated losing so much that it would take him days to make a move. I used to tease him about it.

"Because of all that, I also felt it when he was losing interest. We did everything less—talked, laughed, kissed. I tried to save it, but I couldn't."

Winston waits a while before he says anything. I'm not sure if he's going to. A part of me thinks he's going to remember how uncomfortable all this made him just last night. Then he'll change his mind about helping me at all. I look at my phone. The bell's about to ring. I start to get up, but he stops me, curiosity and maybe a little concern in his eyes.

"How'd you try to save it?"

The bell rings. I jump up. He does too, but he doesn't take a step. He's not going to let me just end this conversation.

"It doesn't matter what I did. It didn't work. But I know never to do it again."

THE END OF 23 DAYS

District Game 1

About an hour and a half before the game, I pull into the Le-Beau parking lot a little haphazardly. I don't use my phone at all while I'm driving. That doesn't mean notifications don't sometimes make me anxious to see what's going on. Everybody I talk to knows where I am and what I'm doing, so this notification means either spam or something super important.

As usual, only Coach's, Meegan's, and Riley's cars are in the lot this early, so I have my pick of spots. Still, I pull into the first available and fish my phone out of my soccer bag. *Winston has sent a video* floats in the middle of my screen. I open it, expecting to see some TikTok he thinks is hilarious or ironic. The kind of thing I'm used to him sending me. But it's just him in his studio, swiveling from side to side in his office chair and staring at his phone's camera.

He's wearing the same black T-shirt he wore to school today. It makes his eyes pop. He bites his bottom lip. I'm not sure if it's actually nerves or if he's trying to act like a flirty boyfriend.

"Hey, Girlfriend." He clears his throat as if calling me that was stressful. "I don't know if you know, but you are the district leader in assists and you have the most goals of anyone in the top ten of that category. If there's any doubt, or if you just need a reminder, you will be the best player on the pitch tonight." He smiles big as if he's super satisfied with his findings. I smile back at the screen as if he's right in front of me. "I won't wish you good luck, because you don't need it. As always, I'll be rooting for you."

I feel like that smiling, eyes-welling-up emoji. It's not just the stats that Boyfriend Winston obviously thought were worth the effort to find. It's the line about me not needing luck. That's a lot of faith to have in me. Pretty sure I don't have that faith in myself.

No boyfriend—not even Jayden—has ever said anything that sweet to me before a game. *Good luck* was the standard. Guess I have a new bar now.

I'm not into pregame rituals, but I can easily see watching this video becoming one. I watch it again and again and a fourth time before I decide to FaceTime him. If this message were from Kai, I'd want to see his face. If this message were from Kai, he'd immediately go from super crush to something even better.

He answers from his studio. I smile, but it feels weird. Not forced, just not enough. Like I should be doing something equally as impactful as his message, but my smile is all I have to work with. "Hey, Boyfriend."

"Hey." He stretches it out questioningly. "You got my video?"

I nod. "Thank you. That...was...the best pregame speech ever. If I don't play like I'm national-team bound after that, then...I don't even know."

"You're welcome, but we don't have to worry about that part.

You're going to play like you play." He says this as convincingly as if he has seen into the future.

"How did you even find those stats?"

He twists at his waist as if he's cracking his back. "I DMed all the teams' pages with a link to my show and asked."

I laugh out loud. "Not you name-dropping yourself."

He drops his head and covers his eyes, but I still hear loud and clear, "Only for you."

I want to say the right thing, give him something solid to critique. But honestly, I don't know what I would say to a boy who admits he'd do something cringy and uncomfortable only for me. No one has ever said anything like that to me before. It's kind of hard to imagine it happening.

"Well, um, only for me is very sweet, Boyfriend." I glance away from the screen and back, barely able to look at a person even pretending to care this much about me. "A million and one kiss kisses."

He smiles a little and nods slowly. "A million and one kiss kisses back."

Meegan and I go rushing toward each other as soon as her shot hits the back of the net and we go up 1–0. There's more than a minute left in the game and at least two minutes of stoppage time, but there is no way anyone on the opposing team or any ball is getting past a LeBeau High Charger.

We fought way too hard for that goal. We earned it, piecing it together from the back. It had to be perfect, and it was. I knew where Meegan was going and sent the ball on time.

It's not too early to celebrate. Once the referee is done taking notes on his card, though, he's ready to get play started again. When he gets flamboyant with his whistle, we calm ourselves down. Nobody wants a yellow card. Especially when it means sitting immediately and for the first half of the next game, per Coach's rules.

I jump as high as I can in the air, trying to refocus before the ball goes back into play. It works well enough, but I'm still playing a little outside myself when we get a lucky bounce. The ball comes to me, and I charge the net like a US national team phenom. I outrun my whole team. It's just me and the goalie. This could be my third goal of the season. It would be an amazing highlight for my reel. And in a playoff game? I couldn't have planned it better in my head.

I know the goalie thinks I'm going left because that's my dominant foot. I could catch her off guard and go right, but if I shoot with my right foot I'm going to miss. If I go where she thinks I'm going, my shot's getting blocked. We're going to win either way, so it doesn't really matter. But it kind of does too. I don't want my miss to be the last thing everybody sees.

I pass back to Meegan with my right. Nobody is expecting that.

It's the back of the net for her again.

Two goals in less than two minutes for Meegan. That's a way more satisfying stat. And if I'm being honest, a little more statistically likely too. I get to celebrate the win with my whole heart without wondering why the ball went haphazardly off my foot or why my textbook shot bounced off the crossbar.

And it was such an easy shot too. I would be replaying a miss in my head frame by frame for weeks.

After I tap the last fist of the opposing team, I find my parents at their usual spot in the stands for our postgame wink-and-wave acknowledgment. There will be a debrief but we always save it for later.

I know what the conversation will be anyway. Dad will note that my assists were great but that I could have kept the ball at my foot a little longer. Then Mom will reiterate for the billionth time that I need to be more dangerous.

This is the thing about having parents who were so good that they accomplished everything I dream of—they never run out of notes. It doesn't matter that neither of them ever watched a soccer game until my first one when I was five. Also, neither of them can dribble a ball five yards.

Right after my eyes connect with my parents', I glance over at the student section. Someone I'm not expecting winks at me. Kai. I've never seen him at one of my games before and I'm really glad I didn't know he'd be here tonight. That definitely would have made me more nervous. I'm so unsure about what my response should be that I don't manage to respond at all before Capri jumps on me, pulling my attention back to the team.

I slink along, lethargic under the extra pounds, toward where Coach always corrals us at the end of the field for a talk. Capri gets me in a headlock, and one of my box braids, somehow loose from my high bun, gets caught between us. When I complain she launches herself off me and back to the turf.

Everyone is ecstatic now. Maybe it's true that winning cures everything. At least for tonight. I've been on varsity three years. I already know Coach's style. He wants to talk us down before our heads get too big and we start thinking we're invincible.

I see his point, but the humble people on this team are going to stay humble. The cocky ones are going to stay cocky. I'm somewhere in between.

When he finally sends everyone else on their way, he calls out to me. His topknot is loosely held together by the time we connect.

"Good win. Celebrate, but you need to figure out what's stopping you from being more aggressive on the field, and what you can do to fix that. You're going to have to attack. When teams key in on Meegan, how do you respond?"

I know Coach isn't picking on me. He'll say this exact thing to the left and right forwards. It just bugs me because I'm always making the right soccer play before anything else. And the right soccer play is to assist the person who's most likely to make the shot. Would it be nice to have the glory of the goal sometimes? Sure, but the good feeling of being the hero will never supersede the horrible feeling of being the disappointment when you miss. It's not worth the risk.

After that, I head back to pack up my stuff. Most of my teammates are already leaving. I keep an eye out for Kai. I can't let my nonresponse be my reaction to him showing up for me. Not that I could do much more, with the pact in effect. I don't want to risk my team's trust.

"Good game."

Those are the perfect postgame words, especially coming from

HIM. I turn in the direction of the voice and drop everything. My backpack lands at HIS feet. My phone hits the track surrounding the field. My ball rolls to the turf. And, as if I've been put in the game after a long stint on the bench, the sweat that threatened to turn me into an icicle a few minutes ago suddenly kicks back up into something warm and persistent.

I go for the phone. Kai trots off for my ball. He comes back with it tucked under his arm and tosses my soccer bag over his shoulder. "I didn't mean to scare you. I tried to make noise as I was coming up."

"Yeah. I was..." I look down at my phone. "Your voice. It's..."

Like your skin. Deep and rich.

He searches my face. Eyes flitting to every corner. If he doesn't stop I'm going to start dropping stuff again.

"Your voice is very authoritative."

He stops searching. His eyes meet mine. "People always tell me that. I don't hear it."

I take a long step, propelling us toward the parking lot. The only people still here are our coaches, the trainer, a few parents locking up concessions, and security.

"I didn't know you were coming. Have you seen me play here before?"

I first saw him play at a national tournament two years ago that hosts boys and girls simultaneously. I was at the end of my club season. He was in the middle of his.

The first thing I noticed about him was his game. Watching him was like taking a personalized course in how to fix all the holes in mine. I keep my head up and have good vision on the field, but Kai always sees the third option, which is usually something opposing defenses aren't ready for. I wanted—want to be that.

The next thing I knew, I was noticing him at school, how cute he is. And when he randomly started following me on social media and sending me soccer clips, I realized he'd noticed my game too. He actually told me to my face, with no hesitation, that I play some of the most crisp balls he's ever seen.

He nods. "This is the first time I caught a whole game, though." He runs a hand along the ticket shack as we pass by. "Is it okay that I came, with the no-dating pact and everything?"

I'm too afraid to look around us to see if anyone's paying attention. From the outside, I don't think we'll look date-y. I'm used to keeping my distance from Kai. Then again, I don't want to make him think he did something wrong by supporting me.

I smile up at him. "I'm really happy you came. But no more winking or waiting for me after."

He smiles and takes a step away. "I knew it was a bad idea. I just wanted to make sure you saw me."

I laugh. "I definitely saw you."

Both of our smiles fade and it's quiet for a while. I know I need to say something but I'm not sure what. This is the most alone we've ever been. I want him to feel like there's something to wait twenty-three more days for. He must be thinking the same thing because we both start talking at the same time. He pulls his lips between his teeth and nods for me to go.

"I just wondered what you thought of the game." I glance quickly to and away from him. "It moves a little slower than club and there are some hacks, but there's some talent too."

"Like you." I look over, expecting to see a flirty smile, but he's serious. It makes me feel good that he's not giving a compliment just for points. He means it. "You know you could've had two goals easy, right? Not even including the one at the end, which I would have passed too because it was fun."

I sigh. "You know how it is. I'm always looking for the best soccer play. Doing what my team needs."

He starts to say something but tries to pass it off as a sound of agreement. I literally see words die in his throat.

I swallow hard. "Say it. Go 'head."

He shakes his head. "No. No. You have to play your game your way. And you know how I feel about your passing."

I stop him at the trunk of my car and take my soccer bag from him. "I'm asking. I value your opinion."

He scratches his hairline and grimaces. "Your team needed the game to be decided before two minutes to go. It was wide open for you."

I don't miss the relief on his face, as if holding this information back was painful.

I start running the game back in my head, mentally checking for the spots he's talking about. "I didn't see it."

"You weren't looking. You never looked at the net as an option the entire game." He leans against my trunk. "I could be wrong, though. If you send me the video I can go through and try to show you. If you want. I mean, I don't know. You really had a good game."

I laugh at how his being uncomfortable with critiquing my game is warring with his need to critique. "I would like it if you could do that for me. Even if it's going to be super embarrassing."

He scrunches his face and stuffs his hands into his pockets. "It would make me look like an asshole, wouldn't it? Like I think I'm an expert or something."

I click my tongue against my teeth and narrow my eyes at him, but I'm smiling. "It would be embarrassing for me. Obviously."

"For *you*? Why?"

"You know why."

He shakes his head slowly and raises his eyebrows. "I don't."

If this boy doesn't realize that I genuinely just want him to think I'm good, then I'm not going to embarrass myself any further by putting the idea in his head. It's not like I don't know there were things I could've done better. There always are, but they're going to stand out to Kai more than they are to the average player.

But then my conversation with Winston from earlier plays in my head. The whole thing about a complete answer. Technically, I haven't really given an answer at all.

I wrestle my key fob from the front pocket of my backpack, unlock my door, and throw everything inside. "It's embarrassing because it's you."

He swallows hard and licks his lips. For the first time ever, he's the one searching for words. I'm not sure yet if this is in a good way or in a *slow down, you've said too much* way.

He looks at me as if I've accused him of something and he's trying to prove his innocence. "I'm really not that big of a deal."

That makes me laugh out loud and I feel a little less exposed.

He smiles. "What's so funny?"

"You're funny," I tell him, and take a deep breath. "Don't worry. You can be completely honest. I can take it."

He studies me again. "Okay, Dru."

"Okay, Kai." I smile. "Thank you for coming."

"You're welcome." He looks around before opening his arms wide, and it's a second before I realize he's asking for a hug. "Just this one time. No more cheating after tonight."

It's new, but instinctively I fall into his very warm body, realizing all the issues too late. "I'm so sorry. I am the sweatiest, stinkiest mess."

He laughs a little. "I assumed that. It doesn't bother me."

He's the typical soccer player—everything from his knees to his core is muscled, lifted, and ripped. His chest and arms, not so much. But still somehow the hug feels comfortable, like something I'll look forward to doing again.

Ugh. This is always how things start, all comfortable and sweet. Then somehow not anymore.

I pull away first. "See you later."

He nods and waits until I'm safely in my car before heading to his own.

22 DAYS REMAINING

Kai: 22 Days

That was his last text at midnight. I didn't see it until this morning when I went to send him a link to last night's game. And when I saw those six characters I was thumb-tied again. Who needs a *good morning* when you're getting a *22 Days*.

Dru: Stop
Dru: Don't actually. I like the countdown.

Kai: 😂 I wasn't going to stop.

Thinking about that conversation makes me excited to get to school just to see him.

That in mind, as I pace the kitchen waiting for the chance to talk to my dad alone, I send to Winston what I would've sent to Kai had he not texted me first. I have to let Boyfriend know I'm thinking about him.

Dru: Girlfriend Dru: Hey. 😍

Then I stuff my phone in my back pocket so I can't see it. I'm expecting anxiety about the potential romantic back-and-forth with my friend but it doesn't come.

That's probably because after all Winston's stressing and the ick I felt when he first tried out being my boyfriend, playing our roles wasn't actually that hard. Our conversation during me-and-you time was to be expected. He's a good listener.

The pregame message was a whole other thing. And he did it without too much flinching. I'm about to watch the video again when he texts me back.

> **Winston:** Boyfriend Winston: Thinking about you too.

That would be the perfect first thing to hear in the morning from a guy I like. I imagine Kai's name at the top of the screen. If a message like that were from him, I would be a puddle of speechless nothing right now. I respond with all I would have the capacity for.

> **Dru:** Girlfriend Dru: ☺ I was just about to replay your pregame message from yesterday.

> **Winston:** Were you?

Was I?
I was.

The floor creaks in the second-floor hallway. I head toward the stairs to see who's coming down. I'm relieved to see my dad all by himself in a T-shirt and jogging pants.

He smiles when he sees me. "Hey, baby. It's just me. Your mom will—"

"Dad," I whisper yell and press my finger to my lips.

He pulls his lips between his teeth and bites down to let me know that he understands we need to have a private conversation. Then for some reason, as if Mom doesn't know we're home, he tiptoes, taking each step like he just learned how. I motion for him to come on. Still, as he follows me to the laundry room, he stops in the kitchen to grab a banana.

Once we're inside I try to close the door, but this is a one-person kind of space and my dad's frame screams *I used to play football*. It gets in the way until we're playing a game of Twister. I give up, but not without peeking out the door to make sure Mom hasn't somehow come downstairs without us hearing.

I hold my phone in front of him and point at the screen, where I've pulled up the broadcasting summer program web page. Dad isn't wearing his readers, so he has to push the phone farther away from us and even still tilt his head slightly back. I hold as he scrolls.

"I don't know anything about this one." He shakes his head. "But there are so many programs on campus, and unless there's a problem, it's mostly athletics that come my way, you know."

I look at him seriously. "This is just between me and you, like forever. No pillow talk. No predinner-drinks conversation. No small talk in the car."

He scratches his face, just outside his goatee. "Don't tell your mother. I can handle that."

I want to, but I don't have time right now to question exactly how he plans to keep a secret from her. "Winston has been rejected from this program three times and he wants to know why."

"Three times?" Dad makes a face that says he's over it. "I say fuck 'em."

My dad can frequently be heard saying a rejection is a *blessing in disguise. When one door closes another one opens. Go where you're wanted. They don't know what they're missing...* Just to name a few. *Fuck 'em* is no surprise to me.

I roll my eyes. "That's not what he wants to say, Dad. He just wants to know why so that maybe he can correct the problem when he applies this last time. He doesn't want you pulling any strings or anything. He wants to do this himself."

Dad nods. "I get where he's coming from, but using a resource isn't a bad thing. Even if I make some calls, he still has to show up ready."

"I tried to tell him that, but he has his reasons." Reasons that I get more than anybody would probably realize. When I think about the way he couldn't even look me in the eye yesterday, it makes me want to make sure this is handled exactly the way he thinks it should be. "He especially doesn't want his family to know he's been rejected all those times."

"Okay. I got it." Dad rubs his hands together and I know an assignment is coming. "I'm going to make sure it's looked into and get back to him. But I need him to do something for me. This thing is so important he's willing to risk being rejected again, he has to have something he wants to get out of it. Five specific goals. Order of importance. In my inbox by tomorrow."

At school, Aubrey and I are sitting on the floor in front of my locker and she's venting to me about her SAT prep course and how her projected math score isn't improving. Somehow, listening to my friend is helping me relax. I'm a little nervous for the second district game tomorrow.

"I'm just trying to understand what I'm doing wrong that other people with worse grades are scoring higher than me."

Before I say anything, I really think about this because I'm one of the worsers. "I don't feel like I did anything special. What does the tutor say? Does she help at all?"

She looks between me and the test prep book on her lap several times. "What she's saying doesn't make any sense."

I side-eye her. "What's she saying?"

Aubrey does this sort of nod/shake thing that makes her look like a bobblehead. "She said we should take a break."

"Wait." I pause, holding my palms up like a superhero stopping the force of something. "Did your tutor quit you?"

Aubrey's bobblehead thing is still going.

My eyes go wide as I point at the test prep book. "Ma'am. Taking pretests constantly, spending every spare second you can thinking about the SAT, is the opposite of a break."

She looks at me like she's never heard a less intelligent argument. "I can't take a break, Dru." Her voice is calm, but her chest is heaving like it's taking everything she has to keep her feelings in. "My parents can only help out so much. I need to qualify for more scholarships."

But then I get an idea. "LeArra might have some advice. She did really well on all the standardized tests. She might not even respond to me, but I can ask."

I take out my phone and start a text to my sister. I ignore her last message confirming I saw that another day of wedding dress shopping has been added to the calendar for this weekend. I want to look forward to that. I did the first time. But if I said I was now, I'd be lying to myself.

Aubrey sighs next to me and says in an exhausted voice, "Here comes your boyfriend."

This isn't the first time she's said those words to me. It's been teasingly before, but now it seems really plausible. Since Kai asked me out and came to a game it feels more like we're working toward some mutually agreed-upon thing. And that thing is scary.

"Hey, Kai," Aubrey sings as we both stand.

He gives Aubrey a nod and turns to me. "Hey, Dru."

I try to speak, but my voice skitters around until I clear my throat. Even after all the flirty texts and the hug, he makes me so nervous. "Hey."

Aubrey thanks me for messaging LeArra and gives a cute little wave to us both, and announces she has a long walk to class. She couldn't be more obvious. Normally that would be fine, but I need her to stay. I can't have my teammates thinking something is going on. Not that I expect Kai to hug me again or anything, but I have to be very careful.

I give her a look. I try to put begging in it, but she doesn't seem to get it.

All he's doing is standing here. It's harmless, nothing anyone can question, but still, I glance up and down the hall, looking for my teammates. Riley's first period is in this area. If anybody has the chance to spot us, she's the one.

"Hey," he says again.

"Hey," I say again.

Like last night, we both laugh and then try to speak at the same time and then both go quiet. Maybe it's wishful thinking, but I let myself go there. Could he be nervous too?

I nod at him to talk.

It's still a second before he says anything, as if he doesn't trust either of us not to ruin the opportunity. "I took a look at the game, and I marked where I thought you could've taken a shot."

"Oh." I try to shake my head clear of the nerves I feel just having him in my space, and shift into my game mindset. "Already?"

He presses his lips into a straight line. "Too eager, huh?"

Heat rushes to my face. He *is* nervous. "Not at all, or if it is, I like it, so it's okay."

He breathes out a laugh as he holds his phone up between us. He watches me as I scoot in close to see. "Are you sure you want my feedback? I don't want you to think I go around trying to tell people how to play."

I blink at him but can't hold any eye contact because I know I'm about to sound like his number one fan again. "You can tell me how to play. It's fine."

He nods, then shakes his head. "Don't worry. Your game is near perfect."

That's obviously an overexaggeration. No matter how many times I see him play I don't have any suggestions. *That's* near perfect. Still, I blush. "Thank you for saying that."

He looks me in the eyes. "I'm going to get you to believe me too."

Heat creeps up my neck. He waits a second like he knows that's what's happening and is giving it a chance to pass. "Here we go."

He slides his finger along the screen, stopping the playback to show me five opportunities for me to shoot where I chose not to. I don't disagree with any of them, except it's not just a matter of having a shot. Something I've tried to explain to people before.

I shift away from him. "Shooting might not be a part of my game."

His forehead wrinkles. "What do you mean?"

I stretch into an arch, the whole of what I'm about to say making me uncomfortable. "I mean I practice shooting all the time, but it never plays out in the games."

"Oh. I can help with that." He nods and unzips the front pocket of his backpack to slide his phone in, all nervousness undetectable now. "I used to go to this training when I was younger. It changed how I looked at shooting and finishing. I still remember and use everything they taught me. I can show you."

I play with the strap adjustments of my backpack. This is a very nice offer that I'm going to accept. But since it's coming from Kai, the person I want to impress the most, it's a little overwhelming.

He must view this as a no-brainer because he starts solidifying plans. "I have a game tonight. You could come and I could show you some of the drills after that. I'm sure one of the fields'll be open."

I tilt my head down in case I can't tamp my smile as much as I intend to. "You want me to come to your game?"

Inviting someone to your high school game is an overture, yes. Going is reciprocating interest, definitely. But club games are attended mostly by family, and if you're lucky, college coaches. Whenever anybody beyond that shows up, I assume the connection is a little more serious. And way beyond the bounds I suggested for my team during this playoff season.

At the same time, this *is* for my team. It could maybe help.

He looks down the hall, thinking. "Unless you think it's breaking the pact or something?"

"No," I say quickly. "This is for and about soccer. It's fine. Maybe I'll invite one of them if that's okay. And we'll probably be a little late. We have practice."

"Yeah that's fine." His eyes connect with mine. "See you tonight, then."

" 'Kay." I smile.

He smiles back.

22 DAYS REMAINING, PART 2

Winston's leaning back against his locker with one foot up, holding court with a group of guys. They would probably be his best friends if he didn't already have Jake, who's sitting on the ground with his laptop on his knees.

When I'm a few steps away, Winston arrives at what must be the punch line because everyone busts out laughing. He stands up straight when he notices me. After goodbyes to Winston and nods to me, everyone disperses.

He leans close to my ear, smiling. "Boyfriend likes your side braid."

Immediately, my free hand goes to my shoulder where my box braids meet in a thick, messy, interwoven mass. It's my answer to relief from my heavy soccer bun, but also not wanting to feel hair all over my neck. It's designed to be functional, not noticed or liked.

Still, it's nice that he noticed what no one else did. Kai didn't. Not that I'm comparing.

I—Girlfriend Dru smiles back.

His smile gets bigger. It's hypnotizing. He leans back against the locker and puts his foot up again, like he owns the hallway. This is the confidence most people see. Probably the only two people who know he doesn't feel that all the way through to the inside are with him right now.

I'm surprised to hear myself say, "Girlfriend Dru likes when you smile like that."

"Really?" His voice is high, and his eyebrows go up in surprise. "Is that why you were going to replay the video I sent? To see me smile?"

I step closer and shake my head. *"Girlfriend Dru"*—I, for some reason, feel the need to stress the POV—"liked your smile, but mostly she just wanted to hear that part again about not needing any luck."

His smile and the glint in his eye turn mischievous, and he's not leaning back relaxed anymore. Whatever he's about to say next is something he can't *not* say. "How many times has she rewatched it?"

Apparently, the same thing that has him caught up has me too, because I say, "Still counting."

Winston blinks at me, surprised. Shoot, I'm surprised. But it's true. She's going to watch it again.

There's a shift below, reminding me that Jake is there. My smile fades immediately. There's no way Jake didn't hear the last few minutes. Out of context, it's weird. Then again, maybe he'll think we're just joking around. Winston and I would never talk to each other the way we just did. Even though I kind of meant what I said. His smile *was* nice.

I look down at Jake and then up at Winston very pointedly, signaling that we can't keep going on like this with Jake here. But Jake seems to be the one to know what's expected, even though he's not looking at me.

"I'll go. I have to stop in my advisory before class anyway," Jake says.

I look between them. Winston shrugs as Jake walks away.

"Is that some twin telepathy or did you send him a sign I couldn't see?"

Winston leans back against the locker and puts his foot up again. "I have no idea. As soon as I registered the look you gave me, he got up."

"That's weird." I'm running my hand over my braid again, wishing I had a mirror to verify that there's actually something to like about it, when a thought occurs to me. I grab him by his sleeve. "It didn't seem like he thought that conversation was any different than normal. Did you tell him what you're helping me with?"

He glances at where I have him and chuckles. "I didn't. But can I? Please?"

I frown and rock back on my heels.

"You know how Jake is. He won't even care." He shrugs. "But I'll be better at this if I'm not tiptoeing around him. We live together. I'm going to slip."

Despite the fact that he didn't seem to be tiptoeing a minute ago, that makes sense. And I want Winston to be able to do his best.

I stare him down threateningly and let him go. "Fine. You can tell Jake, but nobody else. Aubrey is the only other person who knows."

He steps closer, protecting our circle. "I promise. I won't tell anybody else."

I keep my stare. "I'll know if you do."

That makes him laugh.

I blow out a puff of air, pretending to be irritated even though his smile makes me want to smile too. "Anyway. My dad's going to look into that thing for you."

His teasing smile fades, and he stands up straight.

"But now you have an assignment." I frown, expecting at least a little pushback, but Winston just nods for me to continue. "My dad is really into goal setting. By tomorrow, he wants you to email him five specific goals for the summer program if you get in. And when he says specific, he means specific. He will come back at you about not being able to achieve something you can't even wholly visualize."

Winston looks off into space as if already writing the goals in his head. "That makes sense. I can do that."

"So." My hands start to tremble a little and I lace my fingers together and hold them still on my thighs. What I'm about to say next is what I'm here for, but that doesn't stop me from being nervous.

I see him notice my hands. Immediately, lines appear between his eyebrows like he's going from thoughtful about his own future to concerned. I put my hands in my pockets.

"I know it's barely been twenty-four hours, but do you have any theories about me yet? I'm supposed to be going to Kai's game tonight. I don't want to be grooming him to be perfect for somebody else already without even knowing it."

He bites his bottom lip and stares somewhere over my head. "Is that...a date? I thought—"

"It's not a date. It's soccer," I say sternly. "He's helping me work on shooting. I'm going to see if Capri or someone will go with me."

He lifts his eyebrows and nods. "You been taking my advice? Giving Dru answers?"

I keep my face as neutral as possible so he doesn't get too full of himself.

It doesn't work.

He tilts his head back and looks over his nose at me. "And he still wants to spend time with you. Weird. I'll take my thank-you in chocolate."

"Have *you* tried *my* advice?" I shoot back a little teasingly, but also with a little attitude. He can't be getting full of himself because he thinks he's figured me out.

His face lights up. "I did. Jake sent me the latest draft of his book. It's really good so far." But then his face goes soft as he leans in. "He said he didn't think any of us would want to read his book and he didn't want us to feel obligated if he asked. I don't understand how he was thinking any of that."

"You're welcome," I say smugly, and shake my head.

I turn to take a step in the opposite direction, almost running right into Riley. I stop on my tiptoes, nearly tripping. She doesn't have the same problem. It's like she was waiting there.

"Hey, Dru." Her words carry a singsongy peppiness I'm not really used to hearing from her. I love it when the winning feeling carries over into the next day.

I still feel it too. "Hey, girl. Practice better be chill today."

"Doubt it." She looks from me to Winston, drawing my attention to the fact that he's still right behind me for some reason. She looks back at me. I wave. She throws me the peace sign. Then she's gone.

I love it when we're able to just be ourselves without all the tension. Hopefully it lasts at least through the next game.

I smile to myself and take another step but stop when I realize Winston is at my side.

He sniffs a laugh. "Boyfriend is walking you to class. Is that okay?"

I roll my eyes at myself and start toward my classroom. "Yes, it's fine. Sorry, Boyfriend."

We turn the corner into the next hall and end up trailing none other than Jayden and Malia. The most recent couple to spawn from my failed relationships. They've been together nine months.

Out of the three months Jayden and I were together, two of them were perfect. I had started to forget all my fails and what they might mean. But by the end, when I decided to break up with him, I couldn't figure out if he even liked me. I got my answer three days later when he was holding hands with Malia in the halls. She was smiling at him, and he wasn't even speaking or emoting. She was just happy about his face and its proximity to hers.

And I understood it. Jayden is sweet, and he has the cutest gap-toothed smile.

Malia is short, hourglass shaped, and soft-spoken. I wanted to be mad at her, but how can you be mad at someone you have to lean toward to hear.

I wonder if Jayden ever suggests just-me-and-you time. He never said anything like that to me. Does he send encouraging videos before her important events? Or just wish her good luck?

Winston made it seem so easy and logical to ask Jayden why things unfolded the way they did. But he doesn't know the whole story. If he did, he'd understand why, of all my boyfriends, Jayden is the one I'm most afraid to ask.

Curiosity doesn't feel like enough to approach somebody I rarely speak to. Why would he even remember why things changed between us? Maybe to him things had just run their course and that was it. It's possible that this was only earth-shattering to me. After all, I'm the person this keeps happening to. Jayden is obviously happy and has no issues riding off into the sunset.

They're walking so close, they're touching from shoulder to wrist, and every step or two his jeans make a swish sound against her tennis skirt. The accidental brush of the back of Winston's hand against mine tells me we've drifted almost as close as they are.

"You walk behind them like this every day?" he whispers.

"If I'm lucky they're behind me."

"Maybe you should—"

I lean away from him when a snippet of their conversation is clear to me. I don't mean to listen, but I can't help it. Jayden's voice is cautious and gentle. "If it doesn't work out I'm still going to be here."

She's staring at him the way I used to, all admiration.

She grabs his hand and squeezes it, letting him know that he's said the perfect thing, or at least that she appreciates him trying. And I don't know how I know, but I'm confident now that every minute they spend together has a just-me-and-you-time vibe.

Winston slows our pace and leans into me again, letting our closeness tell me that what he's about to say is sensitive. "Is that how you guys were?"

Something pulls my attention to their connected hands. I watch them as I think. "A little bit, yeah. I mean, she never looks like she's trying, and I definitely tried sometimes. I didn't want to be oh and eight. And he told me things that made me have to talk to him the way he just talked to her, yeah."

He told me a lot in the beginning. He was mostly worried about his grades or his parents. I got good at knowing which one was on his mind just by watching his facial expressions.

"Did you give him Dru answers?"

My stomach drops a little at the memory of getting comfortable enough to tell Jayden certain things, and in the end, being wrong. But also knowing the reason I was wrong was me, not him.

I shrug. I don't feel like answering that.

Winston nods up ahead in Jayden and Malia's direction.

"If you wanted what they have, I don't think you were wrong to try. Even if it didn't work out." He nudges my shoulder and gives me a small smile that makes me want to believe what he's saying. "And I don't think you'd be wrong if you decided to try again."

I don't have a way to let him know as effortlessly as Malia showed Jayden, but that's exactly what I needed to hear.

I turn toward my class.

"Hey, Girlfriend."

I look at him over my shoulder. "Yeah."

He looks a little hesitant. "Me-and-you time at lunch?"

"Yes, Boyfriend."

22 DAYS REMAINING, PART 3

When I get to Kai's game, I'm still thinking about what Winston said earlier. I have been all day. I'm not wrong if I decide to try again.

This is my favorite kind of night for soccer. And I'm not just saying that because I'm at Kai's game. It's sixty degrees and dark enough that the lights are coming up, but the sun is also setting across from the bleachers. There's just enough of a breeze that if I was playing I wouldn't have to worry about overheating. And it's not so cold that my joints would feel stiff.

This game would be worth it no matter the weather, though. The defense on both sides has been a wall, and it's three minutes away from ending in a tie. Now things are getting a little more urgent with everyone, including defenders, looking for shots.

I tuck my hands between myself and the metal bench of the three-tiered bleachers. I'm alone. No one on my team wanted to add even more soccer to their day when they didn't have to. They also encouraged me to get some tips from someone known to be good at shooting. I'm feeling a little bit out of place among so many parents, with nobody my age to make me look normal.

Assuming Kai belongs to one of the two sets of Black families here, I sit as far away from them as possible. I don't want to be the weird, random girl hovering. No matter how I'm introduced there's going to be an appraisal. If my family had any sons, my mother and sisters would do it. I would like to avoid that for as long as I can.

It would be just my luck that I've made all the wrong assumptions and I'm sitting next to his white adoptive father or stepfather right now. The way my eyes have been glued to Kai, it would be obvious why I'm here to anyone who's paid attention. *Most* people's eyes are probably glued to him, though. He's the best player on the field.

If the lesson is to try to give your team what it needs most, then Kai's providing the best example. The only issue is that the rest of his team isn't quite ready for his ability to see things before they've fully developed.

His teammates' inability to keep up has turned him all attack. He's taken five shots in five minutes, and they've been good ones. But the opposing team's goalie has made two unbelievable saves, defenders blocked two shots, and the other one deflected off Kai's own teammate.

Somehow, he doesn't look defeated or less determined after any of it. He's still looking for his shot when he comes up the field. After those five in five, he never finds it again, though. Still, when he sits through the postgame and says goodbye to his teammates, he looks upbeat.

But once he gets to his family—thankfully, I guessed right—I can tell by the high pitch of their voices, they're trying to build him up. He's let them see his real disappointment. Not everything that happened in the game just rolled off him.

When they turn to leave and he points in my direction, I assume he's letting his family know he's staying with me. I pretend to be looking at something else as opposed to being deeply engrossed in their family business. Still, I can feel it. I don't get to avoid that appraisal after all.

I hope that their looks and whatever they say to him don't make this training session date-y. I've been able to sit here and watch him as a player and not as a guy who makes me speechless. I'd like to keep it that way.

I move to the last row on the bleachers and smile as he swaggers over. Even in a loss, that confidence—the way his shoulders sway a little but never fall as he walks, how long he can maintain eye contact without even a flinch—never goes away.

He sets his bag down next to me and uses his jersey to wipe sweat from his forehead. I'm not sure how much it helps. His jersey is so wet the dark blue looks jet-black. Now I don't feel so bad about the state I was in after my game.

"I should've invited you to a game I knew we'd win."

I nod at him enthusiastically. "It was a really good game. And I love watching you play so..."

He shifts a little and smiles at the ground. Somehow, I think I made him blush. Then it makes me blush.

He juggles the ball between both feet. Then one foot, up to his knees. Then to his head and catches it in his hands. Then he proceeds to do an Around the World, something you would never do in an actual soccer game, but definitely in warm-ups if you're trying to intimidate the other team. Having this skill usually means impeccable touch. I can't even do it consistently.

"You're not showing off, are you?" I try not to sound impressed, but it doesn't work.

He does another Around the World and traps the ball under his foot. I guess I have my answer.

I shake my head and laugh as I pull out of my slides and step into my cleats. I hop off the bench and kick the ball from under his foot.

He laughs and chases me onto the field. "I just played a whole game. Go easy on me."

"Nope. I had a very hard practice. You don't see me asking for special treatment," I tease. "Who was that you were talking to after the game?"

"My mom and her sister."

I look up at him. "Are they really into the game?"

He moves his hand from side to side between us, indicating *kind of.* "They're into *me.* Thinking I'm the best player in every game. Accusing the refs of not calling fouls for me or wrongly on me. Questioning my teammates for what they see as deliberately not passing to me when I'm open. But they don't get much about the actual game."

I laugh a little and stop the ball with my foot. "That sounds like a dream. My parents never played but *over*stand everything. They know all the kinks in my game, how to fix them, and how good I can be."

"I saw them the other day." He nods appreciatively. "When you get the ball, they lean in. They're into you. Your mom wears your number."

I smack my lips at him. "I never said they didn't represent. But I'll call you the next time they're giving me a postgame critique. You can hear it for yourself."

I take a few steps back from the ball and shoot it recklessly from where I'm standing outside the penalty box. I make it. Upper ninety. Perfect placement.

Kai's eyes go wide. "Hold on a second. Be right back."

He trots off and comes back with a bag of balls he had in his trunk, like any good soccer player. Meanwhile, I get my ball out of the net.

He unleashes the bag of balls and steps back. "Do it again."

I shrug and shoot all nineteen balls. I call where a few of them are going to go into the net. A few times he tells me where to send them. I only miss once.

When I'm done, Kai tilts his head and stares at me. "If I could shoot like that, we would've won today. Your leg is powerful as hell."

His eyes travel up my lower half in a curious way. Of course my body takes it some other kind of way. I tense.

His eyes come back up to mine. "If you wanted to hang out and pretend it's about soccer so you don't feel guilty, you could've just said that. You could teach *me* something about shooting from outside the box."

I smack my lips again. "*You* invited *me*."

He shrugs one shoulder as if to say he couldn't help it.

I follow him to the net to pick up all the balls I've shot.

"So why don't you shoot?"

"Um..." I think about giving him the answer I always give. The one that's true about half the time, and I stand by it. I don't shoot because I put what's best for my team first. And what's best for my team is a midfielder who distributes the ball, not one who looks for her own shot. But the Dru answer hasn't failed me yet with Kai.

This is me deciding to try again.

I walk two of the balls I've picked up over to the bag as I try to figure out how to word this. Everything happens in my head. Bringing it outside of there is like actually trying to crack through my own skull.

"Before the games, I always think I'm going to shoot, try to be dangerous at least." I hold the bag open so he can put in the few balls he's collected. Then he takes the bag from me so we can be more efficient about collecting the rest. I barely get the next part out before I stop myself. "But then I can't do it."

We stop at the net and both bend down to pick up several balls, casting long shadows on the turf. "You mean like you can't get open?"

"No." I drag the word out as I think about how to explain it without looking like an idiot in front of him.

"Yeah. Because you look pretty open a lot to me. You don't need as much space as you think you do." He tilts his head as he closes the bag with its drawstring. "Is it a prep touch issue? It's hard to simulate game speed but we can try if you think that'll help."

I put my hand up for him to pause. I know what I want to say. "I mean my leg is refusing to follow the signal my brain is sending it."

He scratches behind his ear. The look on his face says he's really trying to absorb my words. And honestly, I'm kind of afraid of what will happen if he does. What will he think of me? Everything about him says he's never had my kind of problem. "But wouldn't that mean you're not sending the signal? Your leg can't refuse."

"I meant that figuratively, not literally." I busy myself with checking that all the balls have been put in the bag, so I don't have to maintain eye contact when I say the next part. "But I guess you're right. I'm obviously not sending the signal."

We both turn back toward where we've left our soccer bags in the bleachers. "Why don't you send the signal? Not to keep repeating myself, but you have a great shot."

"Yeah, when it's just you here. But this isn't a game." I look around the field, drawing his attention to the absence of players.

He turns to me, walking backward. "And when there is a goalie, and defenders?"

"The net gets really small or something."

"That's easier to fix than touch or technique."

I've actually heard that before, from my coaches and at special training my parents have sent me to. You can't learn talent or athleticism, but you can build confidence. It's one of those things that make sense, I can see that it is, but it just doesn't play out that way. Confidence isn't easy to build.

I make a noncommittal noise.

"You just have to get out of your head," he says as we approach the bleachers. He pulls his phone out of his backpack. "I read these a long time ago, but I think they can help you. I'll send you the titles."

My phone buzzes in my backpack with texts. "Books?"

He looks at me over his phone. "You don't like to read?"

I look from him to the field and back. "It's fine."

And that's the absolute truth. I don't love or hate reading. I don't seek it out, but if someone puts something interesting in front of me, I'll give it my attention. If there was any tone in my response, it's because if there's a book about the mental side of sports that I haven't read, it hasn't been written yet.

If there's a TED talk or some autobiography by some GOAT, I've read it, watched it, or at least attempted to. There are shelves upon shelves of these books at my house, and when my parents see an issue—not just in sports but in life—they are happy to give me some wisdom first and then back it up with a PhD or athlete POV.

It's worked for them and my sisters, but not for me. At least not yet.

And even if they were going to help, I don't have time to read anything that isn't assigned by a teacher. I have the second district game tomorrow and then the district final three days after that.

I take my phone out of my bag and check his recommendations. Just as I thought, I've read every single one. I don't want to tell him that, though. I don't want him to think I don't appreciate him trying to help, because I do. Also, the more we talk about this, the more likely he is to ask me questions I don't have answers to yet. I'll end up feeling like a loser. He might even think I'm one.

This isn't like talking to Winston, where he can come to some conclusions, somehow overlooking my loser because he knows me. I have to come up with the words to make Kai get it. I don't have them yet. I can't hold it against *him*, though. Maybe we just need to find something else to talk about besides soccer. But what?

"You have a lot of homework tonight?"

He chuckles as we both sit down to unlace our cleats. That was the worst subject change ever. "Are you asking me if I'm busy? Because I think us hanging out anywhere other than here would be hard to explain to your team."

I smile. I guess that question could've sounded like I was on my way to asking him to hang out tonight. "I—"

"For the record, I'm free to go get something to eat. Just putting that out there if you're on the fence."

I bite my bottom lip as heat rises up the back of my neck. "I was really just asking about homework."

He scratches the side of his face and does something between a grimace and a smile. "Oh. Misfire. My bad."

I laugh.

Kai stands up, offering his hand to help me off the bench. I don't need it. He knows I don't. But I take it. "Very close to twenty-one days."

I don't know if it's because those words remind me of how my time to figure out my issues is dwindling or what, but they feel like a backhanded whack against the crown of my head. I just nod.

We're quiet as we walk to my car. I don't know what he's thinking, but I'm looking for something else to talk about that won't lead to talking about my shooting. Just like the night he came to see me play, when we get there, Kai opens his arms. "Just one more cheat."

I smile up at him. Just one more.

20 DAYS LEFT, BUT HOPEFULLY THE LAST DAY OF WEDDING DRESS SHOPPING

Kai: 20 Days

Dru: 😉

Winston: Boyfriend Winston hopes everything goes okay today.

Dru: Tell him don't bother.

Winston: Dru . . .

Dru: What? I just don't want my boyfriend to waste his time.

Winston: 😳

We're dress shopping…again. This time, we're at Bridal Magnifique, a salon we've never been to before, about an hour away from LeBeau. It's huge, but somehow still has the boutique vibe with two dedicated salespeople, champagne, tiny crudités, and a private salon for each of the three brides by appointment and their entourages. Somehow, we haven't exhausted all the bridal brands and dress types, but up to this point, I'm only getting half the dresses confused with those Moriah tried on before she decided on the gown formerly known as The One.

Luckily, we have pictures of not just the two finalist gowns but every dress she ever seriously considered. There's a total of eleven and the goal is to end with a top two—again. To streamline the process, we're comparing every dress she tries on today to the top eleven. Any gown in the top eleven falling short of a gown she tries on today will be displaced.

If it wasn't for the fact that I haven't had any champagne, I'd wonder if it was the drink making everything look good, because Moriah is perfect in every dress.

At the sight of her in a lacy mermaid-bottom gown, Mom fans herself and pinches the bridge of her nose to prevent tears from falling. LeArra steps up to get pictures from the front and back. Pictures means we're escalating the dress to the next level of comparison.

I tilt my head as I walk around the platform Moriah stands on. "It's pretty, but we don't like the heart-shaped necklines, right?"

Moriah whirls on me fast enough that the dress becomes a maze with its long train, and I expect her to fall right on top of me. "Who's 'we'?"

With those words, I swear the entire place goes silent. I'm surprised the ventilation system doesn't power down.

I look up at my sister, the pupils of her deep brown eyes nearly fully dilated and red creeping up in her golden-amber skin. I replay my words in my head. I have to be careful with the next thing that comes out of my mouth. I have to clarify without backtracking. Walking back a statement is a criminal offense in this family, even if your new stance means you agree with everyone else.

I spot motion in my peripheral. LeArra is suddenly not an attentive photographer anymore. She's beckoning with her fingers, pantomiming the need for more details. LeArra does this a lot when she's prepping to verbally fillet someone who has said something she considers poorly thought out. This particular *come hither* is for me. I'm about to be filleted.

She points all five fingers quickly toward me as if she's reached the end of a spell and has set it to taking shape. "Please, Dru. Clarify."

I side-eye them all. There's nothing more to what I've said than what I've said. "I meant the collective 'we' that Moriah, as the bride, is the leader of. What she doesn't like, we all don't like."

As she looks up at the white fabric-draped ceiling, Moriah slowly traces the heart that makes up the neckline of the dress with her finger. "Is that what you've been basing your opinion on all this time, what you think I like?"

I find myself following her eyes to the ceiling. "Well, yeah. It's about what you want. Your choice."

I'm not looking at any of them, but I feel Mom's attention turn to me. "Dru, we wouldn't be here if our opinion wasn't valued."

I take them all in, but only make significant eye contact with Mom. "I'm trying to help. She looks good in everything. If I don't remind her of her preferences, she'll never be able to choose." I point at my sister. "Look at her."

This is not an exaggeration. Moriah models every dress like it was meant for her. It helps that she's equally proportioned on top and bottom and perfectly fits the sample dresses. That isn't to say she doesn't have the Eason family signature thighs. It just means they're less muscular because she's the only one who isn't an athlete. Unlike me and LeArra, and unfortunately as far as she is concerned, her butt is never in the way of anything fitting just right.

We can't have everything, but Moriah has made it clear several times that she doesn't appreciate being the recipient of some dormant family body-type gene.

To add insult to her perceived exclusion, Moriah's coloring is from Mom, while LeArra and I are reddish-brown, like Dad. Even with that, she and LeArra are often mistaken for twins. My features are mixed up enough—I'm the only one with Mom's doe eyes and square jaw—that it doesn't register to strangers that it's not a duo but a trio unless it's explained.

Sometimes I wonder if people would stop comparing us physically if we were more alike in some other nonphysical way.

"This is making me feel like you might like sweetheart necklines but haven't been saying so because you think *I* don't like them." Moriah huffs, balling up the train behind her. The movement spurs the salesperson who follows her in and out of the fitting room into action.

I knew it. There was absolutely nothing I could say to make this better. There never is. That's why I keep my mouth shut around them.

I sigh. "It's not like how you're trying to make it sound."

LeArra sighs exasperatedly. "Who does this surprise? Dru was the tiebreaker for the poll and couldn't be bothered to find her opinion. This is a constant with her. Bet she was all into her soccer game last night, though."

I was. I had to be in order for us to win. But as much as I want to be into today with my sisters, I don't have to be for Moriah to win. They will win without me. Always.

"LeArra." By the way my oldest sister's name seeps from Mom's mouth, I know her eyes are closed without even looking. She's trying not to embarrass us all. Mom brags about how we're all smarter than her, but then she'll say something that makes us all feel apologetic and petty. She's trying not to do that in a room full of people.

Moriah throws her hands in the air. "LeArra, you have to take that back and apologize. Even if you're right. You can't expect Dru to be on our level all the time. She's seventeen. Think about when you were seventeen."

LeArra forcefully taps her hand against her chest. "I had to think about you guys. All the time. You don't get that."

Mom gives LeArra a threatening look.

"I'm not invalidating you. I get it." Moriah delivers this sympathetic look to LeArra. "We were both late for school when Dru had a diaper blowout, or a tantrum, or needed to be fed. We both had to forfeit our rooms. It's not just you."

"Girls," Mom warns. "I was late whenever any one of you had a blowout. I had to forfeit my *body*. Yet, I've managed to move past it somehow." Her voice is softer than normal. I can tell she's trying really hard not to ruin the day for Moriah but also wants to put an end to the back-and-forth.

I'm all for that. I'm not sure why I'm being faulted for things outside my control.

I slouch against the mirror. I never asked to take anyone's room. Moriah was moved into LeArra's room after our *parents* decided it was better not to have an infant interrupting their established routines. And then there's the whole thing about my mother realizing she was pregnant with me, nearly six months in and well after The Girls had been cast in, accepted, and excelled at their roles. This is why every mention of me comes with a *she's a mistake/she's in the way* undertone.

Everybody conveniently forgets none of us were planned. My parents started living by *if it happens, it happens* a few years into their marriage. Two years later came LeArra. Two years after that came Moriah. Nobody questions the timing of their arrival in any way, but I have to answer for showing up eight years after their world seemed set.

Actually, I'm not even a hundred percent sure what I've done today. LeArra thinks I'm too selfish to offer an opinion, Moriah thinks I'm what...too dishonest or people-pleasing, and my mom thinks I should give my opinion without being worried about the outcome. Any response I had would've made at least two of the other people in this room angry at me.

Mumbling about being even more confused than she was earlier, Moriah hops down off the pedestal, the salesperson shifting quickly behind her to protect the dress first and my sister from a spill second.

LeArra rolls her eyes over to me. "And, Dru, please don't start with that victim stuff. Can today just be about Moriah?"

I haven't even said anything. I try to change the look on my face because I know that's what she's reacting to. I've eliminated everything else they can pick at. My face is the only thing I can't see and honestly have very little control over.

"I was trying to let this be about Moriah. That's what got me in trouble."

"We'll talk when we get home." Mom makes direct eye contact with the two of us separately. This is a top-ten Momism. We don't act up in public. Period. "If we're going to get through today, you're all going to have to be quiet. Yes or no on the dresses. Anything else, keep your mouths closed."

"But, Mom, she hasn't even been updating the spreadsheet with RSVPs for the shower," LeArra starts in.

"Yes, I have," I whisper shriek. "Every day. I told you."

My oldest sister holds up her phone screen for all to see. "Not one update from you yesterday."

I lift my shoulders to my ears and put my palms out. "That's because there were no RSVPs yesterday."

LeArra mockingly imitates my movements. "How would I know that?"

Why wouldn't she just assume that? Why would she assume I'm slacking? And I've said it before, though I won't say it again because what's the point, but it doesn't make sense to give me a job she doesn't even trust me to do.

"What did I just say?" Mom looks pointedly at the door to the dressing room as if protecting the bride from this conversation is the most important thing she'll do today. "We'll talk when we get home."

LeArra leans in closer to Mom. "You always say that, but we never talk when we get home."

"Because usually you've come to your twenty-seven-year-old senses by then. But when we get home, if you still want to talk, let's."

Mom and LeArra stare each other down for a few seconds before LeArra withers. I pull my phone from the pocket of my cropped denim jacket. I don't want a stare-down with anyone, even though LeArra deserves worse than Mom effectively muting her by calling her immature. That worse thing would have to come from someone else, though. Anything I put out there has the efficacy of baby aspirin.

20 DAYS LEFT, PART 2

Winston's mom, aka my soon-to-be brother-in-law Rashid's mother, Ms. Teddy, comes rushing through the door with apologies for being late. She had other plans today and said she would do her best to make this weekend's impromptu dress-shopping trip. She has latched on to Moriah like the daughter she never had but always wanted.

We all love Ms. Teddy, and I'm sure it's nice for her to have some feminine energy around. It's her and four guys. The exact opposite of my family.

She and my mom look more like sisters than friends, down to the bone-straight hair pulled into a ponytail at the nape of their necks. The only difference is their style. My mom is classic—trousers and a blouse. Ms. Teddy is in a long, formless navy dress with spaghetti straps, an animal-print button down underneath, and wooden earrings that resemble wind chimes.

As I hug her, I get a text.

Winston: I'm here. Can you come out?

When the focus is clearly off me and on to welcoming her, I walk over to the glass storefront and spot Winston in the parking lot.

He's sitting in the driver's seat of his mom's car. Bobbing his head to music.

My last text to him, not Boyfriend Winston, was *I hate it here*. I'm not sure why either of them would show up. Doesn't sound like a good time to be had by any. I *am* happy to see him, though. I need to get out of here for a minute.

Come to think of it, maybe he has something to tell me about the camp at Midwestern. It's been a few days. Maybe he's heard back. If that's why he's come all this way, it has to be good news.

I angle toward the driver's door to see what he wants, but he motions for me to get in on the passenger's side. When I open the door, he pushes the volume button on the steering wheel until the music is a murmur of bass.

I fall into the car and look at him hopefully. I could use something to bring my energy up. "Did you hear back from Midwestern?"

His eyes go wide. "No. I haven't heard anything. Why? Did your dad say something? We've been emailing and he said he was looking into it, but that's it."

"Oh. No. Sorry." I grimace. "I haven't heard anything. I was just hoping. I'm ready to be happy for you, I guess."

"Me too." His face brightens. "Your dad's that guy, though. Love him."

"Just so you know. You're one of many to love Keith," I tell him with mock seriousness.

He deep sighs. "Yeah, I figured I wasn't the only one."

I laugh a little.

He pulls a pack of gum from the center console and offers it to me. We each take a piece and chew loudly, enjoying those first few moments before the flavor leaves and you're left with chewing out of obligation, then just sit there looking into nothing

"Boyfriend Winston would've been here sooner, but he had to convince his mom to come all the way back over to our side of town to pick him up after her appointment because Jake has the car."

I spot a pair of sunglasses in the cup holder. They must be Winston's, since Ms. Teddy came in with hers on the top of her head. I try them on and pull down the visor mirror. They're too big but also perfect. When I pull one leg up in the seat and face him, he gives an appreciative nod.

When the sunglasses slide down my nose a little, I peer at him over the top of the frame. "Is Girlfriend supposed to be expecting you?"

He stops mid-chew, making his dimples pop extra. "I wouldn't say expecting. But she should know that I would try to help relieve her stress if I could, and her text sounded very stressed."

That text was from regular old Dru, but I let him play his boyfriend card. So far I've been better at responding to than initiating Boyfriend Winston/Girlfriend Dru scenarios.

He reaches into the back seat, angling himself far enough back that his plain black T-shirt reveals a sliver of skin above the waistband of his jeans. He's not trying to give me a show but sometimes clothes that are long enough for him are also too roomy everywhere else. Winston isn't a fan of that. He thinks it makes him look thin. Given that he *is* pretty much a string bean, I don't think this can be avoided no matter what he wears. "I brought you something."

I raise an eyebrow when I see what he has.

He places crayons and a spring-themed coloring book, with a basket of flowers and birds flying around on the cover, in my lap. He taps his fingers on the gearshift and bites his bottom lip. "I looked it up. These are supposed to help with stress and anxiety. I hope this one isn't too young. I didn't want to get the really intricate kind and add to your frustration."

I know this is a Boyfriend thing, but since it's something meant to actually help real Dru, I can't help but get caught up in how sweet it is.

He's blindingly shiny as a make-believe boyfriend. Way shinier than any of my exes, even in the beginning.

He's supposed to be critiquing me, not the other way around. But still, I have to ask. "You—Boyfriend Winston researched stress relievers and drove an hour all the way here because his girlfriend was kind of having a bad day. You couldn't have just sent a cute meme or something?"

He laces his fingers together in front of his chest and tilts his head slightly. "I could've, but...I want to believe that me showing up would be the thing that really made her feel better. The coloring book would be a bonus."

I tilt my head too. "The *just-you-and-me* vibe. That's what would turn her day around?"

"I hope so."

I fold the book's cover back and tuck his sunglasses into my braids to better ponder which of the twenty colors I'll make a momma bird. "I think it would work. Her day would go from a three to a ten. You'd get another million kisses."

I know it would work. I don't just feel better; I feel really good.

It makes me wonder if Kai would be this sweet if I had texted him instead. Not that *sweet* is a word I'd use to describe Kai. He's a little more matter-of-fact. Practical.

"Good to know," Winston says thoughtfully.

I look over at him. "What?"

As he leans back in his seat and stares me down, a smile slowly builds on his face until it's a full-on Winston special. "You're too easy to impress."

I smack my tongue against my teeth. "No, I'm not."

He snickers. "Yes, you are."

"I have standards."

"Let me be the judge of that."

I roll my eyes.

"They're going to get stuck like that. Then what?"

I smirk. "Then you won't get the million *kiss kiss*es for all your trouble. How 'bout that?" I slam the crayons into my lap. "Maybe that's the problem. I've been giving the kisses out too willy-nilly and now you're acting up."

"Are you trying this out for our experiment? Or is kisses unlimited just how you are?" He raises his eyebrows.

"I mean"—I shrug my shoulders until they reach my ears—"I'm an affectionate person."

"For example?"

"For example..." I look up at the ceiling. "Had I actually been Girlfriend Dru, I would've made you roll down your window and hit you with a kiss or a hug before I even came around to the passenger's side. Before I even knew you brought me something."

His eyes go so big with surprise that I can't decide whether to classify the expression as teasing or real. I don't even know what I want it to be. "What kind of kiss?"

I look around, as if analyzing our surroundings. "It depends on the situation, the people present, and what we've built up to."

"Dru." This he says like a person who would clutch pearls, and places a hand at his chest. "Are you saying I'd be pulling you into this car by the mouth if I was Kai?"

"I—" My brain does this thing where it creates a visual of exactly what he just said. Winston—not Kai—is pulling me into the car by the mouth. It's impossible to finish my thought. Is he actually seeing that scene too? Is Winston imagining *us* kissing?

For some reason, the smile Winston's been wearing for most of this conversation dissolves, and I think maybe he is having the same visual and cringing. But then he says, "Just hearing his name makes you speechless?"

He's somehow managed to keep who's kissing who straight, obviously.

Before I can clear my head enough to tell him he's wrong, he goes back to tapping on the gearshift. "Speaking of. You never told me what happened at his game. Any more chances to take my advice?"

"Kind of."

"Kind of?" He blinks at me. "Is that you buying time to look for a loophole? Because you can't best me at that. I know all the tricks."

I finally pick a soft blue crayon and start to outline the bird. "Kind of, meaning I gave him a complete answer, but I don't think he really got it. So I just left it at that."

He swallows hard and taps on the gearshift. "Because it would have made you feel stupid to try and help him get it?"

I pause my coloring to think before I answer. "I was more worried about *him* thinking *I* was stupid, actually."

"Yeah. Somebody you like not seeing you how you want them to doesn't feel good. I can see why you'd try to avoid that."

Still looking at my work, I nod a little. As hard as it is to admit that, Winston's one of two people I would ever even consider telling this to. Maybe it's because I don't feel any less about myself after having said it. And I don't think he feels any less about me.

Just to be sure I look over at him. He's focused on my artwork too, at first, but eventually looks over at me. He smiles. Not one of his Winston Portis, made-for-TV smiles, but something softer. One that I can kind of see his heart in. Inexplicably, my stomach flips.

Our phones vibrate at the same time. He looks away first and pulls his from the cup holder to check it. Confused by the moment, wanting it to last a little longer so I can make it make sense, I find it hard to change my focus. But the face he pulls makes me curious.

I take my phone out of my jacket pocket. Holding my breath, I click on the notification from the twenty-one-member Eason-Portis wedding group chat. The notification is from the general channel and not the private invite-only channel. It can't be too distressing. Nothing like the poll about the dresses. So far the general channel just has all the who, what, when, where info. There are a lot of notes, but they're harmless. Things like wedding party dance instructions and ordering fabric for dresses.

But Moriah is in the middle of dress shopping. What information could be so important that it couldn't wait until we're done?

Apparently one that goes right for the sisterly jugular. A link to a sign-up sheet to help with the wedding planning by "securing a breadth of honest and objective opinions and recommendations" because her sisters, namely me, appear to be incapable of providing these things for the bride. Here's the list of what Moriah's trusted advisors can sign up for:

- Cake Tasting
- Food Tasting & Signature Drink Selection
- Venue Decorations
- Wedding Vocalist Selection
- Flower Selection & Bouquet Design

I don't bother to look for open slots. Not signing up doesn't get me out of anything. This I know without even asking. I'll be expected to be everywhere. At first, when Moriah and Rashid got engaged, that was okay. I had high hopes for being everywhere with my sisters. I thought this wedding was one thing they couldn't exclude me from because of things I can't help, like my age, where I fall in the birth order, or my lack of experience. Not even any of Moriah's friends have planned a wedding. So I should've been able to find a way to make myself useful.

But somehow, this wedding and the more time we spend together have only made things worse. And I don't have a clue how to make them better.

When I look up from my phone, Winston is watching me. "This has something to do with the message you sent me earlier?"

I put my hand on the car door to let myself out. If I stay here a minute longer, I'm asking for another berating from my betters, one even worse than this sign-up of shame.

"It has *everything* to do with the message I sent you earlier"—I smile at him—"but nothing to do with Girlfriend Dru and Boyfriend Winston. She really appreciates him trying to make her feel better and is giving him the biggest kiss kiss goodbye. Not even caring if her mom might be watching from the window."

He focuses his eyes on the storefront, but not before I spot the beginnings of a smile. "Gold star for Girlfriend Dru."

I step out of the car, but just before I close the door, I lean back inside. I have to let him know that *I* appreciate him too. Add this to the pregame video, the just-me-and-you time that never feels long enough even though we talk about nothing, and Girlfriend Dru feels kind of special. *I* feel kind of special that he would go through all this effort just for research.

He's pressed against the headrest looking up at the ceiling like he needs to work out something before he drives away. Slowly his head falls in my direction. He doesn't say a word. He just lets our eyes meet and waits.

There's a flicker of something in my stomach.

I look at his face. Flicker. I look at anything else—the dashboard, the storefront, the radio—just to test a theory. But when I finally put my focus on him again, the feeling comes back. It's like one of those trick birthday candles that you think you've blown out but then it just reignites somehow. That's what's happening in my belly right now.

I focus on the passenger's seat as I let out a slow breath. "Nothing."

"You sure?"

The concern in his voice pulls my eyes up to his. Flicker. I check the time on my phone just to have something else to focus on. If I don't look at him—into his eyes or at his smile—nothing will happen.

"I can stay longer if you want me to."

Flicker.

Welp. There goes that theory. I don't have to be looking at him. Winston just has to be here.

"Nope. I'm good. Thanks. Bye." Quickly, I slam the door closed and don't look back.

What the hell was that all about?

18 DAYS

Eighteen Days."

He didn't send a text, but that's what Kai says when he meets me at my locker Monday morning. It's kind of a whisper. Something only for us to know. But that just makes me feel guilty when I've spent all weekend trying to figure out what happened when Winston showed up at dress shopping. How did Boyfriend Winston making Girlfriend Dru feel better turn into whatever happened inside me?

Boyfriend Winston is not a real person. And maybe real Winston was right. I'm too easily impressed. All that flickering was just some weird, misdirected feelings. When I see him again, everything will turn back to normal.

Kai must pick up on my energy, but for the wrong reason. He positions himself closer to Aubrey. "I'm not going to get you in trouble. Especially on a game day. This is about soccer."

Aubrey must misread me the same way because she looks between us doubtfully. "Mmm-hmm. I'll stay."

Kai maintains a serious face. "Were you able to read any of the books? Did you find anything useful?"

I feel my smile fade. Uh-oh. Of course he would want to talk about the books. He expected me to be taking his advice this weekend.

He continues. "I wanted to tell you which one to start with, but then I figured it was better to let you start with whichever one sounded the most interesting to you."

I nod slowly. Aubrey looks down at her phone, obviously disinterested in this turn of conversation. But I know that won't last for long. It's about to be a real page-turner in here.

I had told myself that I would just never bring up the books again. And I wouldn't have, but my conversation with Winston at his dress-shopping rescue has me reconsidering. It's not going to be all Dru answers all the time, but I should at least be able to say I'd already read all the books he recommended. I would tell Winston.

And boyfriend answers and friend answers aren't always conscious decisions, but they are always true. Never the whole picture, but true. Not telling him I've read the books is basically a lie.

Could I be with somebody I feel like I have to lie to in order for him to think highly of me? And it's not like Kai did anything to make me feel that way. It's just me, doing it to myself. If I want me and Kai to have a chance—which why wouldn't I—it's something I need to work out.

If he asks questions, I'll answer them. I do with Winston, and it works out fine, even when he doesn't agree. And me having already read books Kai recommended gives us something in common. It's a positive that will hopefully keep him from taking my omission personally.

He tilts his head, defeated. He must be taking my pause to choose my words wisely as something bad. Which...that's a great instinct. I start from the beginning.

"Do you know that both of my parents were college athletes? All-American. Everything. Both of them."

He jerks his head back. "Really. That's cool. I didn't know but it makes sense. Which sports?"

"Um..." This question throws me off my run toward the truth enough that I have to think before answering. "Football and volleyball. And it doesn't make *that* much sense. I should be way better than I am. The genes didn't quite live up to their expectations. At least not with me. My older sister was a volleyball phenom and she's not even that tall. I got a little more size, but not as many gifts."

He eyes me. "I guess I'll have to take your word for it."

I clear my throat. "Anyway. My dad's the athletic director at Midwestern, and even though my mom is a financial advisor, they can both find a way to apply athletic or team principles to anything."

Aubrey's looking at me now, her face twisted in confusion, which actually isn't helping at all.

"And they're both very cerebral about their game." I nod passionately. "Like you."

Kai nods along with me. "Of course. I think you have to be to earn accolades at that level."

"Well, I hope not." I laugh nervously. "I'm not really like that, and I want to do all the things too."

He nods even harder now. "I know and you *can*. That's why I recommended the books. If you just apply some of the concepts, even ones that don't seem like they'll help, it'll take your game to another level."

I tap my thumbnail on my lips and look at the ground. "That's exactly what my parents said when they recommended those books and at least two dozen others over my whole life."

Aubrey's mouth drops into an O as she looks between us. I think she gets what I'm saying before Kai does.

"Girl. Did—"

I shush her. If there's going to be scandal, I don't need her adding to it.

"So you've read all these books before?" He puts his palm to his forehead. "That's why you got that look on your face when I first brought it up. I knew it was something. You could've just told me."

"I know. I should have. But I just..." I sigh and look him in the eye. "I didn't want to tell you that kind of stuff doesn't work for me."

"Why do you think that is?" He looks like a professor now. Arms crossed. Shoulders raised.

I catch my bottom lip between the nails of my pointer finger and thumb and pinch. For at least a second, the pain overshadows the anxiety of saying what I know is true. This is past the point I wanted to go just the other day, but Winston's right: I can't give certain answers to certain people. It's even worse than lying to them. It's kind of invalidating myself.

Because I'm scared. I can't outthink scared. It's that simple. It's what I should say.

But somebody with the ice Kai appears to have in his veins when he plays wouldn't get it. How do I even explain scared?

"I'm scared, I guess," I blurt.

He scratches his chin. "What do you mean?"

I side-eye him. "You know, like, afraid. Fearful."

He rolls his eyes to the ceiling, looking genuinely confused.

Aubrey glances at me and then back to him. I've never admitted this even to her, but she's ready with the synonyms. "Panicked. Terrified. Stricken. Petrified."

He buries one of his hands in his hair and scratches. "I know what all those words mean, like, by definition. I'm just thinking about what happens when I get scared. I jump. My skin crawls. I scream. My heart beats really fast. Does all of that happen to you on the field? Is that even possible? Is it happening every single game?"

The reason I have certain answers for certain people is coming back to me now as I actually experience a few of those symptoms he's describing.

This is how it starts, or at least how it went with Jayden. I share something really personal, thinking it will somehow help the relationship. He asks questions because, yeah, what I've just told him is wild. It makes me think he cares. But in reality he's just curious or he feels bad for me. I answer the questions because I think he gets it. Then later I find out he didn't hear me at all.

I see curiosity and a little bit of pity developing in Kai's eyes. If I keep talking I'll just look weak, which is not what he's supposed to get out of this. Luckily, I'm not in so deep that I can't backpedal. Maybe I'll explain it all once we get to know each other better, but this isn't the right time.

I force a chuckle. "It's not all like that. I should have just said I'm a little unfocused sometimes."

"Oh. Okay. I was about to say..." He looks so relieved that my issues aren't harder than anything he can imagine.

Aubrey looks between us. I swear I see relief on her face too.

He puts up his hands like he's claiming innocence. "I won't give you any books about meditation. I mean, I have them if you need them, but I'll wait for you to ask."

This makes both me and Aubrey crack up.

"You catch on quick," she says with an eye roll in my direction.

The bell rings and his face turns sincere in a way that makes me put all jokes aside. "Maybe just try to be more logical about it. You miss a hundred percent of the shots you don't take."

Aubrey smacks her teeth. "That's not logical. That's corny."

He points a finger at her as if he's about to deliver a defining point. "But you can't say it's not true." He turns back to me and lowers his voice. "I'm going to be there tonight. But no winking and I'll leave right after."

I don't know why but relief washes over me. That just makes me feel guilty all over again. It isn't that I don't want him to come to my game. I have no reason not to want him there.

"Okay. Cool." I watch him walk away, which somehow he knows because he turns around and mouths *Eighteen days.*

Eighteen days until I finally get to go out with Kai, which is what I've wanted for so long.

18 DAYS, PART 2

I can barely stand to sit with my team at lunch for longer than five minutes before I get a big anxiety ball in the pit of my stomach. It's a game day and the tension at the team table is thick. I don't really want to go into the game that way. I want to go in feeling like if we all do what got us here, we'll be fine. On to the next one.

I get up, throw away my half-eaten tray of food, and look for Winston. I haven't even texted him to meet me at the stairwell, but I find him with his paper lunch bag balled up in one hand on his way to a trash can. It's early for Girlfriend Dru and Boyfriend Winston to meet. This will be more like forty minutes, or most of our lunch. It's a big ask considering how much of his time I took up last week and the way I've avoided him all day just because my wires got twisted. But I've been thinking about it since I talked to Kai. Boyfriend Winston's whole purpose is to help me do away with the boyfriend-launcher part of me. I need to focus on that.

Winston meets me at the door. I'm prepared for something weird based on what happened the last time we made eye contact this close. But nothing happens.

Well, nothing like the flicker.

I do immediately feel like I missed out on something by avoiding him, because Winston looks very cute today. I'm not sure what it is. His haircut isn't fresh. He's wearing his normal T-shirt and athletic pants. He's not even smiling. Just Winston, but glowing or something. Even under these bright, flattering-to-absolutely-nobody fluorescent lights.

I mean, he's cute in general under the variety of different lights I've seen him under. I just...I don't know what I mean. And whatever I mean, I don't know why I'm thinking it.

His look turns cautious, probably because of what I now realize is a stare coming from me. I think I just CIA investigated every part of him.

"Are we hanging out?"

The question and the realization of what I've been doing makes *me* cautious. "If you want to. If you're not busy. It *is* early."

"Why would I not want to hang out with my girlfriend?" He opens the door so we can go through.

That easy Boyfriend Winston comment finally settles it. The flicker wasn't real. There's no way I could've been the only one to feel that if it was. And if he felt even half of what I felt, he'd be a little nervous, or scared to look me in the eye, like I was with him on Saturday. I don't pick up on any of that.

"Yeah, but—" I look both ways down the hall to make sure nobody's around. "You're not actually my boyfriend. You could have something better to do. And not sitting with my team on game days is like not showing up for the game."

He looks behind us as if checking the table for me, even though we're in the hallway. "You're not at the table *now*."

For some reason, I look behind me too. "They're stressing me out. We're team trauma bonding and everyone's nerves are getting to me. Before big games, I always wake up a little anxious, but I can talk myself out of it until warm-up, when I'm a mess. When I'm with my team lately, though, I'm anxious no matter what time of day it is." I let out a puff of air. "I have Meegan in one ear doing a critical review of our game and the other team's game and preaching to me about shooting more. Capri in the other complaining about Meegan. Lauren stress eating everybody's food. Riley literally bullying everybody about trivial things like the way they chew. By the time lunch is over I'm doing all those things at once."

Add to that my earlier conversation with Kai that has me questioning myself even more, and I'm useless.

Winston laughs. "Sounds like it would be fun to watch."

I roll my eyes. "You wouldn't last a minute at that table. Meegan would probably do a critical review of your show, and Lauren would dunk on your hair, kink by kink. She's ruthless."

"I think I could take it, or I'd let you be my protector." He puts on this lopsided grin and looks me up and down like he's really trying to decide who'd win the battle between me and either of them. He looks to be thinking way too hard, not even an inch of me going unnoticed.

Suddenly, he tilts his head as if something just came to him. He looks around again. This time for privacy. "We've spent a few lunches alone together. How are you getting away with that, with the pact?"

I shrug. "Oh. My team literally calls you my brother-in-law."

As soon as those last three words are out, I frown, and I'm pretty sure it's not because it's technically incorrect.

He scratches the side of his face, suddenly and unusually irritated for some reason. "That's not how that works."

"I know. You-you're right," I stutter. "I'm going to stop telling people that."

He pauses for a second and stares at me like he's waiting for me to say I'm joking, which is a valid expectation, since I've liked the sound of calling him my brother so much before. I don't like it at all now.

When I don't say anything, he confirms with a high-pitched, "You are?"

"Yeah. Sure." I try to keep it light, but it doesn't feel that way. It feels like something inside me is trying to rewrite a story that I had no issue with until I had to have Winston's help.

He's watching me very closely, but I pretend not to notice. My body isn't wholly in game like my mind. I feel physically caught in his stare. Kind of like the way I was the other day. It's then that I realize we've walked past the door that leads to our quiet stairwell, and he isn't trying to turn us back. I don't ask any questions. I don't mind him redirecting me-and-you time. He hasn't led me wrong up to this point.

He trots ahead of me to a set of doors that leads to the student parking lot and opens one when I catch up to him. I squint into the sun. It's going to be the best game day. No chance of rain, warm enough that I don't need layers that affect my movement, but not so warm that I'm winded from going up the field once.

"Okay." He pauses for effect, and nods at something that seems to be going on in his head.

I mimic his nod. "What are you doing?"

He puts a finger up, asking for time as he looks off into space. I wait impatiently.

He gives a final nod and turns back to me. "Six-team Disney show all-star tournament. Ready?"

Disney TV. Second only to Roblox in time spent with Winston when we were little. I still stream some of my favorite episodes sometimes. I bet he still does too, but he'd probably never admit it.

I laugh to myself. "Ready."

He walks backward, looking down at me as he sets the tournament up in his head. *"Andi Mack* versus *Phineas and Ferb."*

"Phineas and Ferb. I liked Andi, but Jonah Beck had to be the worst love interest ever. We were in elementary, and I knew that."

"Wow. Very strong feelings in the first round." He chuckles. *"Phineas and Ferb* versus *That's So Raven."*

"Oooh. That's a good one. Mischief everywhere." I take a deep breath. "I'm going with Raven."

"That's So Raven versus *Doc McStuffins."*

I sing the *Doc McStuffins* theme song full out. He doesn't try to stop me even when we notice people looking at us. He just becomes my piano and background chorus.

"Doc McStuffins versus *Good Luck Charlie."*

"I, no lie, can quote *Good Luck Charlie* episodes. It was such a good show. Not a single unlikable character. Gotta be the Doc for me, though."

He turns around and we step into the parking lot. I assume we're going to his car. Mine is in the opposite direction of where he's leading me.

He rubs his hands together like an evil scientist. "*Doc McStuffins* versus *Sofia the First*."

I gasp. "You did that on purpose. And I can't believe I didn't see it coming. That's just...I'm not choosing."

"You have to."

"I don't."

"Just do it."

"I won't."

"We don't have time to watch both."

The thought that he had even considered that there might be a *need* to watch both makes me smile a little, inside and out.

He takes his keys out of his pocket and unlocks the door of the white car he shares with his brother. I'm always amazed at how clean they keep it inside and out. I have stuff everywhere and sometimes my car is a victim of athlete smell.

"We're watching TV?" I clap my hands, and I fling the passenger's door open. I catch it just before it hits the car parked in the next spot. "Which episode?"

"Which show?"

I plop into the passenger's seat and close the door behind me. "This is not me choosing for life. This is me choosing for the day."

He gets in next to me. I can tell by the way the driver's seat is pushed all the way back that he's the one who drove to school this morning. "Okay. Nobody wins the tournament. Everybody gets a trophy."

"Thank you." I cover my face. "Sofia. You pick the episode. I could be here all day trying to do that... But none of the ones where Amber is mean. I don't want to be mad at Amber."

He nods and props his phone up on the dashboard just as the music starts. I sing the theme song like I wrote it. Instead of joining in this time, Winston watches as if I truly am the entertainment.

I clap my hands. "A Cedric episode."

Winston smiles. "He was my favorite character."

"Top two and not two."

We almost bump faces when we both lean into the middle console to see better. I startle back but he doesn't move.

"I can see over your head. You're good."

But when I go back to prop myself up on my elbow, we're pretty much attached from the elbow on. It's not the first time I've ever been this close to Winston, just the first time I've ever noticed it. He's the kind of warm I'd snuggle up to if I was cold. It makes me feel just as comfortable as if I were at home on my couch. Honestly, that's how it is a lot of the time when we're around each other lately.

It's how I felt when he told me to come out to the car when we were dress shopping. I knew I would feel that way. That's why I was so happy to see his text.

And I can feel every single breath he takes. For some reason it feels like a lot of them. Like he's coming down from a light workout.

He stays where he is, so I stay where I am. Sofia is already mini-size on a phone screen. I'm not moving any farther away from her.

As we watch, I have to double-take Winston a couple times when he speaks with the characters and in character. I guess maybe he might admit he has an old-school Disney habit.

When the end credits come up, Winston backs away and scrutinizes me. "Did you tear up?"

I scrunch my face at him in disgust. I absolutely did tear up. Sofia does that to me. But that's not his business to broadcast.

"I was smiling the whole time. What are you talking about?"

He raises an eyebrow. "I'm not saying they weren't happy tears, but something was going on."

I click my tongue against my teeth. "I don't know what you're talking about."

"It's not a bad thing." His voice goes soft. "I was trying to give you a break from thinking about everything else and I did a good job." He rubs his hand over the center of his chest. "I keep my happy tears in here."

"Silly." I turn away from him, but then I feel what he's just talked about in my own chest. Not the flicker, thank God. Just happiness. He *did* give me a break. And he *does* look happy about it. Happy about making me happy? Maybe he's the one who's too easy. I turn back to him. "Thank you for even trying."

He shifts in the seat and lowers his head before he shyly gazes at me. It's like I've said something way better than thanks. "You're welcome. Thanks for letting me try."

It wasn't a matter of letting him try. I knew time with Winston would be a good thing no matter how we spent it. I always know that.

It's why I got up from the team table on game day and hoped he'd see me. Why would I do that unless I thought something would be better in the end?

"Yeah. And one billion and one kiss kisses, too."

18 DAYS, PART 3

We almost lost the district final today. If not for a heroic last-second shot by Meegan it would all have been over. No regionals. No semis. No championship.

When I get home, the only lights that are still on are the ones that will help me get in the house and upstairs to my bedroom safely.

I'm thankful my parents didn't wait up to talk about the game. If they had and started critiquing my play, I might cry. I did not have a great game. Tomorrow would be a much better time for a conversation if it has to happen.

I do have a message from Kai, though, which is really nice. I appreciate him thinking about me even after he found out I neglected to tell him I'd already read all the books he suggested. That detail seems to be forgotten.

> **Kai:** You looked great. But that was a tough one. Is the whole team in their heads??

Is the whole team in their heads *like you are?*

I know that's more what I'm thinking than what he's saying. I sigh. I think I need to invoke the twenty-four-hour rule before getting in too deep a conversation with him about this. I don't want him to think I don't appreciate his interest, though.

Dru: Thank you for coming.

Kai: You're welcome. I hope you're not
taking it too hard. You guys won.

Dru: I know. You're right. I hope you had
a good day.

Kai: ☺ I did.

Dru: Good night.

Kai: Good night.

And I do mean what I wrote. Logically, I know he's right. Winning was the goal. Still, somehow I feel more stressed than happy. If I had brought that up to Kai, I know he'd want a reason. Something I can pinpoint other than that my team isn't behaving like a team and I didn't feel connected to them today. *I* didn't connect them today. That's literally my job.

I can't give him anything other than *I thought so much that by the time I had to actually act, it was too late.* The other team's defense knew where I was going with the ball every single time.

The more I think about how close we came to losing and how

this wasn't a night where winning cured everything, the more I feel on the verge of crying. I do everything I can to fight it. I breathe deeply. I take the longest, hottest shower. I put on my favorite body spray, even though I'm not leaving the house tonight. The pressure behind my eyes just won't go away, but tears won't fall either.

I start with my body pillow and stack several pillows on top of it against my headboard. Comfortable, but not so comfortable that I end up reviewing the back of my eyelids. I open my computer with the intention of logging in to my Spanish class and studying for a quiz. But then I just stare.

And somehow I end up thinking about *Sofia the First*, which leads me to thinking about Winston.

He sent me a pregame playlist that actually did get me very hype and feeling very invincible. And he sent me a congratulations text after the game, telling me to call him if I wanted to talk. I haven't responded to him yet because I'm not in the mood to play Girlfriend Dru. I *do* want to talk to him, though. I don't have anything in particular to say, I just want to.

It's late, but I take a chance and FaceTime him.

When he answers, the only light in the room is the glow of his phone screen. With his bonnet sitting on his head like a chef's hat and his T-shirt twisted around his chest, he looks a little disoriented. He didn't take a second to change anything before he answered. It makes me feel like he trusts me not to find fault in anything about him. And I don't.

He reaches away from the phone and a dim light comes on. Then he sits up in bed with a pillow behind his head.

"Why did you answer if you were asleep?" I ask.

He smirks but also rolls his tired eyes like the question is testing his patience. "What you doing?"

I shrug. "Wondering what you doing."

He laughs.

I smile. "Thank you for my playlist."

His eyes light up. "It *was* fire, huh. Had you playing up to your full potential. I saw you."

I grimace. "The quality of my play is debatable. And either way, how are you taking credit for it?"

"You know, behind every good woman is a good man and all that." Then he gives me a face like, obviously he's taking at least *some* credit, which makes me laugh. It also kind of startles me into remembering he's Boyfriend Winston right now. I should've established right when I called that this is regular Dru and regular Winston. But since Boyfriend Winston makes me feel good, I don't bother resetting the scene.

"Who's debating your play?"

I hum. "I don't feel like talking about it."

He nods slowly. "Cool, but I'm curious. Would you want to talk about it if I was a friend and not a boyfriend?"

I shake my head. I don't care who it is. I don't want to talk about it. "Did you have a good day?"

He sniffs and wipes at his eyes as if he's just decided to stay awake for a while. "I'm actually trying to figure that out."

I laugh. "It's almost tomorrow. When will you know?"

He looks thoughtfully away from the camera and I'm not sure if he's joking anymore. "Professor Apter from the Communication

Arts School at Midwestern emailed me today. She said"—he clears his throat and lifts his chin high—"'Hello Winston. Thank you so much for your inquiry about our summer program. If you're available, I'd like to set up some time to discuss your experience. I have availability Wednesday of next week. Please let me know if this could work for you. Regards, Jorda.'"

Before he gets through what I believe is the email word for word, I'm laughing. "Why does she sound sultry and snobby at the same time?"

He shrugs. "She said 'regards.' And every time I read it, I just imagine somebody wearing red bottoms and a fur, but like on a yacht in a hot climate."

"You need to have that psychoanalyzed. What did you want her to say? 'Bye Boo'?" I laugh harder. "And when did you get the email? Why did I have to call you at almost midnight to find out about it? Did my dad say anything? And why is the email bad? You wanted answers. Sounds like you're about to get them."

"'Regards' is harsh. That's all I'm saying." He pauses, looking into the phone as if waiting for me to agree, but all I can do is look back at him real skeptically. "I got the email after school. I didn't know if I was telling *anybody*. And you needed to focus on your game anyway. Now that you've called, I realize, yeah, I want to tell Dru. She's the only person I want to tell."

He doesn't say this like it's some special admission. There's no pause or change in his voice. It's just a continuation of the last thought he had. He might not be fazed by saying I'm the only person he wanted to tell, but I'm fazed by hearing it. My breathing stops for like a second before I come back to my senses. It checks out. I'm the only person who knows about this whole thing other than my dad. Who would he tell other than me?

When I come back from working that out in my head, he's waxing poetic about my dad. "You've been holding out. I mean, I get it. You don't want to share. But that man of a man has me thinking I can do things. I thought I had a plot for my life, but in one email, Keith revealed that I didn't and helped me get one. In one email. I'm thinking of buying him something and asking him to be my mentor."

I throw my head back against my pillows and laugh. "I don't think you need to buy him anything."

He puts his hand to his chest. "But I want to, though."

I shake my head. "Forget about my dad for a second. Why is the email bad?"

"So"—he sucks his teeth—"I want answers, but the dream scenario is her telling me that they've reviewed my previous applications, and someone made a mistake. Discussing my experience doesn't sound like it's going to be that."

"There's still a chance it could be good. But if you really want to Keith Eason it"—I make a fist with one hand and tap it into the palm of the other—"you decide the call's going to be a win and you make it a win."

He nods deeply. "I really want to Keith Eason it. How?"

For the next hour, I get deep into my Keith, knowing what my dad would tell me, and what I rarely do. Most importantly, we set an intention for the call. And then we decide how to get it met. That way, Winston gets something out of it regardless. He decides on the obvious. Convincing this professor that he should be in the program. And even after the three rejections, I support that intention. He's talented and he spends so much time with his show. It's obvious he's the real thing.

There's no downside to Winston Portis. Never has been.

He narrows his eyes at the screen, and I think I've said that out loud.

He sits up on his pillows. "It's rude to argue, so I won't."

I laugh. He is probably more likely to argue the point. And I don't think, even knowing him as I do for as long as I have, that I realized this about him. Winston isn't this guy who just knows he has it. He's far from that.

"You can argue if you want. You'd lose."

"I'd let you win. That's not the same thing."

"Okay." I look challengingly at the screen. "Give me a downside to Winston Portis."

He shrugs. "I have a rap sheet."

"I'm not sure you can call it a rap sheet if the judicial body is LeBeau Community Schools. Plus, your résumé's longer. Thousands of people watch your show live and you talk about local youth sports. You can't say that isn't a big deal."

"It's cool, I guess."

I give him the stink eye. "Say it's a big deal."

He lifts his eyebrows as if I'm the one with the problem. "It's a big deal?"

"Zero enthusiasm and it sounded like a question. But okay if that's the best you can do."

He blows raspberries and looks off camera. "It's kind of hard to be enthusiastic about what's going on right now when everyone else is enthusiastic about what happened before."

I wait for him to look back at me. I want to see if the embarrassment that comes off him in waves when his past is brought up is visible now. If it is, I'll keep my questions to myself.

Before I have it figured out, he takes a deep breath and says, "You want to know why I got into trouble all the time?"

I push myself up on my pillows and nod. "If you want to tell me."

He tugs on his ear as if he's taking his time to get his words just perfect. "I'm the last person to get things a lot of the time."

"No—"

"I *am*. It's a fact. And it's not all bad. Sometimes once I get things I'm better at them than the people who got them first." He takes off his bonnet, and his hair starts to slowly expand. He pulls on it as if the expansion isn't happening fast enough. "That voice that tells you something is a bad idea didn't really start talking to me until late. It took me a while to actually start listening to it.

"Being in trouble didn't really bother me like it bothered other people. I didn't love having my parents upset with me, but they always got over it. At least when I was younger."

"Is that what made you start listening to your voice? Your parents not getting over it?"

He puts both hands behind his head and stretches, buying himself time for getting the words just right again. I hate that he thinks he needs the perfect words for me.

"You can just say whatever it is, how it is. I'm not going to think anything bad," I tell him.

I try to sound as upbeat and encouraging as I can, but that doesn't stop him from looking at me suspiciously, which kind of hurts my feelings. Does he really think I'd have bad thoughts about him? Would I be asking for his help all the time if I did?

I search his face for answers. "We can talk about something else if you want. You asked me if I wanted to know, so I thought you wanted to tell me. But you don't have to."

His face softens. "I'm sorry. That's not about you. None of this has ever been outside my own head. I think I'm just trying to figure out how it sounds to *me*. I definitely want to tell you."

This is the second time in one conversation that he's said he wants to share something with me. The feeling that it sets off in my belly goes flicker to flame in less than a second. I snuggle deeper into my comforter and lie on my side to try to put it out. But I'm looking at him, so it doesn't work.

He pulls his blankets closer around himself too, relaxing a little. "I do care about how my parents feel. I don't like it when I can see them struggling not to think the worst. I know that should have something to do with why I decided to listen to that voice more, but it doesn't. It's more selfish."

He licks his lips and lets out a big breath as words start to spill out. "When I was expelled and had to do online school, I missed *people*. Jake would go to school and my parents would go to work. I would sit through my classes and then wait for them to come home so I could have real people to talk to.

"I couldn't drive. And I couldn't do the things that other people who were enrolled online could. I couldn't join clubs or go to games, nothing."

I frown at the screen. "You could've called me. I barely heard from you during that time."

"You were busy. Everybody was busy. Or at least that's what it felt like."

The sadness in his eyes makes me wonder if he's having one of those moments I have on the field. You know one thing is true, but all you can believe is some story your brain has written on its own. I hate seeing that look on another person. Especially Winston.

"It was five months of school and then the summer where I didn't know how to get back into things. I watched all these shows online. I started to think I could do it. I picked the thing I liked talking about most at the time and started talking about it." He smiles, mostly to himself. "The first time I got a comment, it was mean, but I felt like I was with people again. I slid into that dude's DMs. We're still friends to this day."

I laugh out loud.

He shakes his head. "Now, if there's anything getting in the way of any of that, I won't do it."

"I had no idea it was like that for you. I was busy, but I would've made time just like how we do now."

"I know that *now*." He gestures with his hands as if he's trying to bring the right words to him physically this time. "But you know how it is when you're in the middle of something and you don't realize what's really going on around you or what you're headed for."

I look at him thoughtfully. "Yeah, I mean, you found something you love, something you might not have come to otherwise."

He turns very serious all of a sudden. "I think that's what's going to happen to you."

"You think I'm going to start a podcast?" I snicker.

He stays serious, looking like a wise old uncle. "I think something's going to happen to make you not hate your boyfriend-launcher phase so much."

"That would have to be something miraculous."

I sigh and slide out of bed to turn off my overhead light. It's decidedly not the vibe. This is LED lights–only time.

"Wait. What's on your wall?"

He's looking at my wall of complete coloring pages. I turn my camera toward it.

His face brightens immediately. "That looks like the whole coloring book."

"Except one." I frown just thinking about it. "The color choices were bottom tier."

"Get closer. I want to see the details."

I move the phone, focusing on a few at a time.

"Nice." He nods approvingly. "I hope this doesn't mean you've been *hating it here* seventeen times since I gave you the book. It's only been two days."

"My sisters were here the whole weekend, and I got texts and audio from The Girls all day today." I put the camera back on me as I turn off my light. "Why are you smiling like that?"

"Because every time you open that book for a little stress relief, you have to be thinking about the person who gave it to you."

I settle back in bed and pull up the covers. I know Boyfriend

Winston is the one who said that, but real Dru is the one opening the book. That feels like a lot of Winston living rent-free in my head time. This whole thing does.

In theory. But in reality, I'm not thinking about Winston.

I'm thinking about the sweet things that Boyfriend Winston— an imaginary person—does. And I'm thinking about them a lot. How could I not get these little excited feelings? I look at Winston all snuggled in bed. Maybe I should ask him for some tips. He looks completely unfazed. No flickers for him, just friends.

Winston's eyes are barely open now, but his smile never wavers. "Feeding Boyfriend's ego by letting him know something he did actually helped her. That's two gold stars. Infinite kiss kisses."

Gold stars *and* kiss kisses. Together they sound like a bedtime story. The perfect thing to go to sleep thinking about.

I check the time on my phone. It's after two somehow. I sigh, still not really sure if I'm unwound enough to sleep, but I'm not thinking about crying anymore. I'm just thinking about Winston and looking at Winston.

I should be doing all these things with Kai. Then again, it was my choice not to. I've set this whole thing in motion.

I deep sigh. "I'll let you go to sleep. Thanks for picking up."

And I really do mean that, regardless of how angry I am at whatever my body and mind are trying to do. I'm glad Winston's here.

His eyes linger on spots around the screen as if he's really registering every part of my face. "You're welcome. Good night."

"Good night." I'm about to press end, but then I can't. I have to know something. "Winston. Wait."

He blinks at me groggily. "Yeah?"

"Did you decide yet? If it was a good day? Did I help you figure it out?"

He smiles. "Oh, yeah. It was a very good day. Thanks for your help with that."

I smile, feeling relieved somehow. "Good. That's great. Okay."

"Okay. See y—"

"You know what I just realized?" I don't have to tell him this now. It could probably wait. But, again, I can't press end.

Creases form between his eyebrows like he's actually trying to solve the riddle. After a few seconds, he gives up. "What did you just realize?"

"I just realized that the regional final, if we make it, is next Wednesday too. It could be a big day for both of us. Maybe *I'll* make *you* a playlist."

Why would I say that? Why would I *do* that?

"I mean Girlfriend Dru will…Boyfriend Winston. You get what I mean."

He shrugs. "*Somebody* brought it up and now I'm looking forward to it. So somebody *has* to make one for me now. It can't be a maybe."

"Maybe."

I say this playfully and expect him to laugh but he doesn't. He just watches me, eyes glassy from being open too long. My stomach does a flip.

I sigh. "Good night."

He nods and we both just sit there. Quietly examining each other is weird in theory, but in practice, I don't mind it at all. It's worth losing sleep for.

Without losing eye contact with the screen, I shift out of my blankets. It's getting really hot in here. I should check the thermostat. "Why aren't you hanging up?"

He shrugs one shoulder. "I didn't think I should. In case you had more to say again."

"I said good night."

"You said that before."

I sigh deeply and shut my eyes. "I guess I did, but I mean it this time. Good night."

"Good night." Again, he doesn't hit end. He's really just watching the screen. Watching me.

"Seriously. It's late. I'm going to hang up."

"You swear I'm trying to stop you."

He isn't trying to stop me. He isn't doing anything except waiting for me to end the conversation I started and have not been able to shut down.

"Okay, then. Good night," I say with finality.

Winston gives a tiny nod. "Okay, then."

I push end, fall back onto the bed, and pull my covers over my head as if I can hide from the butterflies finding their way to my stomach.

17 DAYS

Kai: 17 Days

          Dru: You're not making this any easier.

Kai: I'm not trying to.

Winston: Did you sleep good?

          Dru: Yes. I was knocked out. HBU

Winston: Couldn't go back to sleep. I was
thinking about my girlfriend.

Oh.

          Dru: That's sweet. You should've told me.

Winston: I'm telling you now.

Dru: No. I mean you should wake me up when you're thinking about me.

Winston: You wouldn't be saying that if you knew how many nights I think about you.

Dru: Maybe next time you won't let me hang up so easily.

Winston: Yeah, that was a mistake. Do you forgive me?

Dru: As long as you're thinking about me, I can't be mad.

Winston:  I hope you have a good day today.

Dru:  I hope you have a good day too.

❖ ❖ ❖

Today's practice is already intense after last night. We don't need Coach to call for a team film review right after. But that doesn't stop him from doing it. I don't mind reviewing film. It's useful. But we're all sweaty, stinky, and tired as we sit in one of the small rooms of our athletic building. And he's told us to review and discuss on our own and report back to him, because obviously we aren't interested in following his directions.

I'm not sure if Coach is back out on the field, in the next room, or on his way home. Either way, we're only five minutes into playback when Meegan gets out of her seat and shuts off the game.

"Everybody who gets in the game knows how to play." Meegan's hands are on her hips and she's glaring at all of us. "Knowing how to play isn't the problem. Playing the way we know how is the problem."

"You have the authority to override Coach, huh? Whatever Meegan says, goes," Capri says. Her chin is resting in her palm like her head truly needs the help staying up. I'm not sure if that's practice or Meegan-caused exhaustion.

Meegan ignores Capri's comment. "We've been practicing every day for months and Westfield has had the same starting lineup for the last three years. We know who they play and how they play." Meegan looks up at the ceiling like she's asking for help being kind with her words. "We were terrible last night. Backups should have been playing by halftime. The rest of us should have been resting. We're not focused."

"I thought the pact was all about more focus." Riley pins me with a stare. "Wonder what could be going wrong there?"

My cheeks get hot. It's not fun to be called out, especially on something that really has nothing to do with the game. The worst part is, Riley could be onto something. Winston isn't impacting my play. My performance last night had nothing to do with him. But I have to admit that most of the day soccer has been warring with him for my attention.

All I've been thinking about since I pulled myself groggily out of bed this morning is how the feelings from dress shopping somehow carried over into yesterday. How that made me not want to hang up on Winston last night. It wasn't part of the Girlfriend Dru/Boyfriend Winston experiment. I, just regular old Dru, didn't want good night to be good night.

I fell asleep telling myself that everything was fine, but then there were the texts this morning. Boyfriend Winston literally doing his job shouldn't have me lying in bed staring up at the ceiling. The suggestion that he thinks about Girlfriend Dru every night shouldn't have melted me. But it did.

Am I coming close to breaching the pact? I definitely breached the lines of friendship. I may have even crossed something unestablished between me and Kai.

That's why I put a little distance between Girlfriend Dru and Boyfriend Winston for the second time. No stopping by his locker or me-and-you time at lunch. I needed to get myself right.

I clear my throat. "It's not just about focus. It's actually supposed to help bring us closer too, as teammates."

"Clearly that's working." Riley's face is stone, but there are a few snickers around the room.

"We shouldn't have won that game," Meegan declares as she rests a hip on a table.

Lauren speaks up. "I don't know if I would say *shouldn't* have won, but it definitely shouldn't have come down to the last minute."

"It shouldn't have come down to me." Meegan's knee bounces.

She's not wrong. She saved us, as the most valuable players on teams do, but she shouldn't have had to.

"Well, yeah"—I sit up in my seat—"everybody could have done something better. That's always true."

"Great point." Meegan stands and crosses her arms. "Let's start with you, Dru, and go around the room. What could you have done better? If you don't come up with something, I will."

"I—"

"No," Capri says. "We're not doing this. Not with everyone upset about yesterday and you looking like you want a fight. You trashing everybody isn't going to help anything."

I appreciate Capri for getting the attention off me. Also, I kind of feel like a coward. I should be the one putting an end to anything that isn't constructive. But it always feels so much easier to just let Meegan take the lead.

"I'm not trashing anybody." She shrugs. "But if people are feeling like that, then maybe they need to consider whether they're playing like trash."

"Wait," Charlotte says from behind me. "You do realize that one of the reasons you look so good is because of the team around you. You aren't doing this on your own. What if Dru decides not to pass the ball to you?"

Meegan's chest is heaving. "You're going to ice me? Is that what you talk about in your group chat?"

"Hold on. There's no…" I'm about to say there's no group chat, but I catch Capri's grimace. I look around the room. There are a few other guilty faces. So I stick to the facts I know, because unless the team ices me, I'm going to get the ball to Meegan. "There are no plans to ice anybody. Period."

I haven't said anything earth-shattering. Everyone knows I'm all about making the best play for the team.

I look around the room again, wondering how we got to the point of starting group chats about each other. "This isn't getting us anywhere. Maybe we should end for today."

Capri stands to leave. Slowly the rest of the team trickles out. I don't look at Meegan or Riley or Lauren, who are all staying back. It feels like official notice that we're not all on the same page.

I meet Capri in the hall. There's mumbling and grumbling before everyone goes their separate ways. It's hard to tell anything except that we're really tired. It makes sense. The season is long even without making it all the way through to the championship game. Captains' practices in June. Camp in July. Tryouts with a scrimmage two days after cuts are made. Then practice every day, with two to three games a week for almost three months, plus school.

To be still standing this far into the postseason is a feat. Making it to the end isn't just talent. It's luck. It's making it through moments like this. We did it last year. We made it to the semifinal, when no one expected us to. But the loudest voices in the room were different.

Capri shakes her head. "She needs to get ahold of herself. We can't disrespect each other and then go out and play hard together. If I want to beat my teammates more than I want to beat the other players, how is that going to work?"

"It's not going to. You're right." I swallow hard. "But, Capri? A group chat? Are you guys trashing her in it?"

Capri shrugs, which I take as a yes. "It's either say it there or say it to her face."

"Or maybe just leave it alone for now."

She raises an eyebrow. "Why?"

I shrug. "Because, like you said, we can't want to beat each other more than we want to beat the other team."

Capri shakes her head but says, "If you think that'll help fix things."

"I think we should try."

She nods and leans in. I'm afraid of what she might say next. "You do know you have to keep your stuff together too. Meegan isn't the only one everybody's looking at."

I nod. This is a way more respectful way of telling me to take a few risks on the field if we're going all the way. I hate being spammed about it, but noted. "I know the competition is getting harder, so I have to be more versatile. I get it."

"Not just that, Dru." She stops and looks at me. "Everything."

It takes me a second before I catch on. But then I get it. Capri behaved more like a captain than I did a few minutes ago. I should've been the one to tell Meegan that what she wanted to do wasn't a bad idea. It was just the wrong time. I don't know why I couldn't just say that to her. I need to be more vocal.

"I got it. I know."

"Okay, good. You know I got your back, but I can only do so much."

We bump shoulders as we start walking again. "I know. I appreciate it."

And I really do, but it seems like we're in a situation where somebody needs to be looked out for or talked down way too often. It's not a good team atmosphere. It pulls us down.

I can't be the only one frustrated with hearing the same things over and over. Shoot, even Meegan was tired of it. That's what started the whole situation. I know when I have this feeling with my own sisters, all I want to do is get away from them. They call it running, but I usually feel better. It's not like we don't all have to go back to each other anyway. Just like now. We have to keep playing together.

We're halfway to our cars when I think I know what we need to do. "I'm going to talk to Coach. I think we all need some time apart. A break. One day."

She looks at me, surprised. "That sounds like a captain's plan. I like it."

14 DAYS AND NO CLOSER TO AN ANSWER THAN WHEN I STARTED

(AKA Opening Night of Wedding Planning Weekend)

Kai: 14 Days

Dru: 14 Days

Winston: 6 days until my meeting. I hope
you've started on my playlist. I
have high expectations.

Dru: I said MAYBE.

Winston: Let me speak to my girlfriend.
She'll say yes.

Dru: She's getting ready for school.

Winston: Tell her I can't wait to see her.

Dru: It's still a maybe.

If ambience means anything, then I and eleven of Moriah's closest confidants are about to be in wedding cake heaven. The back room of this brick-walled bakery probably has its own following on Instagram. Every post is of the room from some previously undiscovered angle.

There's a long banquet table set for us with two bouquets of white and deep yellow roses arranged in matte silver vases. Altogether it's the perfect representation of the silver and gold palette Moriah is going for. It's no surprise that even after her attempt to book months ago, the bakery was barely able to fit in this tasting. With the wedding only a few months away, Moriah is late on checking this task off. There's no doubt in my mind, though. This place is worth the wait.

Me, Mom, Dad, and LeArra are the first to arrive. LeArra drove two hours to LeBeau today. When I got home from school she was in virtual meetings about her PhD project, leaving the rest of us to whisper and tiptoe around her.

The four of us stand around the table. Without speaking, we all seem to know that committing to a chair could be a disaster once everyone else gets here.

I'm about to give in to the urge to pick up one of the arrangements and smell it, likely leading to my hand being smacked, when Dad says, "There he is."

The smile in his voice and on his face, the hugging, handshaking, and back-patting give the impression that he and Rashid Portis Sr. are the best of friends. In reality, they're merely side characters to Mom and Ms. Teddy's sisterhood, whose greeting is a continuation of the last conversation they had. Mr. Portis gives simple, meaningful nods that barely reveal the dimples he gave to only one son.

The Twins are right behind them. Jake has his hands in his pockets, and his eyes spend at least a few seconds on everything in the room. Not like he's making a judgment, but like he might write about it later. Winston is of course all smiles toward everyone. But when he looks at me, his smile falters a little and he ducks his head, almost like he's trying to hide from something. That look makes me feel like someone's punched me right through the chest from the inside.

When they get closer, I also notice he has a small plastic grocery bag.

"Which is which?" LeArra says as the two approach us.

This is one of those times I'm reminded of how different my childhood was from my oldest sister's. She left for college when we were nine. The Twins haven't been as much a part of her life as they have been mine.

Even though she hasn't directed the question at me, the answer that comes to my head is *The fine one is Winston*. And, even without her question, it would be hard not to notice how cute Winston is.

One of the twists right at his hairline is unraveling into two perfect coils. I want to wrap them around my fingers. I thought about it all day at school after seeing him at his locker in the morning.

Maybe that's what he's hiding from. What he can see all over my face. We've both realized that I think he's sigh-worthy, and it scares him.

That idea forces reasonable words from me. "They don't even look that much alike."

As she studies Winston's face, LeArra fusses with the halo braid she had me put in her hair this morning. "All I know is one of them was always following you around. The mischievous one who was always into something."

I shake my head. "LeArra, what—"

"That's me. Winston." Somehow he says that graciously and with a straight face. As if my sister didn't say "always" like just the thought of past Winston annoys her. Like Winston was just walking around setting things on fire or leaving disaster in his wake. I think the correct word would be *curious* or *adventurous*. I mean, damn, we hadn't even hit puberty yet.

And Winston has never followed me around. We were friends. Like, people who walk in unison. "Following you around" makes it sound like a whole different thing. Like he wanted to be my friend, and I was oblivious.

And his use of present tense is bananas. I would have been dreading this tasting if I hadn't known he was going to be here. Who else will give me something to focus on when my sisters judge me?

If anything, *I'll* be following *him* around.

She nods up at him appraisingly. "It's been three, maybe four, years since I've seen either of you. Somebody had a glow-up."

Winston points an unsure finger at himself and looks at Jake. Jake gives his twin a quick appraisal followed by a slow nod that says, *yes, you're the one she's talking about.* There's still confusion showing between Winston's brows when he turns back to LeArra. "Thank you?"

She doesn't even say "you're welcome." My sister's attention is already refocused on Jake. "And you're the author, then, right. In high school. That's fantastic."

Jake smiles. Winston puts his arm around his brother, in agreement that Jake is in fact fantastic.

She looks between me and Jake. "Dru has such accomplished friends. You and Aubrey should be coaching her up. She should be feeding off this energy."

I do a double take. What would she know about Aubrey? She never responded to my text about helping her.

"I didn't tell you?" Her nose crinkles like she's thinking really hard. "I finally had time to talk to her this morning. She's so driven and smart. I sent her some resources, but let her know she can call me anytime."

"Oh. Okay. I didn't know. Thanks."

She waves me off as if it's no big deal. I could never imagine her helping me with anything. But okay. Whatever.

She turns back to Jake. "I can see myself publishing one day. Definitely nonfiction, though." She says this more seriously than a comment like that deserves.

Jake looks up at Winston, performing the same checks as his twin. Should he start talking about his book? Winston smiles and nods as he glances up to my sister and back at his brother proudly.

"It's a masterpiece. Had me on the edge of my seat for three whole days straight."

Since I know how much this means to both brothers, I'm unapologetically beaming too. I might just have to learn to live vicariously through their sibling vibe.

Jake clears his throat. "My book is alternate history, so I do stick to nonfictional, historical events. I know it's not the same as history or nonfiction, but I didn't make up a whole world or anything."

LeArra nods. "Alternate history? I hadn't even heard what the book was about."

Without any prompting this time, Jake goes on to describe his book to my sister. As they talk, my sister moves closer to Jake until Winston and I are kind of on the outskirts of the circle.

Winston takes a step past my sister to stand next to me. I check my phone to find a text from Aubrey thanking me for having LeArra get in touch with her. I just send her a heart back.

Winston rests against the back of a chair, stretching his legs out into a tripping hazard. Then he crosses his arms over his chest and raises one eyebrow. He looks carefully curated by some very talented person whose job is to secure and maintain attention. I vote for that person to get a raise. Expectations exceeded.

"Where's the cake, though?" he says, unaware that in my mind he's become artwork.

I blink at him, bringing myself back from the alternate universe where I think of my best friend as a thirst trap. But even here, in this real, tangible world, my thoughts are still the same.

I shake my hands out and then clasp them together behind my back. "Probably want to wait for the guests of honor before they bring it out."

He shrugs. "Why? They're not paying for it."

I laugh. "Stop acting like you've never had cake before."

He narrows one eye. "I've never had any *today*."

"Anyway." I roll my eyes, as if he needs to get ahold of himself. In reality, I'm forcing myself to stop looking at him. I pitch my thumb in the direction of my sister. "Sorry about that whole thing."

He tilts his head as if he doesn't know what I'm talking about.

"My sister. The 'mischievous one,'" I put on a formal voice in imitation. "Like you're the bad seed or something."

He looks down at me and blinks. "At least what she said about me was accurate at some point. You don't need anybody coaching you up to do anything. That was mean."

I swallow hard. It was. But it's not new. LeArra thinks she's helping. She can't have her baby sister messing up the legacy of The Girls.

Winston studies me, then holds up the bag he came in with. "I brought you a refill."

I have no idea what he's talking about until he actually takes it out. I laugh lightly in surprise. It's an adult coloring book with intricate pictures and colored pencils. There's a sticky note in his perfect handwriting on the cover. *I figured you need a bigger distraction. XO, BW.*

He goes to take the note off, but I hold the book away from him.

Who cares about Michael's notes to Michaela when I have a note of my own? Not that I need any help keeping Winston on my mind. "I was going to give it to you at school, but I haven't seen you all that much the last few days."

"Everything with my team is critical so…"

He studies my face. I'm not sure what he's looking for. "Yeah, I know."

I flip through the pages. When I look back up at him, he's watching me unblinkingly and nibbling at his bottom lip. Is he nervous about giving this new coloring book to me? Does he think I won't like it? Will it bother him if I don't? I get this feeling in the pit of my stomach. Kind of like the feeling I get right before it's time to break up. I know I know something, but I'm not sure what yet.

This time I do, though. Winston is launching. I have managed to bring out the best boyfriend in a boy who isn't even mine. In a few weeks he's going to be in the halls hand in hand with some girl. She's going to be staring at him like he deserves to be stared at.

I'll probably have launched Kai by then too, and still with no explanation. The only difference between Winston and my exes is that he's launching right in front of my face. That's what's suddenly got me so shook every time he's around. I guess I don't like knowing exactly, specifically what the next girl is getting. It's never happened that way before. But, yay for Winston. Right? I should be happy for him. Maybe even proud. I should encourage him, right?

I don't know where to start. "You know, you're so, um…"

His eyebrows lift like I'm about to say something bad. That look makes me want to find the perfect word to describe him. To let him know that whenever someone catches his eye, he'll be able to make her happy.

"Winston, you're so"—I look away from him and the word comes to me so fast, I almost shout it—"thoughtful."

His eyebrows go from raised to creased between. I've confused him, I guess. So I keep talking. I want to be clear.

"I mean the way you think about me is—not me, Girlfriend Dru—and by 'think' I mean 'consider'—The way you consider me and what I might like or need is...special. Not everybody can do that. Not everybody wants to do that."

"Mmmm," he says, as if he's finally starting to understand. But he tilts his head and a side-eye becomes part of the eyebrow thing.

"You know, like this." I hold up the coloring book. "Everything you do before my games."

"Sure. Sure. Sure." He nods and speaks really fast. The way someone does when they don't really want you to keep going because you're embarrassing them.

But I have to keep going. I'm the one who should be embarrassed, not him.

I touch my hair, pulling it over my shoulder. "You notice my side braid. And you said you liked it. Even though I don't know how you can like it. I look like I'm recovering from a severe weather emergency."

He breathes a small laugh. "What do you mean? I do like it. I like your hair however you wear it."

"No." I squeeze my eyes shut and shake my head. "And the other night, I thought I was going to cry. I had almost accepted it and then I called you and I don't know how you did it, but I didn't want to cry anymore."

He points at me, and his words come out fast again. "Oh, yeah, right. The other night. I remember. I didn't really do anything. I just talked."

"No," I say again. "I mean, yeah, you talked. But when you talk you make me feel like I'm not the only one or something. You let me feel useful or helpful even if I'm not really either one. And it's always like you've listened . . . I don't know how to explain it but it's different from how I feel most of the time."

His head dips lower and lower as I ramble until he's looking at the palms of his hands, laced together at his lap. When I'm done, he taps the pads of his thumbs against each other before he looks up to speak.

"You are very useful and helpful. I don't mean to make you guess about that, if that's what I'm doing. I just assume you know that, based on how much I follow you around and everything." He laughs at himself.

His words skip my brain and go straight to my heart, which just happens to be banging against my rib cage at an inhuman pace.

"And of course I listen," he says softly, looking me right in the eyes. "That's a pretty low bar, Dru."

He's right. When I'm in a conversation, of course I expect the other person to listen. Kai listens. He really does. He tries to get me to think deeper. He *did* give me advice. Advice that the people who love me most in the world give me on a regular basis. But I don't feel better. That's probably on me, though, not him. What do I expect him to do? I'm responsible for how I feel.

I don't know why I'm comparing. This isn't even about Kai. It's about Winston riding off into the sunset.

"I'm probably not explaining it right." I touch my temple and close my eyes. The words are harder to come by but also they keep spilling out. "The point I'm trying to make is, I think you are the bar. You would make the perfect boyfriend."

Oh my God. Did I really just say that?

14 DAYS AND NO CLOSER TO AN ANSWER THAN WHEN I STARTED, PART 2

Behind me, Jake lets out a lung-clearing-fluid cough, followed by wheezing and then another cough. Winston and I both jump and look. LeArra is standing there, startled. Mr. Portis says Winston's name warningly as if *he's* done something.

Winston frowns. "That's not even me."

"Are you choking?" Ms. Teddy says on her way over.

Jake answers that by speaking directly to Winston. "I'm so sorry, dude. I had the water in my mouth and I just got surprised...My bad, man."

He doesn't look like he's choking. His eyes aren't watering or anything. He looks...alarmed. And I'm not sure what he's apologizing for. People thinking the disruption was Winston?

But that's not it. Winston and Jake glance at me and then back at each other. They're doing some twin thing, and I caused it. They're twinning about me. Jake heard me.

Jake heard what I said about Winston making a perfect boyfriend. And he thinks what?

That I want Winston to be *my* perfect boyfriend.

And it made him choke because Winston would never want to be my boyfriend, perfect or otherwise. This is the worst-case scenario, especially for a guy just trying to help out a friend.

That must've been what Winston was afraid of the night I asked for his help. He thought maybe one of us would develop some sort of feelings, and that was the last thing he wanted. He just didn't want to say it because either of us developing feelings was so unlikely. I would've talked him out of that idea in ten seconds.

And I would've been wrong. Because obviously I have feelings for Winston. Undeniable, inescapable, big feelings.

Having romantic feelings for Winston would be the most ill-advised thing I have ever done. Winston is my friend. Anything other than that would probably lead to us being something less than that. If I wanted us to be more than friends and he didn't, we'd be awkward and distant. He would always be afraid that spending time with me or being good to me would make me fall harder. And how would I not? It's not like he's going to become a different person just because he doesn't like me back.

And if he did want something more too, then I would be terrified that I would launch him to his next girlfriend. I know I *should* be happy, but the truth is, I don't want to send Winston off to the real thing. I would rather just never act on any feelings ever again.

And then there's Kai. The whole reason I started doing any of this. If I want there to be a Dru and Winston, I couldn't want there to be a Dru and Kai too. And *he* likes me. He's literally counting the days.

Winston turns back to me. "What were you say—"

I can't look him in the eye now, knowing that later he'll be having some conversation with Jake about how to get out of this experiment with me. I have to let him out now while I can still deny everything. While there's a chance this won't hurt our friendship.

I take a deep breath. "We can probably—"

Before I can finish, the cake designer, a Taiwanese woman with a gray, ear-length bob, and the baker, a light-skinned Black man who could maybe be her grandson, come into the room. Everyone goes quiet and focuses on them. Except Winston. I can feel him scrutinizing me. I don't want him to do that.

I don't know if they planned it this way, but Moriah and Rashid show up last, making a grand entrance. People say all the time how the two are glowing with their love, but no. They're both just flawlessly attractive people. It has nothing to do with love or feelings. If they came in separately or on the arms of other people, heads would turn. Period.

Even if they weren't flawlessly attractive, people would still notice them. It's hard not to notice two people who make each other smile constantly.

They apologize for being right on time and are quick to sit at the center of the table instead of the head. My parents go to the left of Moriah, and Rashid's parents go to his right. The rest of us fill in the other side of the table. Winston slides in next to me, groaning when his knees hit the underside of the table. Jake sits next to him. LeArra sits next to me.

I take a deep breath, determined to behave like I know and accept what Winston and I are: friends.

The designer gives her spiel about how cake choice may affect the design options and leaves the room.

The baker talks about sampling cakes that my sister requested. He also puts in a plug for cakes he feels are his specialties, and reminds us to palate-cleanse between tastes.

A tiny square piece of off-white cake with flecks of something brown is placed in front of us. I decide to split the sample with my fork as opposed to putting the entire thing in my mouth. I'd hate to overcommit and it's nasty.

Winston has only dipped his fork in the frosting and decided against the whole thing. He's writing on the comment card my sister insisted on using to make sure we don't taint each other's opinion. We're not supposed to talk about the cakes until all the cards have been turned in.

I run my tongue along my lips and teeth, trying to figure out what flavors I taste.

I find myself stuffing the second half of cake that isn't good nor terrible in my mouth. As I chew, I catch a glimpse of Winston's card. He's given the sample a zero out of five in all categories for consideration and in the comments written—*Spicy cake? No.*

He catches me peeking and flips his card over.

I scrunch my face. "Don't worry. I'm not going to copy you. Your taste is questionable."

He eyes me as he maneuvers the little yellow pencil between his fingers like a baton. "You wouldn't say that if you knew what I like."

My entire stomach finds reason to flip. Did he really have to say that all buttery and smooth like he's trying to be the embodiment of one of these cake samples?

"Please. Share. What do you like?" I force myself to ask because Friend Dru would definitely challenge him that way.

His face softens, going from playful to something I don't have a lot of experience with as far as he is concerned. I think he's about to tell me a secret, but he just nods toward my comment card. "Worry about figuring out what *you* like."

"I know what I like."

He drops his eyes. "Do you?"

As if we're talking about something other than cake, heat envelops my entire body. "I do."

He keeps his eyes on his comment card. "Write it down, then, and stop looking at me."

He's right. I'm staring. The last thing I want to be doing.

I lower my eyes to my own card. I don't know if it's a sixth sense or inhuman peripheral vision, but I feel his eyes back on me. For some reason, I don't call him out on it. I genuinely do not want to circle back to anything I said or Jake thought earlier.

I rate the cake mid in everything.

Next a chocolate square is placed in front of me. I commit quickly with zero regrets. We're only two in, but the chocolate square wins. I don't need to taste anything else. Like we're in third grade, he covers his card with his arms as he writes his review. Still, I can guess his answer.

From then on, the relative quiet of the room doesn't continue. There's constant murmuring and laughing. Winston rates another cake a zero and slides it away, barely touched. I can't believe he's getting away with that. LeArra would be *tsk*ing all over the place.

He takes a sip of water and slides the last piece of cake closer to him. He dips his fork in the icing. I haven't paid attention to the kind of cake we've been given. I have no idea what to expect. I am pleasantly surprised when I eat the first half. Winston moves on from his icing test to putting the entire piece of cake in his mouth. I look around the room at the responses. This one is coming in a close second.

Suddenly the cake decorator is standing right behind us, holding up a camera. I didn't hear her come in above the murmur of the tasters. "I want to get pictures for the couple. You don't mind?"

"Boyfriend Winston," Winston announces low in my ear as he hooks a finger into the bottom of my chair and pulls me so close, the lengths of our bodies are touching.

There's no time to think it through or consider what he means by that before he shows me and drapes his arm over my shoulders. I lean in and smile up at the camera, but as she takes the picture I can feel his eyes on me.

13 DAYS OUTSTANDING

Kai: 13 Days

Dru: Yep. It's getting really close.

Winston: WYD

Dru: Getting ready to go to Aubrey's.

Winston: Are you going to talk about your
boyfriend?

Dru: Lol. No. Aubrey's SAT prepping. She's
about business.

Winston: No downtime? No breaks? No
chitchat? It's Saturday.

Dru: Maybe.

Winston: I'm going to talk about my girlfriend all day.

Dru: You're going to get on people's
nerves.

Winston: I don't really care.
Winston: Can't wait to see you later.

Man, I really have to put an end to this.

"Your sister's a genius," Aubrey says when she opens her front door. She might think she's exaggerating, but she's not that far from the truth. LeArra's IQ is nearly Mensa level. "I took a practice test using some of the techniques she gave me, and I was actually able to finish in time."

"Yes!" I congratulate her with a hug. It would be overboard for anyone else, but Aubrey has been working so hard. She deserves a breakthrough.

She closes the door behind her, putting us both on the porch, and I realize she has her shoes on and is dressed to go out. Her purple tips are hidden inside a sleek, lumpless bun, and she's wearing a cropped top and shorts. Not her usual SAT practice outfit. She's also smiling and talking about the SAT at the same time. I'm not sure what's happening.

I narrow my eyes at her. "I thought we were doing SAT vocab."

"We were." She shoos me off her porch. "And we might still, but LeArra told me that if I meet a goal I have to celebrate, and I promised I would. So, we're getting tacos."

At the mention of tacos, I get on her excitement level and beat her to her small SUV. I put my seat belt on before she starts the car. She checks her mirrors and shifts into reverse. Aubrey lives on a busy road, so backing out into traffic requires a lot of patience. Patience she doesn't have. I wait for the whole adventure to be over before I speak.

"I'm always up for tacos, but I didn't even know LeArra had called you. She never responded to my text. Like, at all. I told her about you, and the next text was about the shower."

"Yeah." Aubrey shakes her head. "She said she didn't know what kind of friends you have and wanted to vet me before she offered to help."

I click my tongue against my teeth. "Wanted to *vet* you?"

"Yep. She went through all my social media before she sent me a DM." Aubrey takes her eyes completely off the road and looks at me as we approach a traffic light. It takes everything I have not to grab the steering wheel. I never feel like my life is in danger when I'm riding with Aubrey, but she has moments of lack of attention that put me in self-preservation mode a little bit. Luckily she manages to stop safely when the light turns red. "I didn't even care. She had so much great advice. We talked about everything, not just the SAT, and it made me feel so much better."

I tut out a humorless laugh. "The only advice she's ever given me is to be more like her and Moriah and you too now, I guess."

"What?" Aubrey's voice goes high pitched.

I adjust the shoulder strap of my seat belt. It feels too tight around me. "Nothing. She thinks you're as great as you think she is."

I don't want to rain on my best friend's accomplishment with my sibling problems. I am super happy Aubrey is already seeing improvement. I just don't understand why my sister would see so much promise in someone else while seeing so much nothing in me. Is it just because we're different? I truly don't get it.

"And I'm so happy for you." I smile at her. "What's next? What else did she say you should do?"

The green light glows through the windshield. Aubrey refocuses her attention. "No more practice tests after I was finally able to finish one on time. That goes against everything I've been taught, but after her way of taking the test helped me finish for the first time, I'm taking all her advice."

I shrug. "Sounds like a good idea to me. She has all the accolades to back up everything she's saying."

Aubrey puts her hand on her chest and looks away from the road and up at the ceiling for a second. I only get *a little* worried. "Seriously, Dru. Thank you for helping me out, especially when I know you didn't really want to ask her."

I grimace. I hate being that obvious. "You're welcome."

"Now." Aubrey takes both hands off the steering wheel to snap her fingers to a song playing in someone else's car as they ride by. "What's going on with Kai? He break up with you yet for conveniently forgetting you read all those books?"

"No. And he can't break up with me—we're not together." I duck my head. "Even if we were, I don't think he would. He sends me these texts counting down the days until we can go out."

She eyes me as she waits for a chance to turn left into the plaza with our favorite taco spot. "Ugh. That's messed up."

I jerk my head back. "What's messed up about it?"

She shrugs a shoulder and pokes her lips out. "I don't know. You tell me. You're the one who made it sound like he coughs on you and calls it love."

"That is *not* how I made it sound." Her posture says she's about to turn. I don't think the way is clear. I look both ways. I wait until she sees the cars I see and settles back into her seat before I start talking again. "It's sweet. Really, really sweet."

She goes for the turn when, in my opinion, the way still isn't clear. I brace myself against the seat. I swear we barely make it into the parking lot. She's unfazed, though. "Really?"

"Really," I say exasperatedly. I point to someone pulling out of a parking spot in the next row. She nods and zooms in that direction. "I'm just running out of responses. I don't know what to say anymore."

"Running out of responses like you're tongue-tied or like he's getting on your nerves?"

"Um." I hum in thought. "Neither."

She taps her fingers on the steering wheel as we wait for the car to clear the tight spot. "What about Winston?"

I clear my throat, sitting up straight. "What about him?"

"What are his findings"—she pauses to catapult us into the parking spot—"about your launching problem?"

I throw my hands up in exasperation. "Nothing. He keeps giving me gold stars and finding no issues."

She *tsks* and shuts off the car. "He can't find anything wrong with you. That's interesting."

I turn to her. "What do you mean? Do *you* have ideas?"

"Girl. You already know. I would've told you by now." We both get out of the car and walk embarrassingly fast to the restaurant. The closer I get, the more my mouth waters.

I open the door for her, and we both go in. As usual the small space is packed. There are no tables and only a few seats for waiting on food. We figure the owners must like it this way because they don't accept any phone or online orders.

I sigh. "After the cake tasting last night, I'm thinking about calling it."

"What? No. Why?" She presses her lips together. "I mean, what happened last night?"

I look at her. The alarm in her voice is not what I expected. I started to call a bunch of times to tell her what happened, but the more I thought about it, the more delusional I realized I might have been. Maybe even *she* saw how problematic doing this experiment with Winston could be.

She asked me point-blank if I thought he was the right person. I thought she was judging his past. But was she actually questioning my ability not to fall for him? What did she see that I didn't, because clearly, me and Winston in a fake relationship was a bad idea.

I don't even know where to start. She's surprisingly patient as I figure it out.

I know what I'm getting. Still, when the guy in front of us offers the menu, I take it. "He did something really sweet for me yesterday. I was trying to thank him for it. I ended up saying that basically he set the bar and would be a perfect boyfriend."

She frowns as if she's weighing what I've just told her. "You were making an observation?"

I press my lips into a thin line and grip the menu. "I said that after I told him how thoughtful I think he is and how special he makes me feel."

She looks over at me, not even the slightest bit of surprise on her face. "Oh. You were confessing."

My whole body gets hot. "Not on purpose. I just had a lot to say. I had been feeling all these things lately and the words just kept coming out. And I know it's so stupid because he's just playing a role. It's not even real.

"To make a long story short, Jake heard my...confession." Out of embarrassment, I look away from her and up toward the counter. "He literally choked on his bottle of water. Then he and Winston started giving each other these looks like what I'd said was the worst thing they'd ever heard. He felt sorry for Winston."

She blinks and shakes her head. "Or you're really reaching. Maybe the boy just had something in his throat. And you *know* siblings. Guys. The look could have been an inside joke about one of them wearing the other's underwear. Who knows?"

I, personally, don't have a relationship like this with my sisters. They, however, do have that kind of relationship with each other, so I've witnessed that kind of thing. And Winston and Jake are even closer.

"I guess that's a possibility." I shrug. "I mean, Winston would never think I like him. He would think that I value our friendship too much to let anything like that happen."

She side-eyes me. "Do you?"

"Yes, I do. I value our friendship too much to act on anything I'm feeling based on make-believe." I run my hands through my braids and pull them together tightly at the nape of my neck. "Aubrey. Do you know what a disaster it would be if anything happened between us? Because I'm such a great girlfriend, we'd be done with each other before the wedding. He'd inevitably become someone else's real Boyfriend Winston within minutes. And, worst of all, I would lose him as my friend."

Who would I text when my sisters are sistering? Who would notice that my answers depend on my audience and still want to be my friend? Who would think I'm the best soccer player he knows when all anyone else can talk about are the holes in my game? Who would value my trust so much that they'd let me talk them into this stupid experiment? Who would I trust enough to tell me the truth?

She looks at me sternly, and we move up in line. "Not necessarily. Things could work out."

"Even a fifty-fifty chance is too much. Not that I would even be given that chance. If I say anything more than I've already said, things will change." I put my palms out. "And what about Kai? Do I not value him? He's counting down the days as I'm falling for my best friend. What kind of person am I?"

"Dru, I don't know. This is complicated. And I think you need to just think about it more." Aubrey lets out a puff of air. "I'm not saying you shouldn't be concerned about Kai. Like, don't be an asshole about it, but also, make all decisions based on you and your feelings. Not on either of them."

"You're right."

"I know."

I swallow hard. I'm sure about one thing right now. I can't get a clear head when I'm in this thing with Winston and he's being the best boyfriend ever. I have to end this. Tonight.

13 DAYS OUTSTANDING, PART 2

Moriah and Rashid's bridesmaids and groomsmen—including Winston—are all here in the mirrored dance studio where LeArra and Moriah spent a lot of time before they turned thirteen. Today's instructor isn't the one who trained them, but her daughter Monique.

Monique is tall, long legged, and lean. She struts around the room like every minute of her life is a performance. The kind of person you expect to find on a big stage where every show is sold out. At first I felt lucky that she viewed Moriah as sort of a niece and would make sure that the first and wedding-party dances were everything she wanted them to be. She spent the first ten minutes giving us the history of Detroit Ballroom and explaining how the dance has evolved over the years.

While I didn't know the history of the dance, I do know Detroit Ballroom itself. My parents met on a dance floor when well-meaning coworkers worried that they were spending too much time alone in a new city and dragged them out to learn. Needless to say, they're always pulling out their moves. All the Eason girls are good at it.

At least I thought I was until today.

Monique is disappointed in everything I do. I no longer feel lucky.

"Little Eason."

Monique's technically incorrect name for me echoes across the space and over the music. Everyone else keeps dancing. Me and my partner, Peter, stop mid-twirl with my hand clasped in his above my head.

Peter is one of Rashid's closest friends. We've been placed together based on physical traits that Monique has identified but not shared. I've decided it must be mostly height. It definitely can't be anything else. He's white. Greek, I think I heard. I don't really see us doing anything for the other on that note. And there's a white bridesmaid he could've been partnered with if it was about aligning looks.

Also, he played football in college and appears to have continued his strength and conditioning schedule in the three years since. He has muscles popping out everywhere. There's no place to touch him where it doesn't feel like I'm crossing a line. I'm a strong girl, but my strength is more something felt after it's been put on you than something you can see coming.

Peter hasn't had much to say, but when he does speak, his voice is so deep I startle. He's apologized every time, but I'm pretty sure he invented apologizing sincerely while still being annoyed.

Monique slouches her shoulders as gracefully as any person can. "You're apprehensive, especially with turns. You're not loose. You're not having fun with your partner."

Exactly. I'm not having fun or any emotion close to it with my partner. We're learning a routine. Each movement isn't based on his personal whim, like in a normal dancing situation, but it's still his responsibility to lead me into each move. I'm unsure because I'm waiting for him to do his job. Even if I know what's next, it's literally his duty to tell me when to move.

Also, with everyone seemingly comfortable with the basic walk, we've started focusing on turns. He insists on raising my hand way over my head. I'm seriously worried about the future of my rotator cuff.

Peter drops my hand. "I think it's me."

Monique clasps her hands together underneath her chin and tilts her head toward him, kind of like that motion pretentious people use to accept praise. "No. Peter, you have surprised me. You're picking up everything quickly. Maybe you're too demanding a partner for her."

Since I like where her train of thought is going, I try not to be offended by the fact that she just implied I can't keep up. Then again, his being demanding isn't necessarily a compliment either. I think she might've taken us both out at once.

Using her phone, Monique stops the music. "As I said, nothing is permanent. Anyone else feeling like they're not quite a match?" Three people raise their hands. Winston and his partner—a girl from Rashid's side, not mine—and Moriah's best friend since high school.

Honestly, I don't know what to hope for. Winston, who I know I'll have the most fun with because that's what we do, or some random person who I won't have to worry about making sure my feelings aren't getting any deeper for. Someone I won't be afraid is about to give me a friend zone speech. Someone I don't have to breezily end an experiment with when I feel anything but breezy about it.

Aubrey is right: I could be reaching in thinking that Winston and

Jake made assumptions about my feelings and that Winston is now regretting everything. But she could also be reaching in assuming their twin glance had nothing to do with me.

I will feel so much better when I'm able to make it clear that my feelings for Winston are nothing but friendly. Even if that's a lie. Nobody gets hurt but me.

Monique reassigns Peter first, then the girl from Rashid's side, and lastly Moriah's high school best friend. After that, she doesn't even say anything, she just walks away because it's obvious. I'm with "Tall Portis." The reassignment officially debunks my height theory. It also gives me butterflies.

Winston looks as awkward in his basketball shorts and dress shoes as I feel in my running tights and heels. He doesn't hide his smile as I walk over to him. I'm not smiling. I'm actually a little scared. The closer I get, the more I realize it. I don't know if I'm scared to be close to him or scared that he might be wary of me now that I've put things out there that I can't take back. Sometimes when you send a person's mind in a certain direction, it's impossible to send it in any other way.

But he's smiling. Like, grab-everyone-in-the-room's-attention smiling. Maybe Aubrey's right. The twin look had nothing to do with me. Unfortunately, that thought makes butterflies. As warm as my entire body seems to be getting, I would say the butterflies are actually fanning the flicker.

I have to do it. I have to end this so he can stop boyfriending me. This is the perfect time. With other people around, and if I don't make a big deal, he'll think none of this matters to me.

If I could somehow overcome all that, this will be fun, even if Winston is a terrible dancer. I haven't paid attention to anything happening on his side of the dance floor, and his being able to do TikTok dances doesn't mean he can ballroom. But at least Monique won't be able to complain about my lack of obvious enjoyment. I like being with Winston in most situations.

On task, Winston grabs my right hand with his left and places it around his neck as he slinks his right hand around my waist. This approach is more what I'm used to when it comes to being led—an immediate take-charge sort of situation.

But I'm not expecting this from Winston. I freeze. My legs go a little wobbly and every breath of air I take in is like ice going down. Winston is just Winston, with his bottom lip pulled between his teeth for focus. I keep my eyes on his face because when I look at his hand or even think about it, the intensity of everything going on in my body skyrockets.

Monique snaps to a rhythm living only in her head and counts up from five. When she gets to eight I realize my other hand isn't in place around his neck.

Every move I make is a fumble but somehow my hand ends up where it's supposed to be by the time Monique begins again with her verbal instruction.

"My bad. I'm sorry. I wasn't ready," I mumble.

His response is a small smile and a gentle, reassuring press right above my hip. Reassurance that makes me feel like everything's good even though my body insists that it isn't. When the pressure lightens, I want it back.

Even in heels, I'm not tall enough for our cheeks to touch. I fit just under his chin. Somewhere in this area is where he must've sprayed something that smells sweet and clean. I've never been this close to him. I'm not sure if this is a normal thing or if he just wore cologne because he'd be sharing space with someone else today. Whatever the reason, I like it.

"Thank you for rescuing me from dancing with an engaged woman." He slouches a little to be closer to my ear. I feel myself tense, but all over this time. "We can cha-cha freeze or whatever, but I'm not about to be hesitating and dipping her. Makes me feel like a philanderer."

I laugh against his chest. Only he would pull out such a perfect word to describe how he sees the situation. "I ballroom with my dad all the time. It doesn't have to be intimate."

"The way my granddad taught me it does. It's the only way I can do it." His voice is just loud enough to register the bass in every word as it rumbles through me, creating inexplicable little earthquakes. "First rule, make your partner look good. Second rule, be smooth. Third rule, make everybody in the room jealous. I'm not accomplishing all that dancing the way your dad dances with you."

"Well, but..." I laugh nervously because the little earthquakes are turning into one deadly, record-breaking event at the idea of whatever he's going to do to make everybody in the room jealous. "You will be dancing with me *in front* of my dad."

"He'll have his eyes on Moriah, not us," he says, as if he's thought this out. "This would probably be a good time to have Boyfriend Winston privileges."

Monique is at the end of her countdown, and he walks me back in time with the music.

In competition with the earthquake, my heart rate picks up. I laugh again. "Okay."

It's just going to be this one last time because obviously I can't say no without an explanation. Not now.

With all the sweet messages and the times he's made an effort to make me feel better, Girlfriend Dru definitely gave Boyfriend Winston a lot of privileges a long time ago. I'm left wondering which ones he plans to take advantage of when he slowly moves his hands along my arms, tightening the slack that keeps distance between us. I don't think there's as much as a centimeter of space left between our bodies, but when he wraps one of his arms back around my waist he manages to pull us even tighter. We're close enough that even the slightest movement of his body registers in mine.

After the two eight-counts of basic walking, the lead is supposed to pivot and send their partner out into a turn. Half the couples fumble, but Winston does not. When he sends me out his eyes meet mine. Where I'm used to seeing my father's smiling face, I'm staring at a very, very beautiful boy.

I look down at my feet as if I have to concentrate on them to get the steps right as I turn. What I need is to not look at him while he's Boyfriend Winston. If I do I'll look worse than I did dancing with Peter. We complete our partner turn and drop our arms to our sides.

It's clear what he means now about the way his grandfather taught him to dance. It's not necessarily the moves, but how you do them.

Even though we're not touching anymore, I still can't look at him. My eyes drift across the room and connect with LeArra's, of all people's. I don't know why she's eyeing me the way she is. I mean, she's always inspecting me, but this is like a deep investigation into a crime I don't even know I'm committing.

Winston clears his throat. "If you don't look at me, people are going to think you don't like dancing with me and try to take your place."

I force my eyes up to his. There's no piercing stare, just my friend Winston.

I give him a questioning eyebrow and whisper, "Why are you cocky about this?"

He points a finger at himself in surprise as Monique hands out corrections to every couple except us.

I nod aggressively. "Have you been listening to yourself?"

He takes a step closer. My heart starts to beat fast again. Is that fear or anticipation?

"I'm not trying to be cocky." He speaks so low I find myself trying to read his lips. "You seem unsure or something. It makes me want to be sure enough for both of us."

I know he's sensing how disoriented being this close to him makes me. But I hope he thinks he's picking up on me knowing that somehow, some way, one of my sisters will have something critical to say to me about one thing or the other. You'd think knowing I'm constantly being critiqued would've lost its effect by now, but it hasn't.

And I'm confused on who's talking here—Boyfriend Winston or my friend Winston. Wanting to be sure enough for both of us is a very sweet thing to say, no matter who's saying it, but the way I should respond is dependent on the speaker.

I go with my gut, return the look Boyfriend Winston gave me during the dance, and whisper, "Kiss. Kiss."

He blinks, and his eyes drift to my lips. I lick them. Not suggestively, but once he puts my mind on that part of my body I become really self-conscious about it. Are my lips properly conditioned for a real *kiss kiss*?

These are all things I shouldn't be thinking about. Why didn't I just go with friend Winston?

"Looks like this is a better fit." Monique creeps up from behind us. "My only note is don't hunch when you look at her. Little Eason will learn to allow the eye contact."

She doesn't leave room for any sort of waffling on my part. And since, even with the turmoil in my belly, I'm holding my own in a two-way stare now, I think I can hold it together for a three-minute dance routine.

"You two will demonstrate for everyone else."

My eyes shoot automatically back to LeArra, whose investigation continues, then to Moriah, who's hand in hand with a smirking Rashid. Moriah says, "They look really good. When everyone shifts on the dance floor, can we keep them near the front?"

Do we really look that good together? Were other people feeling the earthquakes too? I turn back to Winston, confused. He's just staring at me, like he's waiting for something. Like a thank-you. Like, maybe he *was* really Friend Winston, and the *kiss kiss* confirmed everything he and Jake thought they picked up on last night.

Monique motions us to the front of the studio. When we get there, Winston formally nods and bows, which makes everyone chuckle a little. Then she instructs us to get in the home position, which for the purpose of the routine is Winston and me intertwined. He doesn't waste a second securing us with an arm around my waist.

I inhale the sweet scent I've never smelled on him before and start to laugh. At first, it's small enough that it doesn't affect what we're doing, but then he grabs my hand to put it around his neck. His touch is so light and careful it's making me feel too many things at once. I can't keep the laughter inside.

I pull away from Winston and cover my mouth, but laughter continues to seep out of me. And somehow getting it out makes me feel a little more relaxed, less squeamish. I force a deep breath. "Sorry. That tickled."

"Yeah, I bet," LeArra says from across the room.

That comment whips me into shape real fast. I'm not worried about being in trouble with her, or Moriah, or my parents, or even Monique at this point. I'm feeling a little in trouble with myself. First the earthquakes, then my heart, now embarrassing laughter at the exact wrong time. I'm helpless to anything he does.

Winston swings his arms back and forth at his sides a few times before catching one hand in the other, waiting for me to collect myself. "You ready?"

I nod and he pulls me in again. To avoid more embarrassment, I wrap my arms around him before he can do it for me. Just a walk back and then into the turn people are having issues with. After the walk, we won't have to be so close. In theory, I shouldn't have to hold on to him this way for very long, but this woman starts in about hand placement, leaders developing their own styles, and followers adjusting. All the while, Winston is still holding me close, being the perfect example. It doesn't feel funny at all now. It feels good. Too good.

I have to stop this. It's not good for me. It's not good for him. And it's really bad for our friendship.

I drop my arms, causing him to pull back a little and whisper, "What'd I do?"

My eyes shift from his, giving away the fact that I'm at least a little uncomfortable.

"Wait." He drops his arm from my waist. "Did I do something? Like for real?"

"No, my arms are just getting tired."

He nods but there's a crease between his eyebrows like he wants to believe me but he's not sure if he does.

I crane my neck to see if the talking has caught Monique's attention. She's going on now about learning the steps without a partner first. I glance over at LeArra for the same reason. She's listening intently to Monique though none of the movements are new to her.

This is a good time to end this whole thing. I'll have to figure out some other method for solving my problem. Or not, I guess, but I can't go on with him doing the Boyfriend Winston thing. I can't.

My focus shifts from his face to my feet as I think about how to say this. I think I'm starting to sweat, which is weird because this isn't a real breakup. I'm not Girlfriend Dru. He's not Boyfriend Winston.

He looks at me, searching my face for clues. "What's up?"

"Nothing. Really. It's not that serious." I force a breezy laugh. "I was just thinking that I've been taking up so much of your time with all my issues and we're not really solving anything. I'm still doomed. You probably want a break from the whole fake boyfriend/girlfriend thing."

He tries to put his hands in his pockets, but his shorts don't have any. He just ends up tapping his fingers on his thighs and then eventually crossing his arms over his chest. "Yeah, I've been thinking a lot about that too. We haven't really been coming up with anything."

All the earthquakes and the butterflies and the flickers die out. I'm just left with a hollow feeling in the pit of my stomach. How long has he been dreading being Boyfriend Winston? At what point did he know he wanted to stop? And why didn't he? Guilt or obligation? Do I even want to know?

I put my hands behind my back and latch them together. "Why didn't you say anything? I know you have a life, and I just might be unsolvable. We could've stopped whenever you wanted. I would've been okay with that. I'm okay with that *now*. No more Girlfriend Dru/Boyfriend Winston."

Blurting it out doesn't make it any easier to hear. I feel winded and cold. My palms are sweaty. Every time I swallow it just feels like I need to do it again. Maybe I like Winston even more than I realized. Or is this just embarrassment over Winston being annoyed by our arrangement and not telling me?

He's working through something. His face changes every time he gets a new idea and then discards it. I don't ask him to share anything. For the first time that I can remember, I don't want to know what Winston's thinking.

He uncrosses his arms and swings them back and forth a few times. "We could quit, you know. Whatever. We tried but got nothing."

My hands are actually trembling now. It's one thing for our experiment to be over. It's another for it to be over but way after it should've been. I wish Monique would start counting up again. I wish we could just dance.

"Or"—he puts a finger up—"we could try one last thing. It's more of a Winston type of idea." He smiles shyly. "No pigs or stink bombs or anything like that, but probably a little more than you were originally thinking of."

I shake my head and wave my hands in front of us. "No. It's fine. You don't have to."

He puts his hands on my shoulders, and his thumbs do these soft circles on my collarbone like he's trying to calm me down. This isn't how Winston touches me, or at least not before today. It's like a weird spell, the way it feels good but at the same time makes my heart rate pick up again.

I don't want to laugh or shift out of his reach. I figure I might as well enjoy this. Because I know I'm going to miss it when he lets me go.

"Listen." He looks me steadily in the eye. "I never said I don't want to help you anymore. I just said what we're doing isn't getting you anywhere."

I let his eyes hold mine. "What do you think we should do?"

He takes his hands off me, and just like I thought, I wish he would put them back. "We should do a real date always in character as Boyfriend Winston and Girlfriend Dru. See what comes up."

I look away from him and massage the back of my neck. That is a very bad idea. At least I can be sure now that he doesn't think I like him, because if he did he would never suggest this. He would know that being around him that way might potentially hurt me in the end and only make me like him more.

But if I say no, what excuse can I make sound believable after I badgered the shit out of him to help me in the first place? I basically told him that he had no valid reason not to let me show him my girl-friend skills.

"I'm not saying we have to do that. I'm just throwing it out there." He crosses his arms over his chest again. "Just an idea because I know if you don't get some sort of resolution or final conclusion, you're going to be thinking about this launcher thing forever."

He *does* have a point there. I have fixed nothing and therefore nothing will change. I'm destined to stay the girl you date right before you fall in love. If there's any chance at finding a solution to that, I still want to do it. And, most importantly, he's still the only person to help.

And now that I have all these feelings, being Girlfriend Dru will be easier than it's ever been. Getting to my flaws shouldn't be a problem.

After that, I can move on. Get over whatever this thing is with Winston and maybe have a better chance at a failed launch with Kai.

"S-sure," I stutter out. "Why wouldn't we at least try it?"

Other than that going out with him would be an undeniable breach of my team pact. But how can I explain that to Winston? The team pact doesn't apply to platonic situations. And that's what we are to him. Platonic. Nothing more than an extension of what we agreed to in the beginning.

Monique speaks louder now, and something tells me it's to get our attention. I snap back to this moment and put my arms around Winston. He takes my hand off his neck and instead positions me for a ballroom turn. Good thing one of us was listening.

"We're not getting into any movement yet. We're just watching the demonstration," Monique says. I can't see her unless I peek around Winston, but the length of her quiet tells me she's making eye contact with everyone, ensuring they've registered her words. "It might help if some of you know where you need to be after we complete the basic walk."

She starts to count. I look up at Winston. He smiles at me. I try to smile back but it feels more like a grimace. I've just agreed to a bad idea. A bad idea that I really like. Is this the kind of feeling that Winston used to give in to? If it is, I completely understand. Luckily the only person I can get in trouble with is me...maybe him.

No. I won't let myself get in trouble with Winston. I'm going to put everything I have into this date so that there's nothing left to want after.

Winston starts moving me right on time.

"Perfect," Monique quips. "Once we all have the moves, we'll get focused on the kind of chemistry that Little Eason and Tall Portis have. That's the really hard part."

I stumble. Chemistry? Is that what makes me and Winston look good together? Is that what the flicker is? Something neither of us can really control?

I apologize for my misstep. Luckily, I'm still able to follow the bit of pressure he applies and flow right into my turn and another and another before Monique tells us to go back to the top.

The four-step walk brings us back together again.

We're so close, I have to crane my neck more than I normally would and speak quickly. We're not together long. "What should we do on the date?"

I have to wait a full eight-count before we're back together and I can get my answer.

His swallow is audible, but he doesn't lose a step. "How about you plan something for me, and I plan something for you? That way we see it from both sides."

That makes sense, except I've never actually put thought into a date. Jayden and I went out. He'd just ask if I wanted to hang out. He'd pick me up or we'd meet somewhere.

"That sounds good. We have to be careful, though. I don't want to run into any of my teammates and have to explain."

And what would I explain? Admitting what's happened with all my exes is too embarrassing. Telling my teammates that being with Winston is just friendly, part of a fact-finding mission, would be a bold-faced lie.

I just have to keep reminding myself what this is for. I'm figuring out what makes me the boyfriend launcher. As long as I keep myself focused on that, I should be fine. If we come up with something, I'll use it to help with Kai, like I planned. I'll stop spending so much time with Boyfriend Winston and everything will fade.

Another eight-count passes before we're pressed together again.

"When?" he asks. "I'm free whenever you are."

"Tomorrow," I say without thinking, and then add for good measure, "If you really come up with something, I want to have as long as I can to work things out in my head. It's probably not an overnight-fixable issue."

When we've been told to stop and Monique starts another lecture, Winston looks down at me. "Tomorrow. Sounds perfect to me."

THE HALFWAY MARK

Dru: We're still doing today, right?

Winston: Definitely.

Kai: Halfway there

Dru: Yes we are

That one was bad. The worst so far. He sent that message at midnight last night, and I've taken ten hours to respond because I couldn't figure out how to avoid saying something so lackluster. Yet, here I am.

I sit on my bed passing a soccer ball between my feet, wishing I had more to say. He deserves for me to have something more to say. Not only is it sweet that he keeps counting down, but I still think he's everything he was two weeks ago when he asked me out in Winston's basement.

If he found out that I barely slept last night because I couldn't stop thinking about Winston or that I'm going out with him today, he wouldn't appreciate it. If roles were reversed I would be pissed.

My only saving grace, not that I'm trying to justify anything, is that nothing is actually going to happen between me and Winston. He doesn't want it. Neither of us would let it. I have to have some integrity. If I'm lucky I'll get to the bottom of my issues and use that to help me build a better relationship with Kai.

This date will be all business.

My friendship, my team, and my integrity all matter more than the way Winston makes me feel.

When he rings my doorbell, I don't even look at myself twice in the mirror. I'm wearing my normal, everyday sweatpants and a cropped top. I don't need to put in any extra effort to carry this business out. It'll just confuse my heart.

Before I even answer the door, the flicker, which hasn't bothered to go away since yesterday, makes itself known. When I pull the door open and see him, it's like somebody used that one flicker to ignite everything in my belly.

He's wearing shorts but they're not his normal, oversized basketball ones. His tennis shoes are a pair that don't come out much, based on how pristine they are. His haircut is fresh, and there's not even a second's worth of stubble on his face.

He's smiling his Winston smile, but his head is ducked a little to hide it like maybe he doesn't want Girlfriend Dru to know exactly how happy he is to see her. That's what gets me.

He's giving everything. Complete dedication to the role. Just like we talked about.

I look down at myself. I'm underdressed and a little guilty. He's into this for me as a friend, while I'm so scared of being into him as more that I won't even let myself give the same effort. That attitude defeats the whole purpose of everything. I can't let my feelings get in the way of answers. Either I'm doing this or I'm not.

I'm doing this.

"I should change," I say.

"No, no. You look good. You always look good." He nods in a way that lets me know this isn't just him saying what's expected. He means it. I try not to take it personally. He's just stating what he believes as fact. I've always thought he was cute too. That didn't just creep up on me in the last few weeks, like everything else has. It's possible to have those thoughts without feelings. "I had to step it up a little bit, or else everybody will wonder how I pulled you."

I fiddle with the waistband of my sweatpants. "Now they'll be wondering about *me* pulling *you*."

He raises an eyebrow in challenge. "We both know even you don't believe what you just said. Let's go."

I turn to go back inside. He grabs my wrist. His touch puts a stop to any move I'm about to make. There's no real pressure behind his grip, but the electricity is fast-moving and incapacitating. With his other hand he reaches behind me and grabs the doorknob. When he pulls, it forces me out of the house and us closer together. He's watching me the whole time. I'm hoping he doesn't notice how hard I swallow or how tense I am as we get closer.

He unhands me and takes the four steps down my porch two at a time. Pretty sure real Winston wouldn't have touched me as gently as he just did or hovered that close to me anywhere outside of wedding dance rehearsal. But just so we don't run into any weird situations later, I feel the need to clarify what we are. And, also, if we're not on the same page, I can't trust his critique.

I shuffle behind him. "Today, you're always Boyfriend Winston, right?"

He nods over his shoulder.

"Well, hold on, then."

When he stops to see what I want, I dash past him, reach his driver's side door first, and lean back against it. He looks around suspiciously as if he genuinely feels in danger before making his way over to me.

He bends down a little, still skeptical but smiling. "Yes?"

I've never put much thought into what kissing Winston would actually be like considering our height difference. Even with him bending down to me, I have to press up on my tiptoes. His eyebrows shoot up as if he's afraid of what's about to happen, but I swear, he leans down just a little more to help with my reach.

I try to breathe regularly, but when I go to exhale all I can think about is my breath on him and his breath on me. It's a weird thing to think about, us breathing each other in. I push that thought to the periphery. I can't force it any further. I focus on why I raced him to his door in the first place.

"Kiss." I kiss the air next to his left cheek, thinking he might feel a bit of the vibration if he's open to it, and move slowly to his other side, skimming close enough to graze his lips. But I'm careful not to. That would be way too dangerous for me. The closer we get, the more I know that. If our lips actually touched, I might not turn away. "Kiss."

I like teasing Winston. It makes me feel like I have just a little power in the situation. But when he takes a step closer and presses his fingertips against the car door on either side of me, I realize I miscalculated. Winston is officially the teaser, and I am the teasee.

The worst part is, I'm sure most of his teasing isn't even calculated or intentional. He probably can't imagine that the unraveling twist from the other day is calling to me. Begging me to retwist it. Not because it looks bad, but just so I can touch his hair and know for sure it's as soft as I think it is. My fingers are actually tingling with the compulsion. But I press my hands to the car's frame instead.

On the other hand, he has to know he's giving me soft eyes. You can't accidentally look like you're daydreaming about someone while they're standing right in front of you. Can you?

Intentional or not, my insides feel weightless. I actually might just float away. As it is, our faces seem to be getting closer somehow.

He's close enough to be kissed very deeply. That's too much.

I rest on my heels. He moves with me as if I have him on a string. There's no escaping.

His breath is shaky now, as if he's letting it out in little spurts. "What else?"

I shake my head and try to make a getaway by ducking under one of his arms. He catches me by the waist and doesn't let go. I *do* want to get away, but my effort fizzles. Probably because of the amount of energy my body is using to set me on fire. I never should have thought I'd have the upper hand here.

I clear my throat. "Do *you* have anything else?"

He lets his hand fall from my waist. Even though his smile tells me it's a test, I don't move out of his reach. "Nope. Just making sure you have everything you need. You know how you like to linger."

My "shut up" comes out as a whisper.

I think he's going to pull me closer. Instead, he presses a finger into my side, pushing me easily away from the door handle. Somehow, all the almost-touching and the closeness have made me pliable. He could've pushed me out of the way with less.

As we both get in the car, I accept that my days of teasing Winston Portis are over.

We've been driving for an hour, chatting about school, and shushing each other anytime either of us brings up the wedding of the decade, before it occurs to me to ask where we're going. Navigation is leading us to either a parking lot or a grassy knoll.

"Just a reminder"—I side-eye him—"my parents have a description of you, pictures even, and know the make and model of your car."

He glances at me and shakes his head. "We should be there in a minute."

We suddenly hit a little traffic. I scour the road ahead trying to see what could be a mile away, in a parking lot, on a grassy knoll, and on the more eastern side of metro Detroit in May. I tap my fingers on the dashboard, trying to assemble all the clues he's given me.

Then I see a circular beacon in the distance. I'm pretty sure it's a Ferris wheel.

I laugh at myself for thinking Winston, even the smoldering boyfriend one, would do something as sweet as remember the first date I missed out on in elementary school. Based on his reaction that night at his house, I know he thinks my first launching evidence is trivial.

But as he merges us deeper into the traffic that can only be leading us to one place, I start to believe a little. When he finally gets waved into a makeshift parking area, I know for sure. We haven't even gotten out of the car, and I know it's going to be one of the best days ever.

His setting the boyfriend bar wasn't an overexaggeration. While I wish I'd gotten cute for a someone who would plan a date that means something to me, I'm happy to be in my Jordans rather than the sandals I probably would've worn otherwise.

Once he's parked, he eyes me seriously. "Want me to come around and let you get on my back to keep your shoes out of the mud?"

"What about your shoes?"

He bites his bottom lip and looks toward the sky as if considering it. "If I got on your back, my feet would probably still scrape the ground. But I can scoop *you*, though."

I laugh, then shrug in agreement. My shoes have some love on them, but honestly, I want to see if he's actually going to carry me the quarter mile to the entrance. He walks around to my side and hunches a little as I open the passenger's door. I'm careful not to pull him down as I hop on, clutching my legs tightly to his sides until he secures his hands under me.

My heart thumps. I try to tell myself it's from the effort.

I take in the parking lot and the area as a whole. "Man, this is a great view. Do you even realize how much you see before everyone else?"

His voice is flat when he says, "I never really thought about it."

I smack my lips at his overlooking his blessing. "Seriously, don't take this advantage for granted."

"Dru?"

His voice is serious. I forgo my new view and rest my chin on his shoulder. We're cheek to cheek in a way we couldn't be yesterday. It seems like every day we set a new closeness record.

"What?"

He turns his head a little. I pull back to avoid an accidental kiss. "Is this a good place to bring you?"

"What? Yes. This was the best place to bring me. This is earning you a gazillion of the biggest kiss kisses you will ever get in your whole life, regardless of the crowd." I'm on his back and our mouths are close enough that I probably should have considered going a little easier on the enthusiasm. But, I mean, I am supposed to be narrating what Girlfriend Dru would do, and she would appreciate this. *I* genuinely appreciate this.

He must realize the awkwardness of our proximity too, because he doesn't turn his head the way he did before. "When would I be getting those kisses?"

"There's still a lot to do." I rest my chin on his shoulder again and take a deep breath. "We haven't ridden all the rides, you haven't won anything for me, and I haven't had an elephant ear, and...I'm just playing."

He only moves his eyes this time. "You don't have to be. I can do all that."

I smile. "I'm sure you can, but I hope I didn't undershoot the whole thing and you're not going to be nearly as happy later as you're making me now."

He blinks. I think he's trying to hide disappointment, which is weird. But I guess if I can feel happy right now, even if there are no real stakes, he can feel disappointed. He's still going to be my friend even if he doesn't like my fake date.

"If my girl does something for me, I'm going to find a way to appreciate it."

I groan.

He turns his head and this time I don't pull back. I should because friends move when they're close enough to kiss, but I don't move a muscle. "You don't believe me?"

"Sure. I believe you." I look him deep in the eyes. "But you're giving me this false sense of security. Like if somebody feels a certain type of way about me, they're going to give me extra leeway to be a buffoon. And it's nice to imagine, but nobody's actually going to do that for me."

I do not appreciate the way my voice gives on that last sentence. I'm not even sure why it does, except that if I had thought before I spoke, I wouldn't have let that thought slip.

Winston's pace, which started out leisurely to begin with, has now slowed to nearly a halt between two cars. "You hold your exes' current relationships up as, like, the benchmark, and you don't think they're more considerate to each other than they might be with other people, forgive each other's mistakes, or give each other the benefit of the doubt?"

I adjust my feet around his thighs just in time to avoid crashing into a car's mirror, and apologize. He shrugs it off as an annoying delay to his getting an answer to his question.

I focus my attention out ahead of us and watch the crowd grow by the second. "I don't know what he forgives or accepts or whatever, but as far as I can see, he's a world-class boyfriend to *her*."

Quietly, he goes back to his leisurely pace. He's looking straight ahead but I can tell he's doing more thinking than watching. I'm too scared to ask what's going through his head, but at the same time I really want to know. I wait for my mind to come up with something else to say, the way it always does when I'm with Winston, a nice subject change maybe, but it never happens. My mind is fixated on what he's thinking.

We reach the cement of the parking lot, and he turns us toward a ticket booth. I try to loosen myself, but he holds tighter. I've been watching him think for a while. I have been very much in his space, but the look he gives me makes me feel like I am literally a part of his space. If I tried to let him go right now, I don't think the universe would allow it.

He sighs. "World-class boyfriends exist, but not for you."

It's not a question. It's a statement, but the way he's looking at me says he's expecting a response. I know what he's getting at, but he's off base.

"I know I'm worthy, Winston. I'm surrounded by intelligent, powerful, self-sufficient women constantly. You can't grow up an

Eason woman and not know that basic thing." I laugh humorlessly. "But you can be worthy of things that never find you."

He stares at me until I squeeze him with every part of me because I sense we're about to run into someone. He's forced to check our surroundings. I convince him to let me down before he gets us hurt, noting that he needs to save all his energy for the rides.

I offer to pay for myself, but he's already bought the unlimited ride pass online. All we have to do is pick up our wristbands. When he lifts his wrist to allow me to snap his on, I notice he's wearing three bracelets today, two red and one black, instead of his normal two, and still, I have no idea of the meaning of any of them.

Seeing my hesitation, he gives me his other wrist instead. But when he goes to put mine on for me, he can't hide what he's wearing.

I put my finger through one of them, trying to make out the characters enough to identify the language. "What do they mean?"

He snaps my wristband in place and looks up and away from me so fast it can't even be called a glance. "I have no idea."

I side-eye him. "Are you saying you could be wearing a bracelet that says 'eff Winston'?"

He bites his bottom lip. "That would be messed up, but obviously that would be a reference to a Winston other than myself."

I can't help but smile. "You're good if it's all the other Winstons, just not you?"

"I'm sure there's a few wack Winstons out there." He tilts his head and smiles back. I'm caught up just long enough for him to change the whole trajectory of everything.

He laces our fingers together and raises both of our hands as he points toward a ride that twists, spins, and throws riders high into the air. His hand is warm and a little rougher than I expect. Not in a bad way. It's oddly comforting in a situation where I have no real reason to feel discomfited, except I don't feel like he's telling me the truth. I've never felt like that before with him. "Scariest one first?"

We're nowhere near as close as we were in my driveway or even when he gave me the long piggyback ride, but it feels more intimate somehow. Earlier I had a lot of thoughts about how I could get closer to him physically, but now I'm thinking close in a different way, like closer to his thoughts. I wish I knew why, for a split second, it seemed like there was a lot he's been holding back.

THE HALFWAY MARK, PART 2

I'm still drunk off playing games, and eating all the food, and riding the scariest ride for the third time when I decide we better leave before it gets too dark for my part of the date. I put thought into it, but still cannot compete with him hanging with my thrill level, winning me things we had to actually bring back to the car because they were too big to take everywhere with us, and making sure I had enough elephant ears.

He's held my hand with our forearms brushing for so much of the day that when we have to split to make it to our opposite sides of the car it feels unnatural. I miss it to the point of placing my hand on the console between us, hoping Boyfriend Winston will take the bait. I'm careful not to put it palm up. That would be too obvious. The goal is just to be available, like an option.

As soon as he's done navigating the makeshift parking lot, he slides his fingers right under mine like he missed the contact too. And it's different from when he took my hand earlier. Then it was to pull me along. Now it's just because.

For a while, it's all I can think about, where we're connected and how much I don't like when we aren't. How am I, without looking like an addict, going to keep his hand in mine for the rest of the night?

I can honestly say, I have never spent time with any other guy that has felt this easy. I think it's because, no matter what roles we're playing, he's still my friend Winston. That's why I've been racking up the gold stars and he's been racking up the kiss kisses. No other reason.

With one hand I pull up the directions to the Lower Huron Metropark trail connection on my phone and direct him away from the carnival without giving away where we're going.

My parents used to take me and my sisters to ride our bikes on the portion of the metro trail I'm taking him to. It's pretty and quiet. And if you're not thinking about when you can eat snacks or racing a sister, all you have to think about is the person you're with. The Twins and I went there a few times together when we were little too, but for the water park.

The trail is about forty-five minutes from where we are now. It occurs to me that this drive is actually just-me-and-you time, or at least it could be.

I watch the mirrors just like he does as we merge onto the highway. "At first when you said 'just-me-and-you time'"—I take a breath and then glance at him and then away—"I thought you meant it in a physical way. And I was like *Dang, Boyfriend Winston is a hookup king.*"

Winston frowns. "No. That's not what I was trying to say. I mean, if something happens at any point that's fine, but that's not what I mean."

I raise an eyebrow. "Right. You're just playing unless I'll do it."

"Dru." He squeezes my hand gently, but it doesn't take much to send a tingle up my arm. "That's not me."

I laugh. It comes out hoarse. "I'm messing with you. I know that's not what you mean...now."

He does a double take. "Is that where you're taking me? Somewhere to focus on you? To focus on each other?"

I bite my bottom lip and nod slowly as I check for any signs of disappointment on his face. This could be a fail, meaning it could fail in other, more realistic situations.

"You didn't undershoot. That's a perfect date, and it makes me feel like you've been paying attention. That's a lot of gold stars."

He says this encouragingly and with enough conviction that I have to believe his words. I also have to smile, apparently, because I'm showing all my teeth before I can stop myself. I want to say I'm proud, but it's simpler than that. I'm happy because he's happy.

I single-handedly made him happy. Could be that he's still holding my hand, but I feel the energy of his happiness.

I know that doesn't make any sense. No matter how good a time we're having, Boyfriend Winston and Girlfriend Dru aren't real. At least not as a couple. I think it's just the idea of us being on the same page. This is what we would feel like in something real. Winston doesn't actually send me energy through his touch. But I can't help but wonder if he can feel mine. I can't hold back.

For some reason, acknowledging the difference between his energy and mine deflates me. My smile doesn't hold. I stare out the window.

He runs his thumb along the back of my hand. I look at him. Our eyes meet. Quickly he looks back at the road.

I clear my throat. "So how did you figure out that you just like doing nothing with someone?" I ask.

I feel his eyes on me for just a second. "What do you mean?"

I shrug. "You've never really had a girlfriend. I'm just trying to figure out how you came to this conclusion."

He bites his bottom lip. "It's just a thing I've wanted to happen in certain cases, and it feels good when I think about it, so I know it would be good in real life. I don't have actual experience."

I wipe my free palm on my pants. I hope the hand he's holding doesn't feel as sticky as the rest of me. "Same."

His eyebrows go up and he glances at me.

"Kiss kiss is more of a perfect scenario. What I'm capable of. It hasn't actually happened the way I imagine. And it isn't necessarily getting pulled into the car by your mouth. It's like a hello peck where you don't need the words anymore." I'm not sure how audible I am since the words come out so airy. "And it's not just kissing. It doesn't have to be kissing at all. It could just mean being so close to somebody you can feel it on your face every time they exhale."

"Suddenly it all makes sense." He nods to himself.

I squeeze his hand, hoping I can send him energy too. "You just going to leave me hanging? What makes sense?"

"I wasn't understanding how with the kiss kisses lying in the balance, these exes didn't do more to keep you, but I get it now. They had no idea about the potential." He licks his lips as if he might actually be imaging this scenario in his head. I wish he was imagining me.

If for no other reason than my heart can't tell the difference between a fake date and a real one right now, I try to bring things back to the regular Dru and Winston and pull my hand free to point out his next turn.

He tilts his head as he follows my directions. "Are we going to the park?"

"You're not supposed to guess." I cross my arms over my chest. "But yeah. I really like this part of the trail."

He smiles without teeth, but I still get the dimples, and his nose crinkles like he thinks it's sweet. I don't think he realizes how cute he is. In the silence, it's all I can see, so I find something to say.

"Is being Boyfriend Winston really as effortless as you make it seem?"

He laughs a little. "No. It would be hard to make the same moves in a real situation."

"Really? Why no? That seems kind of backward."

"Because"—he scratches his head and pulls into a lot outside the park that leads up to the trail connector—"in this situation I already know I have an opening to try, but in a real situation I wouldn't know that."

The doors automatically unlock when he puts the car in park, but I don't open mine. I have to hear this logic out. "Wouldn't being my boyfriend be your opening to try?"

He nods slowly. "That makes sense, but real Boyfriend Winston might spend a lot of time wondering how he got here with you."

"Probably by saying things like that. Seems kind of obvious to me. I don't think you'd have any trouble." I laugh nervously, my body's unchecked reaction to the idea that any Winston—boyfriend or otherwise—would question his ability to get me. Or maybe it's my reaction to the realization that if Winston wanted me, all he'd have to do is say so. Could also be that I just implied he can have me, and it doesn't sound as hypothetical as I intend it to.

Winston, on the other hand, is not laughing. He's squinting at me with his head tilted deeply to the left. He's probably going over my words in his head. It feels too late to declare what I've said hypothetical. Instead, I open the door and hop out of the car. He's slower to get out but eventually he joins me on the sidewalk. I don't wait for him to take a hint this time. I just twine our fingers together like it's how they belong. He lets me.

For the second time I find myself thinking he likes it better this way than apart too.

His eyes are still a little quizzical, but his voice is soft when he says "Kiss kiss" and places air kisses on each side of my face. It's suddenly so warm, but I don't know if it's his body heat or my own blush.

"Kiss kiss," I say back because if Winston Portis was my boyfriend, he'd be getting those kisses just for existing and being next to me.

But then he smiles his brightest smile and coughs to cover the next thing he says, which sounds a lot like "easy."

I smack my teeth and push him in the shoulder. "I hate you a lot."

He grabs the hand I pushed him with. We're linked together two ways now. It feels like a cardiac event is happening in my chest the way my heart is trying to pound through it.

He pins our hands to my sides. "Careful. I'll take my kisses back."

I don't make another move. I don't think Girlfriend Dru would want Winston to take his kisses back.

He glances down at the part of me left bare by my crop top. It's like my stomach muscles know they have someone's attention because they clench.

He lets the offending hand go and pulls me back toward the car. He reaches into the back seat, grabs a blue sweatshirt, and holds it out to me. "Just in case?"

I nod and unhand him to use my *just in case* for right now. It's definitely getting a little chilly in that way Michigan air does just to remind you it's far from summer. When I get the sweatshirt over my head and push my arms through the sleeves, Winston untucks my braids from where they're caught at the back of my neck and gently lays them over one shoulder. I'm not sure why he does that for me, but then I remember he's Boyfriend Winston. Boyfriend Winston probably does simple, kind gestures for his girlfriend all the time.

I smile a thank-you. He smiles the best you're-welcome ever. We grab for each other's hands at the exact same time. My heart, the one that's been trying its hardest to come through my chest, does what can't be called anything but an actual skip.

We let a few cyclists pass before we step onto the black pavement of the trail. Immediately, I think of my sisters, Moriah mostly.

"I don't remember how old I was but I couldn't have been more than four." I look up to see if I have his attention before I keep going. He's looking at me with this small smile that makes my chest hum. I have to turn away. "My parents used to bring us here for bike rides. I cried every time because we would get to this particular spot and

Moriah would just take off on her bike. I could keep up for a few feet but that's it. Mom would take off after her and Dad would stay back with me. I'd have snot dripping down my face, and Dad would be like *slow down before you fall*, which I almost always did."

"What was she, like, twelve?"

I nod and look down at the pavement. Even though his legs are miles longer than mine, our steps are perfectly in sync.

"And you had training wheels, right?"

I inhale a sharp intake of air. "Training wheels? Not your girl."

He laughs. "What's wrong with training wheels? I had them until I was seven. It was a party when I got them taken off."

"What's wrong is that neither of my sisters had them. Why should I? Period." I stare up at him, and still he's watching me instead of the beautiful stretch of trees surrounding us. "Didn't you want to be like Rashid?"

"Sure," he says thoughtfully. "But in more of a *someday* way. Like, when I got big. I still feel like that now actually. He's as good as you can get without making everybody else want to beat your ass."

This makes me laugh out loud. It's true, though.

There's a big age difference between Winston and Rashid, just like there is between me and my sisters, but somehow it's worked out for them. Not that there aren't things I admire about my sisters, but it's just different. Is it because we're girls? Or because I have two older siblings and he only has one? Or is he less competitive? Or maybe it's that he has a twin to balance things.

Or maybe it's simply a matter of them having left me nothing to be best or first at.

As if he's reading my mind, he lets out a deep sigh. "Jake is a different story."

I raise an eyebrow at him. Siblings have issues, I know that. The whole misunderstanding about Jake not sharing his book with Winston was minor and easily resolved. Other than little things like that, I've never seen issues between Jake and Winston with my own eyes. And I could never say this out loud because there are things people can say about their own family that others can't, but there's not one thing that Jake has or is that I think Winston should aspire to. I'm not hating on Jake or anything. Jake is great. I just think Winston is great the way he is too.

"I've never wanted to be Jake or be like Jake. I know we're different and it would be a lot if we weren't." He starts to speak, sighs, and then starts again. "I just wanted to be all the things people like about him that make him the less stressful twin. The twin that people don't assume they'll have to make more accommodations for."

I nod, trying to wrap my head around what he's saying.

"Not to take anything from him. I want everything to be easy for him *and* me," he quickly corrects. "Remember how I told you I'm the last to get things a lot but I'm okay with it?"

"Yeah because sometimes you end up better off."

"That's true, but I don't want to hear *everybody gets things in their own time* when I'm the last one. Or know everybody's waiting for me to catch on if for no other reason than they can finally be happy for Jake without hurting my feelings. They don't have to worry that I might not get things at all."

I side-eye him. "I'm sure nobody thinks you're *never* going to get things."

He side-eyes me back and adds a twist of his lips that lets me know he's about to crush my thoughts. "My mom tells this story all the time. It's supposed to be comforting to me but pisses me off."

That makes me slow my pace way down. Ms. Teddy loves her kids. You can actually see it. It's hard to imagine her doing something to cause the look of hurt crossing his face.

"It's about how in third grade I could still barely read, and she and Dad decided to take me out of some program I was in because it was doing more harm than good. They didn't want me to think I was disappointing them if reading never happened for me for a while."

I vaguely remember our moms talking about Winston having some trouble in school when we were little. For some reason I had it in my head that it was all more behavioral, not learning-related. There was a whole thing about some teacher making him her permanent helper with a special desk right next to hers so she could keep a close eye on him. Both dads felt like it was a race thing.

He places the side of his hand on my forearm to let me know he's getting to the good part. "I was never diagnosed with anything. There was no reason they could come up with that I wasn't getting it. And every week I was checking out sixth-grade books on library day and taking them out at home and at carpet time. Everybody thought it was great for me to *interact* with the books."

I shake my head and stop walking. "Wait. Winston, could you actually read? Grade levels ahead? That whole time?"

"Not the *whole* time. I did need the program at first, but once I got it, I got it. There was some good stuff in books." He smacks his lips. "But the people in the program...It was like they pitied me or something. Honestly, now I couldn't tell you if that was how they felt about me or how I felt about myself, but I never wanted to read for them. Nothing they said would make me do it."

I hate to think about anybody pitying themself or being pitied for something they can't do. Not for lack of trying or intelligence or want, but because it just isn't there. The thoughtful look on Winston's face tells me he doesn't love remembering it either. I don't plan on prompting him for the rest of the story, but he tells it anyway.

"One day, my mom starts reading to me from where we'd left off in a book and instead of letting her reread what I'd already read, I showed her where I was in the book." He shakes his head as if she's standing right in front of him. "She was so happy...a little less when my parents realized how long I'd been reading, and that I knew how way before they gave up."

I bite back a smile. It's a story he doesn't like, but it's all very Winston. The best parts of him actually.

"It's kind of amazing how you always find a way to turn things into a positive, and you never give up on yourself."

He hums noncommittally, avoiding looking me in the eye. "I don't know about that."

I ball up my hand and extend a finger with every point. "You missed people, so you made a way to reach them. You made a mean commentor your friend. You're applying to the Midwestern program for a fourth—"

"I'm not sure that's anything to be proud of." He presses his lips together and squints as if carefully examining my points. "And even if it was, it hasn't turned into anything positive."

"Yet." I smile up at him. "But you're working on it."

His eyes are steady on my face long enough that I'm about to ask if something's wrong with it when he murmurs, "Yeah, I'm working on it." Even after he says that he's still watching me, making me so self-conscious I have to look away. It's the only way I'm able to breathe.

I spot a metal bench a few hundred feet away. It's the demarcation for where the path goes from tree-covered on all sides and as far as you can see to wide open for more than a mile. I head for it. He trails me.

I pull his sweatshirt down over my butt as far as it'll go to add some extra cushion before I sit. He sits down next to me and is so hesitant about his next few words that I brace myself for some big reveal about him and Jake. But that's not where this is going.

"You don't mind if I stretch out, do you?"

I don't know what he means by this at first. Where and how does someone as tall as he is "stretch out"? Is he about to start doing yoga right here? I'm for it. I'd join in. It's just a little unexpected.

My question is quickly answered when he turns his back to me, scoots on his butt a little, and rests his legs on the arm of the opposite end of the bench. Then he glances back at my lap as if making sure the space is clear for him. I move my hands up and away as if denying responsibility for any wrongdoing. With a short groan of relief he lies back, closing his eyes.

I have to put my now-empty hands somewhere. One ends up just above his navel. I have the urge to put my other hand in his hair, but that feels like I'd be doing a whole lot that can't be explained away by lack of room. I let my other hand fall to the arm of the bench.

The path hasn't been super busy except for a few cyclists and runners. All that means is that there's not much else to do other than look at Winston.

I clear my throat because I have this feeling my voice is going to come out wobbly if I don't. "Comfy?"

He licks his lips. "Definitely. Thank you."

I don't know if the lip licking was supposed to be a warning or preparatory, but he puts his hand over mine and brings my palm to his lips. It's the most delicate thing that's ever happened to me. Long enough to be out of the peck zone and short enough that I ask myself what I could've done to make it last longer. I have to hold my breath to take it without squirming.

He couldn't have meant to kiss me, though. He just got too comfortable or caught up in the moment, his role. The way he pulls in his bottom lip and lines appear between his eyebrows when he's done gives it away. Slowly, he puts our hands back down together on his belly. I don't know what to make of it, but his lips on me was an in-the-moment thing, not some calculated Boyfriend Winston test. And that's a good thing because I'm frozen. I would get zero stars for everything if he attempted any critique.

To force myself to breathe, I speak. "Did I wear you out already?"

He smiles a little and taps his fingers on the backs of my matching ones, one at a time. "It's more embarrassing than that."

Since I'm breathing now, I actually have the ability to squirm away from his touch, but I don't want to. "What could be more embarrassing than you not being able to keep up with me?"

"I think I'm having a growth spurt." He says this so quickly I have to repeat it in my head before I understand it.

I laugh out loud. "But, why?"

Suddenly, he opens his eyes and lifts himself a little. "That's what I want to know. Don't get me wrong, it's cool to be tall, but I feel like I've already extracted all the height cool points I can without getting docked for a lack of athleticism."

"You're not wrong," I tease.

He slides one hand behind his head, looking about as relaxed as anyone could. Like when he got up this morning he knew he was going to do this very thing. I want him to be relaxed with me; he's my friend. But I'm not relaxed. I'm a little topsy-turvy inside, actually feeling my breaths as they go in and out.

The competitive side of me feels like I'm losing, like I need to rally but I have no idea how.

How can I relax when the reason I'm riled up is Winston Portis—unpredictable, talented, funny, kind, and fine, and thoughtful, and, and, and?

"Dru?" Winston taps his fingers on mine one at a time again, and I realize I've just been sitting here staring down at him for, like, five minutes. I'm not even sure if I've blinked.

"Yeah."

He blinks as his fingers continue to drum mine. "How do people ask you to be their girlfriend?"

I tilt my head to the side. That's not what I was expecting. My heart thumps and I stutter. "Wh-what?"

He looks at me thoughtfully. "I'm serious. It seems like an awkward question to ask. I'm just wondering what route the success stories took."

Careful not to disrupt his comfortable position, I sit up straighter. "Well, Michael said something like 'You're my girl, right?' And I said sure."

"Slick way to get around that. Just that little change and it feels way different coming out. That's clever."

"I guess." I laugh. "I'm still not sure who asked who when it comes to Jayden. We had been talking awhile. I was getting a little impatient. So, I asked if he was going to ask me because I was okay asking him. He said he planned to ask me but wanted to get me something. I told him he didn't have to. Eventually he came to my house with flowers and chocolate and said the actual words. 'Will you be my girlfriend?'"

He smiles. "You liked that one. I can tell."

I smile back. "It was definitely sweet. But honestly, it would be cool to just like somebody so much and have them like you so much that you both just start telling people you're together and neither of you ever questions it. It probably would never work like that, though."

He squeezes my hand and stares up at me so seriously that I'm afraid of what he's going to say. "I think it could work. I think somebody can like you that much."

I take my hand away and rest it on the back of the bench because everywhere we're touching is vibrating and it's the only part of me I can set free without throwing him to the ground. And there's nothing I can do about my chest. He's not touching me at all there, but I feel completely hollowed out. How am I going to come back from this?

I take a deep breath. "Okay, Boyfriend. Are you recovered now? I don't want to miss the sunset."

THE HALFWAY MARK, PART 3

The sunset is beautiful. The fade from barely blue to bright orange with a few wispy clouds in the distance is the perfect ending to any day. I had a million things going through my mind as we watched, realizing that we both would have probably been okay if we'd just stood there the whole day waiting for these few minutes. Because mostly, what makes the perfect date is the company.

All I can think about on the drive home is the beginning of the night in my driveway. I felt an energy brewing but didn't know what I was getting into. I still don't. I'll probably be comparing every date to this one forever. Even though only some parts of it were real. Which parts those are, I'm not sure. I do know that the way I vibrate when Winston touches me isn't something I can manufacture no matter how much I pretend that I'm playing a role.

It doesn't help that today the line between Boyfriend Winston and friend Winston got even blurrier.

There shouldn't be any pressure at the end of a date planned as a last-ditch effort to find my faults, but as he pulls into my driveway I'm not clear how to end things. We're talking about which foods taste better a little bit burnt. It's not a conversation that needs closure, but instead of just putting the car in park, he shuts it off. This makes it clear we aren't in a drop-and-run situation.

"Burnt cheese is good on pizza, but if the cheese gets burnt on mac and cheese, then the noodles do too." I scrunch up my nose like I smell something stinky. "And hard noodles are gross and chewy."

He waves my point away. "That's burnt on accident. I'm talking burnt on purpose. It's different."

"Now you're telling me burning food is a skill."

He jerks his head back and looks from left to right as if my words are a shock. "You didn't know that?"

I open the car door and put one foot out. "I feel like somebody told you that to cover up the fact that they can't cook."

He laughs and mimics my steps until he's waiting for me at the front of the car. I pass him by. As I walk by the garage, the faulty motion-sensor lights blink but ultimately decide not to come alive. I put in the code. The heavy door creaks as it rises.

When I turn to him, I'm surprised at how close he is. He might be a little surprised too, based on the way he startles when our eyes meet. He doesn't look away, though. Neither do I.

He smiles a little. Obviously, I love his smile. I bet if I polled my whole block it would be unanimous that his smile is everything. The way he's looking at me now, I might have to change my opinion on whether he knows that.

"You do know that dimples are just birth defects, right?"

His smile turns into a lip lick that just makes the dimples pop out more. He leans a shoulder against the house in the most Winston way. Like he's simply exhausted with standing up straight. It's just a small move, but he's even closer. I could take a step back. I don't.

"Jake tells me that all the time, but he's jealous. What are you?"

This little bit of confidence seeping off him doesn't feel very Winston in the way I know him, but at the same time it feels real.

"Not Jake."

That's not an answer, but with us just standing here looking at each other with nothing but moon-made shadows all around us, me not being Jake is about the only thing I'm sure of. To my surprise, he lets my nonanswer slide.

He sighs, like he's trying to come up with a way to prolong this fake date.

"Well, Girlfriend Dru, Boyfriend Winston had a good time."

"So did I."

I smile and announce the first of my air kisses. Simultaneously, he does the same. But in explicit un-air-kiss fashion, we don't go in opposing directions. Our lips meet first to my left. Then, as if to fix the problem, we both move to our other side, where our lips meet again. From there, neither of us goes anywhere except further into each other. His hand is just beneath my jaw, holding me in place while his thumb caresses my cheek. Up on my toes to reach him better, I find his other hand and lace our fingers together.

As of this moment, there are a few things I'm sure about. Kissing Winston Portis is dizzyingly good. I don't want to stop.

He is warm and sure, but still careful. Being close to him is scary, but in a way that only makes me want to be closer. If I get closer, he'll hold me tighter and kiss me deeper. I grab at his shirt, but the closer I pull him, the more our height difference makes it difficult to reach him the way I want to. But then he untangles his hands from me in all the ways that we are connected, wraps them around my waist, and lifts me until my feet are off the ground.

If flying humans were a thing, I would be the dictionary illustration inside and out.

We are so close now that I can touch him without worrying about his lips leaving mine. I wrap my hands around his neck and lean into him. Winston Portis's arms are the most comfortable yet unnerving place I have ever been. That vibration I've felt every time we've touched today is a constant hum through my entire body. A hum that feels like it's always been there but I've never been tuned in to it.

My plan is to kiss him forever, but the motion lights flicker again. He pulls back. He's looking at my lips, but when he takes a deep breath, I know he's not coming back to kiss me. In fact, his grip on me is loosening. My only option is to unwrap myself.

When my feet hit the ground, I have to look around to remind myself where we are. I've completely lost track. I am outside my house, just having finished kissing my friend Winston Portis.

I'm shaking. That definitely shouldn't have happened. But, man, I want it to happen again.

And he...I look up at him. His hands are in his pockets, and he isn't saying anything. He's just looking down at me, eyes dazed, waiting for...*something*. An explanation. An apology. The look on his face makes me start talking.

"I didn't mean to do that. But we both went the wrong way."

He nods slowly. "I know. That was on me." He shakes his head. "What I mean is, at first I was trying the air-kiss thing. Then I was like, if I'm critiquing Girlfriend Dru, I have to go all the way. What if kissing is the problem, and I didn't even try and find out, you know?"

"Oh." I cross my arms over myself, the cool sweat of embarrassment quickly beginning to compete with the warmth of what we were just doing. "That makes sense, I guess."

"And there was no voice to stop me"—he runs a hand through his hair—"including yours."

"Yeah, I just figured it was the end of the fake date so—" I cut myself off. Everything that he's just said is registering at different times. Some of it makes me not want to be standing out here talking to him. Was everything that just happened to me not happening to him? Is it possible for that kind of feeling to be one-sided?

Even if it's not going to turn into anything, I just want him to say he feels everything I'm feeling. I can still let it go if he felt it too. I just don't want to feel delusional, like I build relationships and feelings in my head. Like maybe that's my flaw. I feel things that other people don't.

I extend my leg and cover a rock with my foot, maneuvering it the way I would a soccer ball. I keep my eyes there. "You didn't give me a gold star. Am I bad at kissing or something?"

"Dru?" He says my name in a way that forces me to look up at him. And when I do, his sincere expression holds me in place. "Everything about you is a gold star. Any guy who's for you is going to see that. You need to forget about what's happened before. I can't explain that. But if you want something from somebody, whoever that is, you should just tell him."

He says all that in one breath, like he's been holding on to it for a while. For me, it's hard to take in what he's saying after he just kissed me like that. Did he really not feel anything? And does he mean any guy but him?

"Are you talking about Kai?"

He shrugs one shoulder and looks up into the bright lights that brought us out of our moment. "If that's what you want."

So that's my answer. I nod my understanding. The kissing transported me, and only me, to another place in my mind and in my heart. But luckily for both of us, it doesn't take long for me to land back in real time.

I take a step back and nod toward my house. "You coming in?"

He shakes his head and starts walking away from me without even offering an excuse.

"I'll tell my parents you said hi."

He nods at that but keeps on toward his car.

"I'll see you tomorrow at school, then?"

Over his shoulder, he gives me a small smile and he's gone.

11 DAYS REMAINING

Kai: 11 Days

If I start counting from the time Winston picked me up yesterday to the moment I roll out of bed for school this morning, I have thought about Winston for nearly twenty hours straight. He didn't text or call me last night. And even though I invented several reasons, I didn't call him either. I replayed the entire day over and over and over again in my head. I couldn't replay that kiss, though. It made my chest hurt.

Not just because of how good it felt, but because I broke the team pact. The one *I* suggested. I can't call anything that happened yesterday platonic, at least not on my end.

And the kiss didn't even matter at all to Winston. He just walked away like it was nothing. I know I have to accept how he sees me, especially if I want to keep his friendship. That doesn't make it hurt less, though.

Also, am I a cheater?

No, Kai isn't my boyfriend, but I'm pretty sure I'd find kissing a guy—a guy I told him is basically my brother-in-law—pretty hard to explain. If roles were reversed, I would be hurt. Especially knowing that what happened didn't mean anything.

By the time I walk through LeBeau High's doors I know what I have to do. I have to be as nonchalant as Winston was when he left my house last night. I have to fake it until I make it. I have to pretend to only have best-friend feelings for him until that's how it really is.

I really wish I had something to talk to him about just so I can show him that everything is normal and I'm good. But I have nothing—not even chitchat about the wedding—that wouldn't be too random for me to walk down to him and bring up. Considering I've never had to think before speaking to him until recently, that says a lot.

Today is the deadline for shower RSVPs. The emails and texts are coming through back-to-back. I suppose I could talk to him about that, but every time I start really considering it, I get another text. I don't want to waste even a second getting information to my sister. With my luck someone will call her to say they sent a text to RSVP, and she'll be calling me because their name isn't on her list.

I'm in the middle of forwarding one to her now where the invitee is asking if she can come later. I'm not sure what she means, so I want to get it to LeArra ASAP. I'm sending the text when Aubrey strolls up to me.

"How's the SAT pause going? Any shakes or twitches yet?" I ask to ensure the conversation stays off me.

She doesn't fall for it. She looks around her personal space as if to check in with herself about how things are going. "I'm feeling good actually. How'd the date go? You didn't say nothing last night."

"He took me to a carnival. We rode everything multiple times.

Then we hung out at the park." It's hard to give this really bland description of our day. But I'm just describing the way *he* experienced yesterday. The way I know I was supposed to. "At the end, he told me that there was nothing wrong with me and I just need to go get what I want."

I can't tell her about the kiss. She would never let it go. She'll have questions. I'll have to admit what an idiot I am. All she needs to hear is that Winston concluded that I have no fatal flaw and should feel perfectly fine going after what I want.

That's all anyone needs to know.

She turns back to me, face scrunched. "And that's it. He didn't say anything else? You didn't say anything else?"

"Nope."

She can't see Kai coming up behind her, so she doesn't realize we need to end this conversation. "Well, are you going to take his advice? Are you going to go get what you want?"

"Hey," I say to Kai before my best friend gets too specific.

He smiles at us both. "Did you get my message last night?"

I closed-mouth smile back at him. "Yeah, I did."

"I wasn't sure. You didn't say anything."

"Maybe I *didn't* get it." I reach for my phone in my back pocket. "Did you ask me something?"

He puts his hand out to stop me. "I didn't ask anything. Just counting. You normally respond to that."

"Yes, I definitely got that text when I woke up this morning. I'm not sure why I didn't respond." I nod deeply. "Time is going by really fast."

He pulls his lips to one corner. "Not to me. The days are going by really slow. Especially the ones where I don't talk to you."

"Oh." I let out a shaky breath. "It was a really busy weekend. The wedding and stuff. And the pact."

Aubrey's eyes ping-pong between us as we talk. I'm glad she stayed. I know she's protecting my commitment, but even if she wasn't, I wouldn't want her to leave. I still have the potential to stutter or make a fool of myself, but for all the wrong reasons.

I'm such an idiot. Kai likes me and he's so sweet. I've let myself get wrapped up in someone else.

"I understand. I wasn't going to try to get you to break your pact. Not again. I—"

I start. "Again? What do you mean by 'again'?"

"Like the time after my soccer game. I wasn't going to do that again. I was just saying."

Damn, Dru. He's just saying. There's no way his "again" could've meant anything other than what it meant. He couldn't have any idea about yesterday with Winston. I wish *I* had no idea about yesterday.

And just like the way yesterday has had ahold of my mind for twenty hours, time with Kai can take hold the same way. In the past it would take one text from Kai to give me butterflies for the rest of the day. It can't be that hard to get that back. I just have to try. Or I have to leave him alone. It's not fair to drag this on if I don't think it will work. I really believe it can, though.

"I miss talking to you too." All the guilt makes it come out way more serious and confessional than I want it to.

"That's good to hear."

He looks at me thoughtfully. He's wearing his professor face and stance from the other day. "How are you feeling about the game tonight? Regionals. It's getting real."

My energy drops immediately. I want to change the subject to try to get back to all those feelings I used to have when I see him, but I don't necessarily want to talk about shooting. But from one issue to the next we go, I guess. Later I'll find out if the day off I suggested helped anything.

He chuckles. "Don't worry. I don't have any more suggestions." He grimaces. "Well, I do but I won't tell you unless you ask."

He pauses, I assume for me to ask. I remain silent. I don't need anything else in my head. He nods slowly, looking maybe a little disappointed, but a smile plays at his lips, so I know he's not taking it too bad.

"I think you're going to be fine," he says with that Kai confidence that has always drawn me to him.

I jerk my head back. "You do?"

His eyes go big, and he nods. "Some of my best games are when I'm the most nervous and worked up. Maybe it'll be like that for you."

I smile. It's not forced or fake. I appreciate any good soccer thoughts coming my way. "Thank you for saying that."

"No problem." He puts his fist out for a pound. I knock mine against his. He smiles as he walks away backward.

My phone vibrates. I sigh, looking away from him before I normally would. I have another RSVP. I'm going to have to turn my notifications off. LeArra can complain to Mom if she doesn't like it. I lean against my locker, add the RSVP to the spreadsheet, and then answer the nine hundred questions it leads to. When I look up, instead of Aubrey, Winston is standing in front of me.

It's an actual, literal, popcorn-flying-across-the-room jump scare. Which in turn scares him and he flinches suspiciously.

"Where's Aubrey?"

He nods down the hall where Aubrey and Jake are walking away from us together. "Same class, different hour. He said he had a question. You looked too busy to interrupt."

I deep sigh and hold the phone up to him as if that explains everything. "LeArra."

He nods in understanding.

I take a deep breath as I put my phone away and stuff my hands in my pockets. I want to be normal, but the last time Winston was this close to me he was kissing me.

I look back at the lockers to see how far away they are, as if there's a possibility that Winston will press me into them. It won't happen. I know it won't.

He studies my face seriously, but somehow I spot something else behind his eyes. Laughter. It makes me smile.

He tries to fight smiling back, which makes me laugh. It makes me so happy. The Dru and Winston who can look at each other and laugh for no reason is one of my favorite renditions. I don't know what it is. But I never do, and I'm not going to start trying to figure out if this is us or his awkward reaction to seeing me the first time since we kissed. It's a totally different reaction than my reimagining, but I don't mind it. It means that maybe we can get back to our old selves.

I know that's mostly on me. I'm the one who got lost in the process. But this laughter makes me feel good.

He nods his head slowly the way he does when something is coming together in his head. "I know what your pregame surprise is now."

I stare at him, confused. "Pregame...I'm still getting that?"

"Why wouldn't you be? They're a tradition now. I can't stop in the middle."

That makes sense. Leave it to my brain to try to make something more of it. Winston just wants his friend to do well. End of story.

I smile conspiratorially. "What is it?"

He gives me a look that says *nice try.* "Tradition says you don't get to know what it is until you get it."

"But what if it'll help settle me down?" I say this in the softest voice I have, hoping it will lead to empathy.

"You know you're getting something. That should be enough."

"It isn't," I say, matter-of-fact.

"It has to be, because that's what it is. So stop asking me. I didn't come here to talk about that anyway." He says this like a kindergartner teasing another with candy, complete with bobbing and weaving.

I try to hold in a laugh.

He crosses his arms over his chest, all seriousness. "If you didn't want Mufasa, that's all you had to say."

I scrunch my face.

He smacks his tongue against his teeth. "Oh, now you don't even know who he is."

"*The Lion Ki*—" I gasp and then whisper, "The lion you won me last night. You named him?"

"Yeah, I named him because he's mine now." He smirks. "I waited all night and this morning for you to realize something was missing and you just left him in the back of the car. Alone."

"I love Mufasa. His hair is—" I kiss the tips of my fingers. "But I had other things on my mind last night."

That last sentence comes out a little broken. He goes still.

"Like what, Dru? What was on your mind last night?"

I'm so confused. What does he want me to say? I know what I can't say. I can't say kissing him. I can't say him stretching out on my lap. I can't say him giving me a piggyback ride. Because that is all Girlfriend Dru and Boyfriend Winston stuff. And Girlfriend Dru and Boyfriend Winston are over. He has given me his final report.

I point to the pocket where I put my phone. "RSVPs. Today is the deadline so they've been coming in nonstop, and you know how LeArra is all over me about everything."

He doesn't look where I point. He just keeps looking at me. All the humor is gone from his eyes. He looks...disappointed maybe. "Do you want him?"

"Mufasa? Yes." I narrow my eyes.

He takes a step back. "Yeah, you can get him from my car after school."

"Why?"

"Because I won him for you. What else am I going to do with him?" He shrugs. "Just come to my car after school."

"'Kay."

" 'Kay." He takes a few more steps back. "See you later, Dru."

I wave as if he's down the hall when he's literally right in front of me. "See you later, Winston."

I fall back against my locker—not quite the way I was imagining a few minutes ago—and sigh. What am I going to do?

THE FINAL COUNTDOWN

Kai: 9 Days, three more games

Dru: 9 Days, but I don't want to rush the season away

Kai: Oh no. Me either.

Dru: Hey. Today's the day! Maybe turned into a yes. Here's the link to your premeeting playlist.

Winston: You actually made it for me. 😊 I'm going to start listening now. Thank you.

Dru: You're welcome. I hope it makes you feel invincible.

Winston: I hope you feel invincible today too. ♥

I will not read into the heart. I will not read into the heart. I will not read into that heart...

I've been sitting in my car outside my house for the last ten minutes. My goal was to be the first one in the school parking lot so that when my teammates showed up to take the bus to the regional final, I was already there. I wanted to be ready with something positive to say to every single one of them. But I'm kind of stuck. Literally.

I've been cycling through songs on my playlist, looking for the best one to listen to before the final. But none of them are it. I'm having the biggest pregame nerves of my life. Normally this kind of stuff doesn't start until I get to the field.

But never have I been on a team before where it feels like everyone was just tolerating one another. The day off helped some. On Monday, we won the first of the two regional games, even after starting off a little out of sync. But on game day people were missing from the table. After the win, more people showed up, even if it was awkward. Capri enjoyed her lunch on the other side of the cafeteria.

Winston's pregame surprise ended up being a video of himself telling dad jokes, making himself laugh until he cried. I did the same when I watched it. It would probably be giving him too much credit to say that after that laugh I was looser than I've been before a game all season, but that's how it went. Maybe that's what I should listen to. Maybe that'll help get me moving.

I don't have anything from him specifically for today's game. He has his call with the professor today. I know he's busy and probably anxious. I still miss hearing his voice. It's become a pregame ritual.

Even though I'd already sent the playlist, by lunch I felt like I needed to actually say words to him. So I sent him a video saying that no matter what happens, he's talented, and driven, and a risk taker. Nothing anybody says or does can stop somebody with all that going for them. I rambled a lot because I had a lot to say and may have even been holding back.

Instead of just focusing on what he needed to hear, my mind kept dredging up spending the day with him and kissing him like I needed it to live. Then, like a bucket of cold water on my face, I remember the very end of everything, where he told me to go for Kai.

I remind myself that I've wanted an opportunity to get to know Kai better for a very long time. Eventually this is all going to come full circle. Everything will readjust and go back to normal.

The whole process is like waking up in a bed that isn't mine. I have to reorient myself to the fact that the last few weeks were a world I built to find a resolution to a problem. Since there is apparently no problem to solve, that world can now be reduced to nothing. I have to go back to reality.

And Kai's making the thirty-minute drive to the game tonight, to support me. Showing me that when the restrictions of my team pact are over and we sprinkle in the romantic parts of our relationship, things could potentially be great.

Kai's not my experimental anything. He's a real guy being his real self. Making an effort. Offering me tangible help because he sees something in me.

Today, I got a good luck message from him that said, *If you're going to be a winner you have to stop being scared.*

I know he's right. I have to get my stuff together. I close my eyes and take a deep breath. Starting now.

There's a tap on my window.

And if jumping through the roof were an actual thing I would've done it. As it was, my seat belt held me in place.

Winston backs away from the door. "I'm sorry. It looked like you were sleeping. I didn't think you had time for sleeping."

His voice is muffled so I let down the window before deciding to just get out.

Not seeing him up close and in person the last few hours makes his face more like something I've never discovered before and less like that of a boy I've known forever. It's just him and his basketball shorts and sweatshirt, and his dimples, and his cluelessness about the actual impact he has on people around him.

"Hey. Are you looking for me?" I ask.

Winston looks at my house, his car, then back at me. "Uh, yeah."

"Well, you do kind of love my dad. So it was fifty-fifty."

He smiles. "That *is* true. I love Keith with my whole heart."

We both laugh.

"What's…" I suddenly realize my hands are balled into fists. When I undo them, I stuff them into the pockets of my warm-up jacket. After that, I have nothing to do but try to form a clear and concise question. "How did the call go? It was good, right?"

He smiles and nods slowly. "It was so good. Really good."

I laugh shakily and push him in the shoulder. "Well, tell me what happened."

"Jorda actually said I was *too* experienced to participate in Midwestern's program. That's why I'd been rejected." He shakes his head as if he can't believe what he's about to say. "She asked me if I would present instead. Any topic I want. And she recommended me to a more advanced summer program in Chicago. It was crazy. Better than the perfect scenario."

I am a millisecond away from jumping on him in excitement. I just gush instead. "That is amazing. I'm so happy for you. You're going to kill it and meet all kinds of new people and just... Winston everywhere."

He laughs. "Winston everywhere? Like, as an action?"

"I said what I said." I laugh too. "Did you tell your family? What did they say?"

"Jake was home when I had the call, so he heard, of course. He's excited for me. I haven't told my parents yet."

"They're going to be so proud of you. You earned it."

"I actually didn't come over here to talk about me, but since you brought it up, thanks for the video. It made me feel really good. Like I was already winning." He frowns, but his eyes are still smiling. "If I was a crier, you would've got me."

I want to laugh because he's so silly sometimes. Also he said I made him feel like he was already winning. That makes me feel like I'm winning too. I keep it simple, so I don't end up saying too much.

"You're welcome."

"Anyway, I didn't get a chance to create any pregame propaganda for you. I decided to just come over, thinking by the time I got here I'd have something figured out."

He looks down at me. At my jacket pockets. I don't let my eyes leave his. He takes a step toward me, bringing us close enough to touch. He pulls both of my hands out of my pockets and pries them open. Slowly, I spread my fingers until they overlap his palms. I'm still watching him. He's still watching my hands. Our hands.

Surprisingly, my heart rate is slowing down, not speeding up the way it did every time he touched me this past weekend. That's probably because the person standing in front of me isn't pretending to act the way my boyfriend would act. He's just Winston my friend showing up for me.

He rubs the pads of his thumbs over my knuckles and looks at me. "You're really nervous, huh?"

I let out a puff of air. "I know. I'm a disaster right now. Seriously. I can't even drive."

"I was just making an observation." The pace of his thumbs over my knuckles slows. "I don't think there's anything disastrous about being nervous. Everybody feels that way sometimes."

"Yeah, I guess."

He looks at me seriously. "I want to tell you something."

My "okay" is almost inaudible.

He lets go with his right hand and points to the two bracelets on his left, directing my eyes there. "The red one is the Hausa language. It translates to *do it anyway*. The yellow one is Arabic. It says *you have everything you need*."

"Wait." I take a shaky breath. "You said you didn't know what your bracelets mean."

He grimaces. "I do. I just like being the only person who knows unless someone else speaks one of these languages."

"Why?"

"It isn't the coolest thing telling somebody that I special order my accessories and decide which ones to wear based on what feels hard for me or what I need to remind myself of."

I take a step back from him. "You think people will judge you? You think *I* would judge you?"

He closes his eyes as if he's thinking really hard, but then he waves my question away. "I just didn't want you to know, but now you do. Anyway, I randomly picked these two this morning, not knowing why until now. These are your reminders, not mine."

So that's what I'm going to do? I'm going to feel my feelings and do it anyway? I don't even know what to say to that. I'm nervous and I'm scared and that's just it. I'm just going to keep being those things and not fight them. They're just going to be here living in me and I'm going to do what?

Whatever I want?

He slides the bracelets quickly off his wrist and onto mine. I leave them there for now but I'll have to put them on my ankle under socks before the game starts.

I run my fingers over the characters I wouldn't be able to decode if not for him. "I'll give them back to you after the game."

"I have other ones. I'll be fine." He smiles, looking somewhere in the vicinity of my eyes but never quite meeting my gaze. "And at least it was my idea for you to have them this time. Everything else of mine, you just get on some possession-being-nine-tenths-of-the-law thing."

I look at him through my eyelashes and run my finger along the bracelets. "What are you talking about?"

"You really going to act like you don't know you have a whole Winston Portis outfit complete with accessories?" He chuckles again. "Okay."

I mentally look through my closet and drawers. "But I don't, though."

He raises an eyebrow. "The day of the interview you took my pants right off me."

I shrug. "It was cold."

"You took my sunglasses at the dress shop."

I lean forward to make my point. "You agreed they were cute on me."

"Doesn't make them yours. They're cute on me too."

"Boyfriend Winston offered me the sweatshirt."

"To borrow, not to own."

"Wellll." I drag out the word. "They're mine now."

"Guess so." He laughs and checks the time on his phone "You need to go."

He's right. I hop in my car, feeling more energetic and capable and lucky. I can't lie—I want to thank him with a hug or a kiss, but I know for the sake of our friendship, just saying goodbye is better.

THE REST OF THE FINAL COUNTDOWN

I make it to the bus on time, but not early enough to greet everyone the way I had imagined. My seat at the front with a defender who rarely plays means I don't even get a chance to connect with everyone or really feel the vibe of the team. I normally sit next to Capri, but when I first got on the bus and looked down the aisle, I found Lauren sitting next to her instead. They're not talking or even looking at each other, but I take it as a good sign. If they can sit next to each other on the bus, they can work together during the game.

Meegan has kept it business at practice. Everyone is working together the way we should. We're not hanging out after the game or anything, but nothing that happened at film review or lunch or the group chat should be able to touch us. And maybe after the season is over and we've won, we can settle everything.

Once we're on the field, I try to hold on to the energy I felt when I saw Winston. It should be easy on a warm night like tonight, under the stadium lights. This is my favorite time to play. It's just a different kind of energy. If you're really in tune with it, it comes out in every move you make on the field. But it's hard.

We're only in warm-ups and I feel like I've played all ninety minutes already with the way my heart is beating. And every other second I become conscious that my hands are balled into fists again. When I unclench them it feels wrong and kind of excruciating. The only thing keeping me from running off this field and all the way home is knowing that sometimes when I feel this kind of energy before a game, I play better than average.

I can't explain how it works, but once I have an outside place to direct all these feelings, my brain and body go into overdrive. Everything becomes simple.

There are also times when that energy gets trapped inside. Instead of dribbling the ball, I'm tripping over it and causing turnovers that send the other team on the attack.

I tilt my head back and groan. Man, I hope this isn't one of *those* nights. The Lakers aren't better than us, just a really bad matchup. Their back line is bigger than our forwards are fast. This means things are going to get physical and the scoring will have to come from somewhere else on the field. Potentially from me.

I don't know if I'm too deep in thought or what, but I get hit right in the middle of my forehead by a shot someone has cleared. There's a bunch of stifled laughter around me. I hope that's not a sign.

"You awake now?" Capri smiles as she shifts with the rest of the back line, looking for a pass to stop or a shot to block.

There's a laugh inside me, but all this other stuff going on in my brain and body weighs more and won't let it escape. Also, the heat on that ball kind of disorients me a little. "Was that on purpose?"

"Just clearing the ball," she yells.

Even after how hard the last few weeks have been as a team, I watch Capri constantly bouncing, warming up with a smile on her face. She makes some sort of physical contact with every teammate who comes near her, giving a pat on the back or a swat on the butt. That's the player I want to be before every game. Loose and relaxed. Ready.

Not watching the other team go through their drills and sizing up players I've played against for years, as if they've all suddenly developed some new element to their game. Not noticing how full the stands are becoming. I should be focused on me and the team.

Instead, I sway from side to side with nervous energy, waiting for my turn to take a shot. When the time finally comes, I strike the ball. As usual, with no one but my own goalies in the net, the shot is perfect. I decide it's a good sign.

From the second the ball is put in play, the Lakers' strategy is obvious. They're going to pack it in, instead of actively trying to score. This makes scoring nearly impossible for us to do. They'll hold us, get lucky on some counterattack, and win with the lone goal of the game. It's what teams do when they know you're better.

The only way to make them open it up is to score, but we're not getting near the box. These types of games are boring to watch and even worse to play. It's hard to build anything.

For our first few possessions we end up kicking the ball around like some beginner drill. We get near the net and one of the six they're holding back as defenders gets in the passing lane and deflects a pass out of bounds. It's even out of range of their own teammates because they have one person back attempting to play offense. While we're waiting for a new ball to be put in play, Coach motions me and Capri over and tells us to worry less about being safe with the ball and do whatever we have to do to draw them to me. If just one of them is undisciplined enough to get out of position, we should be able to push something through. It might take all ninety minutes, but it only takes one goal.

Playing less safe is the easiest way to make a mistake I can't come back from. A change of possession. A breakaway for the other team. I see it all unfolding in my head. But the minute the ball is put in play, Coach is yelling the same instructions he just gave me over and over. I want to tell him to stop. But I don't have a lot of time for second-guessing.

We start to build from the back again. Capri pushes the ball up to me. Our front line is running around trying to make space where there is none. If nothing else, the Lakers will get tired. Meegan can run in circles all day. I watch them chase her as I dribble.

I swear, there's about a minute where nothing is happening. I pass the ball back to our six. She sends it back to me. Coach is not happy. I hold the ball and start roaming east and west, scanning the field. Everyone is popping out giving me a target, but it's all turnovers waiting to happen.

I haven't roamed too far, maybe a couple dribbles either way, when I decide to go directly downhill, directly at someone. When I see a defender take the bait, I hesitate. She can't switch directions quickly enough and I lose her. I can see the whole frame now. I see a space for my shot. But I'm yards and yards outside the twenty. It has to be a banger and needs every bit of power I have. It also has to be with my nondominant leg.

A cacophony of voices fills my head. So much advice. So much wisdom. So much experience. So many words and ideas and solutions. All exactly what came through for them when *they* needed it. But that's the thing: What they need isn't what I need. I tell them all to be quiet, just for a second, so I can get to what I need.

I set it up as best as I can and take the shot. The ball sails off my foot. Coach yells my name, and I can't tell if it's in admiration or frustration. The force it takes to shoot the ball that far pulls my opposite leg out from under me. I land on my back and someone lands on top of me. I wheeze, gasping for air, but still manage to see the goalie make the save of her life. Fingertips graze the bottom of my perfectly placed ball just enough to send it over the crossbar.

I missed.

And that shot, the shot I chose not to look away from this time, was the only chance we had all game. The Lakers came to play. They knew every move we wanted to make before we made it. We were ready for them too. We rose above all our fights and disagreements and left everything on the field, but a perfect shot from the top of the box ends up sending us home.

I had my team's only shot. Me. I can't help feeling that if it had been anyone else on the team they would've made it. Scoring first would've changed everything. I wasted that chance.

A few of us head toward the bench. Others drop where we are and cry or stare up at the dark sky. The celebration going on around us makes everything so much harder. Every time you sob they yelp in happiness. And sobbing isn't an exaggeration. I hear my teammates, but I don't make eye contact with anyone. Even if we were a team with half the ups and downs we've had, there would be no comfort for this kind of loss. Everyone, including me, just wants a moment in peace.

Both sides understand. That's why the congratulations line comes to us. Handshakes and pats on the back. I accept them all with as much sportsmanship as I can. It surprises me how many people compliment the shot that didn't go in. Even the other team's goalie comes over to tell me that shot was the best challenge she's had in her whole career. She hopes not to see me next year because she isn't sure she can pull off anything like that again.

I just made her highlight reel, so I take it with a grain of salt.

But it's Coach, who comes along encouraging each of us with a hand up or a pat on the back, whose words make me feel one percent better.

He bends down to me. "It was the only chance we had, and you took it. Not the result we wanted, but I'm proud."

"Coach," I say with a watery voice. "I missed."

"That happens." He smiles wryly. "But if you take a few more chances at the net you'll get used to it."

I almost smile. Almost.

Once he's gone, the hurt of the loss that had gone cloudy for only a second comes right back. Especially after I realize that all my teammates, even Capri, are hugging and leaning on one another. Everyone except me.

I want my coach's respect, and I want him to be proud of me and

I want to get better. But the respect of my teammates means way more. I want them to look forward to playing, winning, and even losing next to me.

This moment is anything but that. I look up into the stands. My parents are there. I know when I catch their eye because Dad nods and Mom blows me a kiss.

I don't look for Kai. It feels like the more he sees me play, the more I prove I'm not as good as he thinks I am.

I find Winston too. He's standing at the very top of the bleachers with his hands in his sweatshirt, watching me. Jake and Aubrey are next to him. I don't see the three of them together much, but it's nice that they came together for me.

Jake and Aubrey wave somberly. Winston's not sending me any special greetings. He's just watching me like he's trying to make sure of something. That I'm okay? That I'll be okay?

Then it hits like he's whispered it in my ear. He wants to help me be okay. I don't know how it's possible for an intention to travel that distance, but it does. I wish I could let him be that friend for me, but I can't. It would mean too much to me to let Winston support me like that.

Instead, I mouth *thank you*, and his small smile tells me he knows for what.

I read the room and am the last to make my way to the bench and collect my stuff. Most everyone is gone by then. Capri, a straggler as usual, is within yelling distance. I call out to her. She turns around.

When she doesn't come directly over to me, I go to her. I want to hug her, but I can't tell if she's open to it or not. I put my fist up for a pound. That goes over well.

"I guess everybody knows now why I don't shoot." It's probably too soon for a joke, but if everybody else is saying it, I might as well join in.

Capri takes off her headband and tilts her head. "What are you talking about? That was a great shot, Dru. Perfect placement. Not many people are coming that close from that distance, especially with a defender draped all over them. No one can say anything bad about it. You showed up tonight, in all the ways. I hope you know what you did to yourself. People are never going to stop asking you to shoot now."

It sounds like a joke, but I can tell she's serious. And she's right. I'm going to have to find a way to tap into whatever I tapped into today for just a second every game next season. The team will need it even more. Meegan won't be around.

But if Capri is right about what she's thinking and doesn't believe I cost the team the game, why is no one speaking to me? I ask that question.

"You think it's about the shot?" Capri leans her forehead toward me. "It's more about everything else. You opened the door for people to question you."

I release a shaky breath, swallowing sobs that threaten to take over again. "What?"

She studies my face like she's trying to decide if she can believe I really don't know what's she's talking about. "I don't know if Riley has some kind of radar on you or something, but she's been telling everybody that the pact was just to make Meegan look stupid and—"

I stop walking and turn to her. "How? How could a no-dating pact make Meegan look stupid?"

"Something about you expecting Meegan not to agree to it, which would make her look like she wasn't for the team or something. Girl, I don't know. You're asking me to understand sidekick logic. I can't do it." She pulls her jersey away from her skin and fans it back and forth. "I didn't say anything because—I know it's hard to believe—I wanted to keep things as peaceful as possible. But once Riley pointed it out, I paid closer attention, and I saw you. So did other people on the team." She looks around the field. "I tried to warn you the other day. I told them it was nothing and pointed out that some of them weren't exactly following all the rules either. But not everybody appreciated my defense. You're a captain and it was your idea. Why do you think you can focus better than anyone else?"

She pushes me on the shoulder as if she has to do that to get my attention when I'm hanging on every word. "If people didn't have someone they felt good about calling captain instead of Meegan, we would've been out of this thing a long time ago."

I'm shaking. I can't unclench my hands again. For the last few weeks my teammates have been questioning me about something other than the way I play. Okay, so I probably shouldn't have gone to Kai's soccer game, but I've made him wait. We didn't start anything. Not really. "What did Riley point out? What did you see? What are you talking about? The soccer game?"

She tilts her head and stares at me. "Now you're just telling on yourself. I don't know anything about a soccer game. I just know about the lunchtime hookups where you both just happen to leave the cafeteria at the same time. The texts that you do a terrible job of hiding."

She's talking about Winston? People think I broke the pact with Winston? That's almost a relief. I can defend that.

I jerk my head back. "Lunchtime make-outs? We were working on something, but there were no make-outs."

She squints at me. "So, you haven't messed around with Winston Portis this season?"

"I—" In my head, I see the kiss that went on a little long to be called anything other than a make-out. "It seriously isn't what you think it is. It's so embarrassing that I would rather just let you be mad at me than tell you what actually happened."

Capri smacks her teeth. "There's a group chat about it. Pictures and everything."

My face goes hot, and I take a step back from her. Another group chat? One with my teammates making assumptions about me behind my back? With receipts?

"Yeah, I know." She lets out a huff of air. "I can't put you in the chat. That's just too messy even for me. I'll send you screenshots, though."

I look at her seriously. "Maybe I can't prove it to you right now, but you'll see. There's nothing up between me and Winston. It will never happen."

She shakes her head, not even the slightest bit swayed. "I hope not, because I can't really cover for you anymore. I'm trying to be captain next year too, and it's too hard to earn respect just to give it away over something like this."

I nod and I agree. I have no idea how I'm going to fix this with my teammates, but somehow I have to convince them. There is no me and Winston Portis.

OUT OF TIME

I'm so restless and sad that my body doesn't let me go to sleep until then, I'm just staring at the ceiling, replaying the night in my head. I can't believe we actually lost. No last-minute heroics or even lucky bounces. We just had to hold on for two more games and we were in the final, but we couldn't do it.

It's not that we didn't play our best. We did. But the other team executed their plan better. Even though logically I know that, it still feels like I could've done something. I could've made that shot or found a way to get the ball to Meegan. She would've made the shot.

I don't want to go to school. It's not like everyone at LeBeau is a girls' soccer fan, but my teammates will be hard to face, especially with how quiet the main group chat was. I have to imagine the private ones were going off. And even though I left everything I have on the field last night, and Capri and Coach approved of my choices, I know people talk behind closed doors. Even my own parents do it. All I keep imagining is that in some homes they're talking about my game.

And then the whole Winston thing. For the last couple weeks, I've been adding to the stress of the team? Were we really that careless or was Riley just paying that much attention, looking for my flaws so she could point them out? Not that it changes the mistakes I made. I definitely made them.

And for what? I'm no closer to an answer about my exes. I've kissed one of my best friends and it won't get out of my head. Even though, I have to admit Winston was in my head before that. I didn't tell him he'd be a perfect boyfriend just to be nice. It was true.

But he's not a perfect boyfriend for *me*. The perfect boyfriend for me is one who actually wants me.

Eventually everyone will realize there really was no me and Winston, like I did.

Not that the receipts from the group chat aren't valid if you don't have the context. There are pictures of us in the stairwell from above during lunch. We're not doing anything, obviously, but I get why assumptions are being made. There are pictures of us talking in the hall and you could say that the way he looks at me when he's talking to me isn't exactly friendly. And someone clipped us watching *Sofia*. Even I have to admit we're sitting close, but the screen was tiny.

The only way to come back from that and try to regain the trust of my teammates is to not be caught like that with Winston again. That's a pact I can keep.

Once I finally make myself get out of bed, I take my time getting dressed, hoping I can leave at just the right time to make myself fifteen minutes late.

But that doesn't work. I'm right on time. Still, I don't rush.

When I get inside, I do everything the opposite of how I normally do it. I walk through the doors just as the warning bell rings, barely giving myself enough time to be in class and in my seat on time.

By lunch, Aubrey has found me. She doesn't ask where I've been or remind me that avoiding the world isn't going to solve anything. She just sends me to my car while she goes to the school store and gets us both smoothies and fresh-baked cookies.

I blare the radio as loud as I can until she gets back. We don't say much until after we've both chewed our first bite of cookie.

I sigh, still as restless as I was last night. "Are we on this weekend for studying or lunch?"

"I'm still going to be on hiatus. It's getting easier. I actually feel kind of good." She takes a long swig of her smoothie and swallows. "So I would say lunch, but LeArra told me you guys have a wedding singer audition or something."

"Yeah, but that's not until later in the day. I definitely have time for tacos." I run my finger around one of the bracelets Winston gave me. "You and LeArra talk about a lot to only have spoken once."

"Oh, we've talked a couple times. She's been checking in on me just to make sure I'm not getting overwhelmed again."

I let out a bark of a laugh. I don't know why. Maybe because it feels like it should be a joke. My sister checking in on my best friend while only texting me to give orders and express disappointment. Neither of them has even texted me about the game.

It's sad funny. I'm happy that Aubrey has someone who's helping her the way she needs to be helped. I don't want my best friend constantly stressed out. And I actually despise the way my sisters choose to sister me. It's just the principle, I guess. Like, you have a little sister right here.

Aubrey just looks at me like she's waiting for more.

I pick at my cookie, excavating a chocolate chip. "I'm glad you're not stressing as much anymore, and you feel like you have a better plan of attack. It's going to help."

"And?"

"And what?"

"And you want to beat my ass because I stole your sister or something?"

I side-eye her.

She side-eyes me back, but more exaggerated. "You may not know this, but every time LeArra comes up and your hands are free, you ball up your fists."

I look at my hands as if I've never seen them before. "No, I don't."

"Yes." She emphasizes the word as if it can't be any other way. "You do. And, Dru, I feel so bad. If you want, I'll never talk to—"

I cut her off with a hard shake of my head. "No. Please don't do that. If my sister can help you, I'm happy for you."

I pop a chocolate chip in my mouth and chew as I think of how to say this. She waits. "I guess I wish LeArra saw me like how she sees you, like how *I* see you. Smart and capable and headed toward something special one day. If you stop letting her mentor you or whatever it is you two have going on, it won't change anything for me."

Even if I thought it would, I wouldn't ask my best friend to change anything.

"But you *could* mention her a little less. If she tells you something about me or my family, at least pretend to be hearing it for the first time when I share."

She chuckles and taps her cookie to mine like a toast. "Understood."

We spend the rest of lunch scrolling a very messy side of TikTok and laughing. If there was medicine for feeling bad after losing, hanging out with your best friend would be it. When we make it back into the building, we're both still laughing and looking down at her phone. She's the first to look up and notice Kai coming toward us.

"There's your boyfriend, I guess." It's the first time she's ever said it so exasperatedly and questioningly. "If you're planning on launching him, make sure you wait until I get out of the way."

My mouth falls open.

"I'm just saying." She blows me a kiss. "Love you, though."

I shake my head and watch her walk away as Kai comes toward me.

I turn to Kai. There's no pact. Nothing to stop me from going out with him except me. I expect butterflies when I realize that, but I'm calm. It's not like I didn't know this would eventually be the case. It's what I've been working toward.

I was also working toward answers about me. I can't say I have those, but I'm out of time and excuses.

"I turned my notifications off last night," I say when we fall in step with each other. "Sorry if you texted me or something."

"I texted you, but only to say I get it if you're not talking." He nods. "Losing messes with me for days. I get it. Especially games like yesterday. You were the better team, but they had you guys so well scouted. It was like they knew everybody's favorite move, pass. They played it perfect."

Listening to him talk about it makes my heart drop. I feel like

I want to cry. But it's also good to hear another perspective. It's not that we weren't good or were overmatched. They were just better at preparing. I'm not saying it makes me feel better, but it might in a day or two. I'll remember that next year and not be the senior to get up and stop the film review.

His eyes light up. "Your shot, though. They didn't scout for that. It was magic."

I think he's just given me the biggest compliment he can, and I really respect it coming from him. "Thank you."

"If I had a foot like that, I would never not see my shot."

I chuckle. "You see it a lot as is."

He shrugs unapologetically. "I do, don't I."

We both laugh.

He looks at the clock at the end of the hall. The bell's going to ring soon. "Any other team stuff coming up?"

The question bounces around in my head before I answer. "Just the banquet. You know, all the usual stuff."

We stop in front of my next class. He does this thing where he studies my whole face.

I know what he's going to say. I know what I'm going to say. It must be the shock that's preventing the thrill from coming through. Or maybe it's all the buildup. Sometimes the buildup can ruin the actual moment.

Or maybe it's the fear that I've been dealing with all along. If Kai and I really get to know each other and things work out, is there a chance that I won't ruin it? Can I really trust Winston's opinion? Not just his opinion about me, but his opinion about my guy choices?

Do I just pick wrong? Is that the simple solution to what feels like a complex problem?

Is Kai a good pick? How would I even know that? It's not like there was something *wrong* with my exes.

The eye contact is strong when he leans forward. "Let's go out this weekend. I could take you to get something to eat."

Yes, that's the question. I knew it was going to happen. He's been counting down the days. We were counting down the days together. And the day is here.

What if I just said no?

Then what would I do? Sit around and pine over Winston? That would be so easy to do because he's Winston and so hard because he's never going to feel what I'm feeling.

If my fault is picking the wrong guys, then I just have to do a better job of picking the right one. Winston's my friend and he doesn't see me any other way. He isn't the right guy.

He's the wrong guy. *He* would be just another disaster. *He* would break my heart even more than I already have myself.

"Yeah," I say pushing excitement that I don't feel yet into my voice. I'm sticking with the plan. Eventually it's going to feel like the right thing.

THE END OF THE COUNTDOWN

I'm going out with Kai today.

But I have a lot to do before I get to that. After tacos with Aubrey, we end up at my house. Both of my sisters are in town for the vocalist audition, but luckily—for me at least—they're in the basement working out when Aubrey and I get there.

In my room, we decide between two outfits for my date. I want to look like I'm not trying too hard, but I want him to think I did try a little because that shows I care. And I want him to feel good after this whole saga.

Those two contrary ideas are why I'm sitting on my bed looking up at two polar-opposite outfits hanging from my door. Both are casual, but one is more hot girl—a formfitting belly shirt with denim shorts and flat sandals with straps that go all the way up to my knees—while the other is cute girl—a ribbed-cotton yellow bodycon tank dress with Converse. Both are me, but they're saying different things.

At the same time, both say I tried, but maybe too hard.

According to Aubrey, I look good in both. And if I change the shoes on either, it just becomes the other.

Since I won't have time between the vocalist audition with my family and the date to change, I decide to keep it cute with the yellow dress. It's more appropriate for the restaurant where the audition is.

As I get ready, I turn my speaker up as loud as I can without somebody complaining and play nothing but hype, *Dru you are the shit* songs.

I'm not sure if treating this situation like a pregame is good, but I'm trying it. I want to go into this date feeling like I'm winning. I want to go into it feeling like Dru. Against my own will, I start asking myself a lot of Keith Eason questions.

What do I want out of this date?

Just to get to know Kai better? To prove that everything with Winston was built on us playing roles? Or to remind myself that Winston is a non-option?

At that thought, my stomach drops. I've tried to not think about Winston all the time, but we're still friends, still around each other. Of course, there's been no just-me-and-you time in the six days since we went out. I wonder if he misses that time too.

Every conversation is hard for me. I have to be careful. There are things I want to say but I can't. I'm not sure if they're something I would've said before Boyfriend Winston and Girlfriend Dru. And even with things I know I would've normally said—everyday compliments or teasing—I can't figure out how to say them without sounding like a person who's obsessed with him.

The real twisted, upsetting thing is I actually thought about suggesting me-and-you time with Kai. But that's a Girlfriend Dru/Boyfriend Winston thing. I can't just start filling empty spaces with new people. Kai and I will have to figure out our own things.

If we get that far. The thought that keeps popping up is that even if Winston didn't find my fatal flaw, somewhere along the way I should've learned something. The fact that the only thing I learned is how to fall for a friend worries me.

If Kai and I start to build something, will I unknowingly wreck the foundation? By the time I'm ready to leave, my playlist hasn't convinced me that the answer to that question is no.

The vocalist most highly recommended to my sister performs at a restaurant on Saturday nights. Some people say he brings in just as many people as the food. We couldn't even get a reservation on any of the weekends Moriah and Rashid planned to be in town. We're just going to his warm-up before his real set.

Moriah wants there to be some surprises for my parents, so she asked them not to come tonight. I overheard her and LeArra talking. I think she plans to have the vocalist sing a tribute to my parents and doesn't want it ruined in any way. This is something my sister and I can agree on.

A few of Moriah's friends meet at our house to ride over to the restaurant together. That means I get to drive by myself without having to explain to my sisters that I have a date to make it back home on time for.

When we get to the restaurant, I'm walking slightly behind the older group. At first I don't see who Rashid's brought with him. Two large tables have been pushed together for us. On one side of Rashid is Peter; on the other side is Jake, an empty seat, and then Winston. He's slouched at the waist in his chair like he's trying to make himself at eye level with everyone else. He's wearing a gray, short-sleeved, three-button crew neck. Not dressed up or anything, just different from his normal sweatshirt or T-shirt.

I thought he told me he was only giving input on the food-related decisions. And I know I've brought it up. He never said anything about coming today.

I remember when I used to be happy to see him at family functions, especially anything related to the wedding. I knew he'd make things easier for me just by being around. But now my stomach is tightening. I'm more aware of myself than I am anytime I'm with just my sisters.

No, it's not the same kind of aware as with my sisters. I know Winston's not going to judge me for anything. But I also know he's not going to see me the way I want him to. That just makes me feel foolish.

I hope he doesn't think I'm looking cute for him.

God, Dru. Why would he think that? You didn't even look cute for him on your fake date. He's not thinking about you at all. Not like that. Just relax.

Even if Winston wasn't staring a hole into me right now, I'd know the empty seat is for me. I'd save one for him too. After I hug Rashid and say hi to Peter, I slip around the group, nearly missing a waiter with a tray full of neatly folded napkins. While everyone else hugs and says their hellos, I take my seat.

I greet The Twins with a *hey.*

"What's up?" Jake says.

Winston sits up like he's about to say something, but there's a long pause before he finally spits out, "Damn."

I look back and forth between them, thinking maybe I'm walking in on a conversation and need to catch up.

Jake looks at his brother, but his words are meant for me. "He likes your outfit."

"Yes. Yes, I do." Winston nods deeply. "You look nice. Pretty. Beautiful. Good. You look good."

"Oh. Do I? Thank you." I am super hot all of a sudden. I reach for the glass of water in front of me. Winston and Jake both put up a finger. But I need to cool down before I speak again. Before *he* speaks again. He *cannot* say things like that to me. I take them personally.

The water's good, but it definitely needs more ice. When I'm done, I set the glass down hard.

Their hands go down slowly. Winston winces. "That was my water. I already drank out of it. Sorry."

"Oh. It's okay." I shrug and laugh a little. "It's not like we haven't…"

Kissed is what's about to come out of my mouth. Thankfully, I stop myself. What would I be doing talking about that here? Or anywhere? That is the past. Never to be repeated.

"True," Winston mumbles, as if he's mentally filled in the blank. He sits up in the chair and his knee slams against the bottom of the table. "Man, I keep forgetting that's there."

The entire table stops and laughs at that for a second before the band gives us something else to focus on as they start to assemble on a short stage in front of a wall of windows.

"There's nowhere for you to stretch out," I say at the same time he says, "You have stuff on your eyes."

I'm wearing mascara. I don't often but I'm feeling inspired.

I look at him seriously. "Is it bad? I won't be mad if you say yes."

"I'm saying no." He eyes me for a second and I let him. If he questions anything else, I'm pushing the date back an hour so I can regroup. "And you did the side braid. Are you going somewhere special after this?"

"It's not the where, it's the who."

"Who's the who?"

"Guess."

He rolls his eyes to the ceiling in thought. "Moriah dragging you somewhere else for the wedding and calling it a special occasion?"

I laugh as the band starts. I would think the answer to who I would look nice for on a Saturday in spite of the week I've had would be obvious. Especially to Winston. He verified more than once whether I really like Kai. But maybe all my insecurity and indecision make it hard to believe that Kai and I are actually going out.

"Kai."

He raises an eyebrow in question as if he genuinely has no clue what I'm talking about. "Kai. How'd that happen?"

"Since the season ended early…He asked me." This comes out sounding a little unsure. The look on his face and his confusion about who I could be preparing to see have me questioning myself. Am I saying something wrong? Is this a bad idea? Has Winston uncovered my flaw and sees this date as a failure in the making?

He looks down at my hands. I follow his eyes. Without even

realizing it, I'm tracing a finger around the bracelets he gave me. I haven't taken them off since the game. He sniffs smugly. "He didn't waste any time."

My eyes widen. "I'm glad he didn't. Knowing me, I would've gotten all insecure and in my head."

He puts an elbow on the table and rests his chin in his hand, giving the band his attention as is everyone else. He has to speak louder than a whisper to be heard over the music. "He would've asked eventually, and you would've said yes. Insecure or not. You don't have a reason not to."

Is that a dig, and if so toward who? I can't figure it out. That could be because I'm not used to hearing this tone from Winston.

He presses his lips together but still doesn't look at me. "Where you guys going?"

"Everyway." It comes out like a question even though plans are solidified, and I absolutely know exactly where we're going.

When he has no reaction other than a blink, I have to ask an actual question. "Is that bad?"

His eyes turn slightly toward me but he's still facing the band. "Is what bad?"

I shrug. "I don't know. Going to Everyway on a date."

He takes a deep breath as if he's trying his best to be patient with me. "How can Everyway be a bad place for a date? Lots of other people will be on dates at Everyway."

I turn toward him more to try to get him to turn toward me. I hate having this conversation with the side of his face.

It doesn't work. He stays facing forward. I deflate. "You had this weird reaction when I said Everyway, and I started overthinking. So, I asked your opinion. I ask your opinion all the time. I didn't know it was that big of a deal."

He turns to me and tries to school his face into something friendly and soft, but it doesn't work. "It's not a big deal. I just don't think going on a date is something you need my help with. Your instincts are on point. You should trust them more than you trust me. That's all I'm saying."

He turns back toward the band as if the conversation is over. As if that's something he can just decide.

"Why are you grumpy?"

"I'm not."

"Yes, you are. You're grumpy." I nod aggressively. "One second everything's good and then suddenly it changed. It's uncomfortable and weird with no explanation."

Something that never used to happen between us.

"And you *never* change." There's a bite to the words that comes through most at the very end. "Change" could have been its own separate sentence, a demand even.

I sit up in my seat and lean closer to him. I don't want to miss anything he's about to say. "What are you talking about? What do you mean?"

He turns back to me. "No matter what happens, no matter what you're thinking, no matter what we do, no matter what I do, nothing changes with you." The bite is gone, but the words are just as clear and intentional.

I squint at him and wrap my hand around the back of my neck.

"So, you *did* find my fatal flaw. Might have been easier to just tell me."

"It hasn't even been a whole week since I told you what I thought about your fatal flaw, Dru," he shoots back. "You forgot what I said already?"

I did not forget. He said everything about me is a gold star. He said the right guy was going to see. He also told me to go for the guy. I did that.

When he mentions the day we spent together, my heart fills, and at the same time something inside me sinks too. Kind of like Sunday itself. It was the perfect day and we kissed. I was quickly reminded that it wasn't a real day.

"I didn't forget."

"Good." He slouches in his seat again. "That's the important part. Forget everything else I said. It didn't come out right. I don't want you to change."

I scoff. "You want me to remember you said some things but forget you said others?"

"Yep."

"Why?"

"Because it's a me issue. It doesn't solve your launching problem." His delivery is dry and precise, suggesting facts. Only a person emotionally attached to his words would question them.

I let out a sarcastic laugh. "How could it not?"

Jake clears his throat and shifts next to me. I know we're getting louder, but I'm having a hard time dialing it down.

Winston keeps his eyes trained somewhere other than on me but also not on the band. "Because they were your boyfriends. I'm not your boyfriend. I'm your friend."

"You don't have to say it like that. I know you're not my boyfriend. I know I'm not—"

"Then you understand why my opinion doesn't count. It's different." Those words are soft, but definitive.

I frown at him. He can't just cut me off, not when we're actually getting somewhere with me.

"Okay. Something bothers you as my friend. That matters to me." I take a deep breath, trying to calm myself down again. "I'm not going to be mad. I'm not even saying it's something I'll consider changing. But what is the thing about me that needs changing so much that it puts you in a bad mood?"

"Nothing, Dru." He sighs and presses his lips together. "You're a great friend. I'm the one who needs to change."

"Stop saying *friend*. I get it."

"What do you want me to say? Soon-to-be-sister-in-law? It's a little wordy."

"Now you're being a smart-ass." I huff. "You're mad to the point that you can't even stand to talk to me, and everything is perfectly fine? I'm just supposed to let that slide. You've never been like that with me before. In our whole lives. *We've* never been like this. I must have done something. I just want to know what it is. My friend *would* tell me."

He shrugs. "I don't like being wrong, I guess."

"About what?"

I watch him try to school his face into something neutral,

something very un-Winston. It makes me think that whatever he's about to say isn't going to be the truth. But why would he lie other than to avoid hurting me? With no idea how many different ways he could hurt me, he's bound to do it anyway.

"About whether or not you would follow through with Kai."

I blink at him. He's lost me. "That was the plan. The whole time. Figure out what's wrong with me so things could be different with Kai."

He blinks back at me, speechless.

I turn more toward him. My knees are touching his thigh. "Why are you thinking so hard? Just say whatever it is."

He nods in a way that says *I surrender* more than *yes*. "Yes, it was the plan, but I didn't think it would happen."

Jake clears his throat, louder this time.

"If you didn't think Kai was interested, why'd you say I should ask him out?"

"I didn't think you would actually do it. I didn't think you liked him anymore." He shifts so we're not touching. "But you do. I was wrong."

"I kind of feel like you were too busy judging my feelings to actually help me figure out how the same thing keeps happening to me over and over again." I swallow hard. My words are ringing truer than I expect once I get them out. "Did you even try?"

"Yes, I tried. I gave you real, honest advice. I tried to show you—" He stops himself and sighs. I try to cut in and beg him to finish his thought, but he doesn't let me. "Look. Dru. I can't be your wingman or whatever you're trying to turn me into. And it doesn't even matter.

You're getting what you want. I'm happy for you. Can you just let me listen to the band, please?"

Those last three sentences—*You're getting what you want. I'm happy for you. Can you just let me listen to the band, please*—happen after the band stops playing. And since he's talking loud enough to be heard over their performance, his voice fills the entire restaurant.

The first place I look is at my sisters.

"We should've had a kids table," LeArra mumbles dryly.

I glare at her. "Why? So we could sit you at the head of it?"

My sister jerks her head back like she can't believe that I would dare fix my mouth to speak to her as disrespectfully as she speaks to me. Moriah is just sitting there, hands on the table, eyes closed like she's trying to will this moment away.

Otherwise, it's pin-drop silent for about ten seconds, and based on all the grimaces and sharp intakes of air around the table, everyone's heard the Eason sister drama. But at this point, I don't even care.

My sister has said a lot of mean things to me, in a lot of different situations. It's why I try to stay as invisible as I can when she's around...or maybe even when she's not. I don't know. But this is the worst. That sarcastic remark wasn't just about me. It was about Winston. I let her dip her toes in at the cake tasting, calling him the mischievous one. But today she took a deep dive. I will never let that slide.

Rashid clears his throat and starts to clap for the band. Peter and Jake join in fast. Eventually everyone is giving the band their props. Except me and Winston. We turn to each other.

"I'm sorry," I say at the same time he says, "Are you okay?" We both try again. Neither of us laughs. We just end up looking at each other as the band starts their next song. We're so out of sync now. And I can't help but feel like it's not all my fault.

Quietly, we both turn away from each other and face the band.

When they play their last song, the waitstaff starts clearing off the table immediately. They make it clear that we've had our fun, now we can go. Everyone starts to clump together in the groups they came in and I do the exact opposite of when I got here. I walk out first.

I don't look back to see if Winston is paying me any attention. My head is pounding like someone has it in a stranglehold. The muscles in my shoulders are aching from how tight I've been holding them for the last hour. I need to get outside to my car to breathe. I need to think about what's next.

I don't have the capacity for anything that comes to mind. And it's a long list. I have to go out with Kai. I need to apologize again for LeArra. I have to ask questions that get Winston to explain himself better. Get him to undo the parts of this conversation that make him sound jealous and me hopeful that maybe he is, even when I know better. He can't tell me to go for it one day and then act hurt when he finds out I took his advice.

Not even if his being affected by me hanging out with another guy doesn't exactly make me sad. Not even if the memory of our kiss isn't fading into meaninglessness the way I want to believe it will.

What does any of it even mean?

Is Winston having the same feelings I am? Is that why he went from telling me how pretty I am to not being able to look at me? He didn't want to hear about me on a date with Kai? When he said *But if you want something from somebody, whoever that is, you should just tell him*, did he want that somebody to be himself?

But how can it be him? Even if Winston's been thinking about me the way I've been thinking about him, we can't act on it. At least with any other boy I've liked, when it's over we get to decide to never speak to each other again. With Winston, it's not up to us. We'd be done with each other before the wedding. What will I do when he brings a date? Or when the inevitable happens and he becomes someone's real Boyfriend Winston?

What would I do from the end point of anything with Winston until I moved past it? His family would always be invited. Winston would always be in my life whether nothing happened, and it was for the best, or something happened, and it was for the best, was for the worst, ended quickly, or lasted forever.

Even worse, after we've gone through one of my relationship cycles, I wouldn't be able to talk to him about anything I wanted, hype him up about his show, text him for advice when my sisters and I were having a moment. That would be all gone. It's practically gone now and all we did was an experiment.

I can't lose him in that way.

And even if I was willing to risk it, I'd still have to think about my team. The pact that I brought to the team and got everyone to agree to, and then breached. I promised Capri there would never be a Dru and Winston. I told her that everything was just a big misunderstanding. If I pursued something with Winston, that would make me a liar. My teammates would be done trusting me. And it would be valid.

Next year, when the season begins, we'll be starting from this point. The point where we don't trust each other, and everyone remembers everything I said and how it didn't match what I did.

Me and Winston would be the worst idea either of us has ever had. But I have to believe if we keep talking and we get further away from these last two weeks, we can get *us* back.

But if we went in the other direction and tried to make anything real, Winston and I would be lost forever.

THE END OF THE COUNTDOWN, PART 2

I only have a few minutes to breathe outside my car before everyone else starts to come out of the restaurant. At the first sound of laughter, I get in, putting my phone to my ear and keeping my eyes down. I don't think my sisters or Winston are up for talking to me right now. But just to be sure, I want to make it clear that the feeling is mutual.

It works, but when they're all gone, my head is still pounding. I roll down my window. Not only does it feel like summer on this spring day, but I still need to take a few more deep breaths.

I check the time. I have fifteen minutes before I'm supposed to meet Kai at my house. It's a ten-minute drive from where I am. I'm not sure how long it is for him, but he strikes me as a prompt person. I don't want him to beat me there. That would be rude.

I've kept Kai waiting long enough.

I pull up his number and call. Hopefully he hasn't left yet.

He picks up on the first ring. "Dru? Hey. I was just about to leave."

He sounds happy to hear from me, which is nice. Only, it makes me feel like an asshole. I know there's nothing official and this isn't a breakup, but with all the buildup and the way I've made him wait...

The way he's been okay with everything makes what I'm about to do hard.

"Oh. I forgot to tell you," I blurt, and then sigh when I realize I've shown a little too much enthusiasm for what I'm about to say. But it's probably just my happiness at finding a way to avoid the reason I've called him. I have no clue how to even get into it. "I watched the video you sent this morning."

"Tell me that guy doesn't move around the field like you?" His enthusiasm matches mine. "He came across my suggestions and I went on a deep dive. That is literally your game."

"Yeah, it is."

"If he had your leg—"

I cut him off with a laugh. "He's a professional. I'm sure his leg is a gazillion times better than mine."

He's laughing too. "Well, if I had your leg—"

"You'd make all those shots you take."

He laughs. "I *would*. That would be a dramatic improvement. Five goals a game on average. Forget the MLS, I'm going Premier League."

We both laugh, but when it dies down, I'm not sure what else to say.

After a while, he says curiously, "You need to cancel or something?"

I'm relieved at him saying that part for me, for opening the conversation that has to happen. But that relief only lasts for a second. There's a lot more to say after that.

I pull down the visor to block the sun. I'm even hotter than I was inside the restaurant. "Yes."

"Why? What's going on?"

Of course, I knew that question was coming. That doesn't make putting together the answer any easier. One thing I know is that I want to keep this about me and him. Being around Boyfriend Winston and thinking about my exes has definitely helped me come to some conclusions. But it's not like if I hadn't developed feelings for Winston I wouldn't have eventually realized that Kai and I weren't headed toward the kind of relationship I want. It just would've taken a lot longer.

As I try to find the words, I watch the parking lot fill up all around me with actual dinner customers. He doesn't bail me out this time. I decide to just say what I'm thinking. Hopefully without being mean. The reality is, Kai has been sweet to me. It just doesn't feel the way it should when it's coming from a guy I like.

I clear my throat. "I think we're friends."

"Wow. Okay." He *hmmm*s. "We haven't even been out yet."

"I know, but we've been around each other more and we have a little more information to work with than we did before." I sit up in the car, smoothing my dress over my thighs. "What do you like about me?"

I hear the sound of a door closing in the background like maybe he's going for privacy. He makes the *hmmm* noise again as if he needs it to think. "You're putting me on the spot."

I let out a small breath of air, almost a laugh, but not. Maybe he's right. He is on the spot. But in the same amount of time, I can easily come up with what I like about Winston.

I'm not offended by Kai's hesitation. It lets me know that maybe I'm on the right track to something about myself.

"We make sense." He says this like it's an obvious point no one would miss or deny. "Soccer means a lot to both of us. I'm always excited to talk to you about it and show you game highlights. And I know you won't believe me because anytime I give you a compliment you look doubtful, but I love your game. I actually want to play more like you."

I don't want to be doubtful, but I am. I cover my face. "Why would you want to play like me?"

"All the things I need to work on, you do well," he says. "Then the you-getting-nervous-around-me thing. I took it to mean you were interested and I think you're pretty, obviously. Like I said, we make sense."

My hands are clammy now. I put him on speaker and set the phone on the armrest. "Does just being around me make you feel good?"

When he doesn't immediately answer, I add, "Do you ever want to talk to me about anything other than soccer?"

"I don't know how to answer any of that." His voice is low, thoughtful but a little defensive too. "I haven't thought about it."

"I think if the answer to either one of those questions was yes, you wouldn't have to think about it. You would just know."

"How—"

"But please—" I speak over him. "Don't take this like I'm upset or blaming you. I'm saying all this because I *have* thought about it. I do know the answers to those questions."

We both go quiet. I have to believe he's trying to process everything. I don't have it figured all the way out myself.

"I don't want to sound cheesy, but I think we both really admire each other or something, but not in *that* way."

He sighs. "What you're saying makes sense and I can't answer yes to what you asked me. But a few minutes ago, I was excited to see you. That has to mean something."

I can't argue with that. I think we would have a good time together. That *does* mean something. Just not what we...*I* thought it would.

I'm not sure if I'm underestimating his feelings or if he just needs more time to think it all through. I get it. He doesn't have a Winston for comparison.

He sighs, deeper this time. "I don't know if I agree with everything you've said. But I can admit that the thing I was looking forward to most about today was talking to you about the US men's national team versus Mexico game."

One thing I don't think I would've ever had to worry about here is launching Kai into great boyfriend status. I think he can do that on his own with a girl who's nothing like me. Maybe instead I can launch us into a great friendship.

I smile into my phone and take a deep breath. "Same. Go."

THE END OF THE COUNTDOWN, PART 3

When I come in through the garage after sitting in the parking lot for an hour talking nothing but soccer with Kai, my family is all seriousness over a game of Monopoly in the family room. My sisters are both in sweatpants and T-shirts, but my parents look like they walked right from their dinner plans and into this.

Mom, the luckiest person in the house, is holding a stack of money in her hand that looks larger than the bank's. "That was a quick date. You don't like him?"

I sit next to her on the couch. "Kai is really nice. Super confident."

Dad exchanges a look with Mom before he turns to me. "We won't be officially meeting him. Is what you're trying to say?"

"Dad," I chastise.

Mom scrunches her face. "Well, is he wrong?"

I bite my bottom lip and shake my head. Both of my parents bust out laughing.

"Why were you going out with...whoever? You're obviously obsessed with dimple twin." LeArra looks at Moriah. They're both sitting on the floor at opposite ends of the coffee table. "Remember how she was looking at him at dance rehearsal? And that argument they got into today?" LeArra blinks. "Very embarrassing, by the way. Also very telling. To add to that, disrespectful to me."

I sink further in my seat next to Mom. They're both looking at me all investigative. I don't like it.

I'm not surprised LeArra's bringing up what happened at the table earlier in front of my parents, though. This is her chance to shine bright and have somebody put me in my place. Something no one else was willing to do earlier.

There's a part of me that doesn't want to talk about this again. I want it to go away, even though I know there will just be another thing to set her off. Then there's this other part of me that wants to make it clear that any shade toward Winston—or me—will result in her being embarrassed again, and not the other way around.

"Can my wedding gift be you learning to tell the twins apart? My sister not taking the time could feel like an insult," Moriah says.

"Your wedding gift is the considerable amount of time I'm spending to help make your day special." There's not an ounce of sarcasm in LeArra's voice. Moriah has no choice but to accept it and move on. LeArra turns back to me. "What's the matter, Dru? He doesn't notice you? Doesn't find you attractive? Has a girlfriend?"

I shake my head, but I don't think LeArra notices, because she keeps going. "When I was in high school every single boy I liked asked me to set him up with one of my friends and I did."

"I had crushes on one boy every year, for the entire year." Moriah rolls her eyes to the ceiling. "I never said anything. They never noticed me. Now they're all in my DMs all the time. I had a chance if I would've just spoken up."

"What do you even like about him anyway, other than his face?" LeArra shakes her head and shrugs one shoulder. "That's the real problem with high school. Relationships are hard because they're based on the superficial. If he doesn't like you, just find another cute boy. It's not like they're adding value to your life at this point. Or maybe at any point ever. I don't know."

"My advice is not to hide," Moriah cuts in. "Let your feelings be known and move on if it doesn't work out."

"But that's her problem, though. She hides," LeArra says. "We hid her ourselves when we were at home because we were her protectors. Now she doesn't know how to show herself."

I stand up to leave, but once I'm across the room I can just feel LeArra about to pipe up. I can't stop myself. "You've never protected me. I don't hide from anyone but you guys. I don't have to, because no one else in the entire world bullies me like you do. You are literally the meanest, most disrespectful, invalidating people I've ever been around.

"And the judgment"—I blink at them and shake my head—"it's too much. That's what I'm avoiding. Why I'm staying in the background. But no matter what, you guys find me, and you dig.

"And the worst part is, you don't know anything about me." I lean closer to both of them. "I've had more relationships than either of you did by the time you were seventeen. Actually, I've had more relationships than you up to this point in your life, LeArra. So, you should maybe save some of your good advice for yourself."

I could go on forever. I also feel like I could cry. Nobody here deserves my tears, and the speed of my heart is causing a headache.

LeArra scoffs. "Mom. You have nothing to say when she talks to us like that? This is the second time today."

"What?" Mom deadpans. "We're home."

I can't lie, that almost makes me laugh, but Mom is serious. And Dad is silent and relaxed, which usually means Mom is speaking for both of them. But my sisters don't accept this. As they get into a point-counterpoint with Mom, detailing all my shortcomings, I slip upstairs to my room.

I keep expecting to feel bad about what I said or that I'm not doing whatever I can for Moriah, but once I'm upstairs in my room and my heartbeat is back to normal, I don't feel anything. Both of my parents knock and ask if I'm good. I say that I am because I don't want to talk. I need to rest my brain. This day...this week has been hard. They seem to get it and let me have my peace.

It's too much to hope that no one will ever bring it up again, but I was thinking we could at least leave it alone for the night.

I'm changing into my pajamas when there's a knock at my door. Without waiting for me to answer Moriah opens the door and takes two big steps in. Nothing like my parents.

She examines my room. "Even if it was messy in here it would look clean."

I nod, surprised that she gets it. "That's exactly what I like about it. Clutter makes me cluttered."

She looks at me curiously. "Did something happen between you and Winston?"

That was unexpected. I thought she was about to start in on all my wrongs.

I groan. "Moriah, why are you asking me about this? You don't care. If you're worried we're going to mess up your wedding, we won't."

"Well, that's good to hear." She sits cross-legged at the foot of the bed, facing me. "I don't like seeing either of my sisters upset."

I lean against the dresser. I can't sit right now. "What happened between me and Winston has nothing to do with what I said to you and LeArra. If that's where you're going with this intervention, that's the wrong angle. My anger's in the right place."

She rests her elbows on her knees, laces her hands in front of her face, and sighs. Moriah and I haven't had a real conversation since ever, primarily because she doesn't think I'm a real person. Neither of them do. Her coming in here now, trying to act concerned, is re-igniting the flame in my belly from earlier.

And maybe on a different day I would consider a conversation, but right now it's hard for me to feel like this isn't about the wedding.

I take off my earrings and put them in my jewelry box. "We—my soccer team—lost the other day. We didn't even make it to the semis."

She scratches her head as if trying to figure out what this has to do with anything. "I heard. Mom told me."

"Mom can't tell you how much losing actually hurts me. She can't tell you how disappointed I am in myself." I pick up my phone and scroll with no purpose. "Not only do I have actual ideas and thoughts and feelings, I can even articulate them sometimes."

"And when you do, you don't want to be beat up for it. I get that. I should have asked you how you're feeling and not relied on Mom's interpretation. I'm sorry for that."

I look up at her to make sure she's not smirking or something, though that would be a LeArra move. She looks like she really means what she said, but I'm having a hard time believing there isn't a *but* somewhere. Maybe she just needed to take a breath before she really digs in. "Why are you being apologetic? It's so condescending, especially when I know any second now you're going to cut into me about something."

She covers her face with her hands, making her words come out muffled. "I thought I was the good sister."

There's humor in her voice. I want to laugh, but the absurdity of that statement strangles my vocal cords. I'm just sitting here with my mouth wide open.

"I've been coming to the realization of how unaware, unaccountable, and wrong that thought is." She looks at me intently. Where I can't see the similarities in our features, I see them in our mannerisms. "There's no good sister. We have a screwed-up dynamic that takes all of us. I never realized how much it affected you until that day at Bridal Magnifique. In the moment, I was upset, but once I got back home and talked to Rashid, I could see your side. I realized how much I need to think about in regard to our relationship. And you're right. I still think of you as young. As someone who needs to give respect but not expect it in return until you've earned it. I need to fix that.

"I'm sure LeArra is the way she is because she's always been the smartest person in the room her entire life. Everyone has all these expectations of her." She gives a heavy sigh and shakes her head. "I don't know—I can't figure that out or fix it for her. But what I think I know is that LeArra punches down on me, and I give her all this respect. Then I end up punching down on you. And you just get really small and disappear and you take it, which pisses everybody off."

I take a breath, not wanting the anger from earlier to come back, but it hasn't moved far enough away. It's too accessible. "If I stick up for myself, if I say my opinion, you guys jump on me. The best way to avoid that is just to be quiet. You guys will never like what I say or how I say it. It's easiest to just nod and obey or not be there."

She waits a few seconds before she speaks. I'm not sure if she's choosing her words wisely or giving me time to calm down. "I'm not attacking you or judging how you protect yourself. I'm just—"

"I'm not protecting myself." With those words my voice becomes that of the baby sister they both see me as: whiny and oversensitive. So, I repeat myself, training my voice into the person I actually feel like most of the time. But then the words themselves feel a little untrue.

Moriah shrugs slowly, nodding. "Right. You said 'avoid.' I jumped to conclusions about why you would want to do that, as if you can't speak for yourself. I don't want to do that to you. I don't want it done to me." She looks right into my eyes. "This is probably going to sound really strange to you, but since I got engaged, I've been thinking about kids a lot. I don't even know if I want them, but one of the cons is our relationship dynamic. I want my kids to understand each other. The problem is, I don't think anyone can guarantee that."

She's said a lot. So much that I can't process it all in one sitting, like how maybe the Dru I built here with two sisters comes with me everywhere I go too. And that word: *protect*. I never once thought of the way I deal with my sisters as protecting myself. And as much as I want to be offended by that word, it only caught me off guard because I don't like the idea that I'm afraid of them, and how they make me feel sometimes. But I can't come up with a better description.

The idea that I might be bringing that protection outside the house is a lot. Am I bringing that into every relationship? Has the flaw I've been chasing after outside my house been right here in it the whole time? Is my relationship with my sisters why it's so hard to give a complete Dru answer? Why I'm always so afraid of shooting and missing?

One thing I know for sure is that, yes, I want to be different with at least one of my sisters. Even if it's only because of the wedding, I want to try if she's trying. But I do want to get one thing straight.

"I don't think I need you guys to understand me. Sometimes I don't think *I* understand me. But I don't like feeling like I don't belong in the family. Or that because I don't think like you guys, or I'm not like you, that something is wrong with me."

She nods. "I'll try. I'll apologize when I'm wrong. And I'll talk to LeAr—"

I shake my head. "Don't. I know you guys are closer but nobody can convince her of anything. If you try, she'll probably just think whatever she thinks about me even harder."

"Okay, but can I just say one thing? I don't think she thinks badly of you. I just think she wants to see you reach your full potential."

I roll my eyes and shake my head. "Yeah, that didn't make it any better. A, I know how she acts when she thinks someone has value.

It's way different from how she treats me. B, why does she get to decide what my potential is?"

"Okay. You're right. I'll let you guys work it out." She chuckles and rolls onto her side, where she narrows her eyes at me. "Are you going to tell me about Winston or not? I promise I won't tell Rashid...unless you need me to."

I pace my room, thinking. "There's nothing to tell you about Winston."

"Are y'all okay, at least?" She eyes me. "Rashid and I always talk about how cool it is that you guys are close. And Mom and Ms. Teddy too. You hear all these horror stories about blending families. But we've never had to do much. Everybody clicks."

I know she's just trying to keep the conversation going, or maybe even making a real effort to bring us closer. But that's the worst thing she could've said. It makes me feel like shit. Like I'm about to be a problem again.

This isn't a diaper blowout. I can't say it isn't my choice. I walked right into falling for Winston and potentially ruining our friendship. How fun will it be when we all get together if Winston and I just end up in an argument?

I stop pacing. "If you and Rashid want to keep feeling like that, I don't think I should tell you anything about me and Winston."

She sits up. "Dru, I think that's one of the reasons you should."

Because I do want us to be different and because this feels like what I've always wanted with my sisters, through tons of awkward pauses and even more carefully chosen words, I tell Moriah all about me, my boyfriend protégés, the pact, and the dimpled twin.

COUNTING UP, DAY 1

I didn't sleep last night. The conversation I had with Moriah led me to a place I didn't really see myself going at all. Before that, I never would have wondered if the way I interact with my sisters has anything to do with the way I interact with other people, like my teammates or my exes. But I have to at least question it.

It's why I decide I need to talk to Jayden. That's a relationship I felt like I was doing at least half right as the most current version of myself, and we *did* have chemistry. I felt it. I'm not looking for him to give me a solution, just an answer as to why when I tried to give him complete Dru, he didn't accept it.

It can't wait until Monday at school. I might lose my nerve by then. It has to be now. And I would love to hide behind my phone, but this is a conversation that should be had in person.

I find the last message between me and Jayden. *Yeah. Sure.* It's his response to me asking if we can meet up later...so I can break up with him. I wish I could delete it from both of our phones. Especially since the text I'm about to send is along the same lines.

I try my best at variation.

Dru: Hey Jayden.

Twenty minutes go by. Not seconds. Minutes. I brush my teeth. I wash my face. I sort a load of clothes.

I don't put them in the washer because I hear LeArra's voice downstairs. I don't want to talk to her. Calling this protecting myself doesn't feel as bad as it did last night. It feels accurate.

Jayden: Hey Dru. Everything okay?

That's very Jayden to be concerned even though we haven't spoken at all since we broke up. Only I can wreck things with a guy who shows open concern for strangers.

Dru: Everything's good. I need to run something by you. You can bring Malia.

Saying that last part makes me cringe. I don't want to have this conversation in front of her. But I need to make sure he knows that what I'm asking is harmless to him. I'm not trying to get him back or anything. She's probably sitting next to him right now wondering what I'm trying to do. Those two are tethered.

Jayden: Sure. Are you okay?

Dru: I'm fine. ☺ Coffee?

Neither of us actually drinks coffee, but we love cake pops from

Volcanic Coffee. It doesn't surprise me that by the time I get there—on time—Jayden is sitting at a table with four of them laid out in front of him. He's wearing a three-quarter zip windbreaker and shorts. He's smiling just short of wide enough to show his gapped teeth.

What does surprise me is, he's alone. No Malia anywhere.

I'm winded when I get to the table. More from nerves than anything else. I pull out my chair and sit down.

"Where's Malia?"

He smiles at the thought of her. "Church."

"Oh. We could've waited for her. It's not that serious. At least not for her anyway."

He clears his throat uncomfortably. "I told her everything that happened between us. She knows you don't like me. She's not worried about us catching up."

That derails me. "What do you mean by that? What'd you tell her?"

He nods slowly. "I told her about our relationship."

It's been months, but my heart still sinks. "And she thinks I don't like you now or"—it's hard for me to get this out—"that I didn't even like you when we were together?"

He considers his answer as if he's just now realized what he's said could hurt me. I have all the answer I need without him saying a word.

I focus on the long line and busy barista to avoid looking at him. "I liked you a lot."

When the length of his silence makes me wonder if he's still breathing, I look him in the eye. "Was that not obvious? Why would I have been with you if I didn't like you?"

He's still blinking at me like either he doesn't believe me or he isn't sure he's heard me right.

I make myself push forward even though my heart is beating wildly. I'm on the cusp of something that could actually help me. I have to know. "I'm not trying to get back with you or anything. It's really not like that. You and Malia are perfect together. But I feel like you let me go way before I broke up with you. I mean, you were in a new relationship not even a week later. I just want to know what the breaking point was. I want to avoid it in the future."

He crosses his arms over his chest, which makes me mentally brace myself. "I really wanted to get to know you, but you wouldn't let me. Sometimes when we talked, everything you said seemed really calculated or I could tell you had more to say and you just never would. It made me feel like you didn't trust me."

I'm not sure how he could think that. I did trust him. I showed him I trusted him. But I don't want to interrupt. I let it go for now.

"I stopped trying, thinking it would make you act different. But instead, it made you mad, and you broke up with me."

That almost makes me laugh. Jayden wasn't losing interest in me; he was trying to get a reaction out of me? And when he couldn't get a reaction, he gave up.

"But I did react." I lean in closer to him. I try to keep my voice low, but the words are burning to get out however they can after all this time. "I told you something that before that point I hadn't told anyone else. I tried to explain myself to you."

He shakes his head like he doesn't know what I'm talking about.

"I told you what happens to me in all my relationships. I thought if you knew, you'd at least try to help me stop it from happening again."

"Yeah. Okay." He presses his lips together and sighs. "I thought you were joking when you first told me that. Who calls themselves 'the boyfriend launcher'? Who comes up with that?"

I smack my tongue against my teeth. "Well, me, obviously. And it's accurate. Look at you now."

He grimaces. "Yeah. That's a good point. I saw it once it all played out."

"How could you not?"

"Okay, well, even if you weren't joking, nothing changed after you told me that. I still felt like you were holding back. You were the same. You weren't trying to be more open with me. What was I supposed to do?"

I shake my head. "I don't know. Help me not do it."

"I don't—I didn't know how to do that."

I guess that's fair. I didn't know how to either. I still might not.

"As far as how fast I moved on . . . Malia was the exact opposite of you." He gets this dreamy look on his face that tells the world exactly how much he likes her. "There's nothing she doesn't want me to know about her and she doesn't want to know about me. She makes it obvious how she feels all the time. I never have to guess with her."

I understand what he means, but he took the fact that I couldn't be myself or be open to mean I wasn't interested in him. That wasn't the case at all. I don't even have it all figured out in my head, and

I'm not sure Jayden would even care to hear an explanation, but I do want to clear up one thing.

I look him in the eyes, to get across how serious I am. "I'm not sure it matters anymore, but it wasn't personal."

"It matters and I get what you're trying to say, but I think you're wrong." He scratches his head. "If the right person, the person you really wanted, treated you the way I did, you would react differently. Maybe not at first, but eventually you would show him who you are because you would care enough to take that extra step. And that person would be somebody patient who thinks it's easier to wait on you than lose you. That's very personal."

I jerk my head and smile. "I don't remember you being deep."

He smiles. "That's not me. That's her. She has to overanalyze everything until she has squeezed out all understanding. And she wanted to understand me and you more than anything. It took a while before she believed I was over it."

I know he will relay this entire conversation to her, and the last thing I need is her trying to squeeze understanding out of something I haven't already worked out for myself.

Still, I smile back and stand up to go.

"Thanks for meeting me." I push all four untouched cake pops toward him. "Take those to Malia. Tell her I said hey."

He nods. "It was good talking to you, Dru. Take it easy."

I turn on my heel and I'm out the door. It wasn't as embarrassing as I thought it would be talking to Jayden. It also wasn't a conversation I wanted to drag out.

I wanted to be open with him. I wanted him to know me. But I couldn't. Was it because I didn't care enough to try harder or because he didn't wait long enough? Even with boyfriends before him, which came first? For the most part, I've always thought that simply telling someone you want to be with them is as vulnerable as you can get, but obviously it isn't.

The wild thing is, when I really think about it, everything with Winston has been the opposite. I do let him know me; I've just never told him how I feel. And now I'll probably never get the chance.

COUNTING UP, DAY 1, PART 2

"Winston kissed me. I've been barely lucid ever since." That's what I say when I show up at Aubrey's after talking to Jayden. I didn't tell her I planned to talk to him, just in case I flaked out.

I also didn't tell her anything about yesterday. I was too overwhelmed by it all to give a rundown so soon.

She takes the bag of chips and the dips I brought and waves me inside. "Was that one of those... you know when you're supposed to be thinking of one thing, but you're actually thinking of another. Like you *meant* to say Kai, but you were thinking of Winston."

"Freudian slips," we say in unison.

"No, I said it right. Winston Portis kissed me."

"Damn." Aubrey blinks. "I knew something was up when you didn't let me know how your date with Kai went."

"We didn't go out," I mumble.

"What?" She starts leading me into her family room. "We have to get the carbs going before we go any further."

She sets the bag of tortilla chips on the coffee table and sits on the floor in front of them. Next she opens the queso and salsa. She dips a chip in the queso and then in the salsa, which makes me groan at the concoction we'll end up with if one of us doesn't get bowls. She picks up another chip and I grab the queso.

"Get bowls before you mess this up for everyone else," I tell her. She gets two bowls and spoons. I take care of the rest.

Aubrey puts her hands under her thighs as she stretches her legs out. "Let's start with the kiss. When did this happen? At the vocalist audition?"

I grimace. "When we went out."

Aubrey side-eyes me. "When you went out on your fake date, Winston Portis kissed you and you're just now telling me about it? You acted like the date was meh and completely for scientific purposes. Was the kiss so bad you wanted to scrub it from your brain?"

I let myself fall over onto the couch like somebody pushed me and cover my face. "The date was actually one of the best days of my whole life."

"Feeling a little hyperbolic, are we?"

I laugh at her dropping SAT words into our normal everyday conversation. "Nope. It really was. Remember how I told you he took me to a carnival?"

She nods.

"Well, I had told him about how when I was in sixth grade I broke up with my first boyfriend and two days later he took another girl to the fair and rode all the rides and how I've still never had a date like that and so he took me. And then we hung out at the park and just talked, which is apparently his favorite thing to do."

"Aw. That sounds sweet. And the kiss?"

I sit up. She's leaning forward with her elbows on the table.

"It was soooo rude."

Aubrey snickers. I sigh.

"I'm pretty sure he lifted me off my feet. It was sweet and the opposite of sweet at the same time."

Aubrey puts up a finger. "Wait. So the date was good. The kiss was spectacular. But it still took you more than a week to tell me *and* you turned around and told Kai you'd go out with him? The only thing wilder would be if you had actually carried that out."

"I just..." I let out a shaky breath. "I kind of couldn't believe how I was feeling about Winston. I thought it was just because of all the things we'd been saying to each other. The roles we'd been playing. And afterward he was all nonchalant like, *nothing's wrong with you. Go get your man.* Meanwhile, I was barely breathing."

She narrows her eyes. "He did not say that."

I nod deeply. "Yeah, he did. He said he was just making sure kissing wasn't my fatal flaw."

"And if it was your fatal flaw what was he planning to do? Coach you?"

"Right. Like what was the plan?" I shrug. "And when he told me—and yes, he said this—'If you want something from somebody, whoever that is, you should just tell him,' I thought I'd just gotten caught up and would be back to myself shortly."

Aubrey makes a duh face. "*Somebody* is Winston himself. Obviously."

I cover my face. "That's what I was hoping but I asked him if he meant Kai. He said yes. And I was just embarrassed that I got lost in the whole thing and he was able to keep his head. The next time I saw him he was just normal Winston. The experiment was over and that was it. And then things got really irreversibly messed up."

I get my phone and show her the screenshots Capri sent me.

She swipes through, then looks up at me. "They were all over you, girl."

"With good reason."

"Who has that kind of time? Must be nice." She tosses the phone back to me. "You got those after the game. Why am I just now seeing them? You have too many secrets, Dru. Let me best friend you, please."

I haven't been keeping Aubrey updated, but she's still here. Still all in. Not everybody can be that for me. But she's chosen me for a reason. I hope to never take that for granted.

"I didn't tell you because I don't like to see or talk or think about my teammates not trusting me." I groan. "And it was all supposed to just go away. I was never going to be with Winston. I was going ahead with what I had planned. I thought time away from Winston, and with Kai, would cure me. I told Capri that Winston and I would never. And if we ever did, my teammates would never trust me again."

"Yeah, that's a situation. But before we even go there...what happened with Kai?"

I tell her about my argument with Winston, my awkward conversation with Kai, and even the whole thing with my sisters, which led me to my talk with Jayden.

She narrows one eye. "Are you sure all this Winston stuff isn't because things didn't work out with Kai? I've been thinking you were obsessed with Winston, and you don't look at Kai the way you look at Winston, but I have to bring it up."

"I'm positive," I get out before she's finished asking the question. "I fall asleep thinking about Winston. I wake up thinking about Winston. I always have things I want to tell him. And his face... When I see him I just want to blurt it all out."

Aubrey blinks at me and shakes her head as if she doesn't know what to do with me.

"I've tried to get you to see. I wasn't going to just put it out there, because you never acted like Winston had a chance and I don't like to set people up for failure. But I've thought for a long time that Winston had feelings for you. The way he watches whenever you talk to other guys, not just Kai. He always seems so happy to be around you." She smiles a little. "And the day after the game, when you were in hiding, he was really worried about you. He is obsessed with you."

I whimper. *Obsessed* is probably too strong a word, but at some point during our little experiment, I definitely got under his skin somehow. Unfortunately, it didn't take long for me to see myself out.

"You need to talk to him," Aubrey urges. "After yesterday, he's probably checking his phone every three minutes to make sure he didn't miss your call."

"I need to, but I can't." I groan. "As much as I like him, I don't know if I can be the person he would expect me to be. Jayden thinks I didn't care about him enough to really open up. There are a lot of reasons for that, I think, but his points were valid. How do I know I won't be the same way with Winston?"

"Are you listening?"

I put my forearm over my eyes. "I am, Aubrey. Damn. It's not that easy."

Her silence tells me she's waiting patiently for me to explain myself. I uncover my eyes.

"We're friends. When we break up in a month or three I won't have that anymore. Especially not after he moves on to somebody else." I shake my head. "I don't want to lose him in that way."

And, Jayden's point of view has merit. I could be doomed to ruin things with Winston. He may be patient with me, but everybody has limits.

Eventually, I could disappoint us both.

"You have to at least talk to him about it. Do whatever it takes to make sure you're ready to be uncomfortable because there's a chance it could lead to something great. Make sure he's a person you would do that for. Not like you haven't dated enough to know the difference." She says that last part to herself, but just loud enough for me to hear.

I don't even get offended. She's right. At the very least, I should have a clue about what's not for me. Moving slower with Kai definitely helped.

Winston is worth me being sure. And once I am sure, either way, I have to let him know. These are things that have to be said. Questions I think he needs answers to as much as I do. Luckily, I can figure that out without him being absent. He's not going to ignore me. He has given me that.

I perk up and smile at her. "You're right."

Without even a second's thought, my best friend says, "I know. Call him."

"What about my team?"

She shrugs. "That has to be secondary. I know they're important to you, but you don't want to admit to stuff before you know if you and Winston can work things out. That would make things worse for no reason. But if you guys can work it out, you have to own your shit, Dru. There's no way around it if you're going to be with him and try to rebuild with your team." She pushes my phone toward me. "Call him."

WHAT'S LEFT OF DAY 1

I can't call Winston right away. He has a live interview tonight. I wanted to let him focus on doing his thing before I come at him with a hard conversation about us. Aubrey's entire family is home now so we watch from her bedroom. As soon as it's over, Aubrey demands I call him. I want to have the conversation as much as she wants me to, but the anticipation I've built up over the last few hours, and the fact that the last time we spoke we argued, paralyzes me a little.

She actually picks up my phone and holds it up to my face to unlock my screen, finds him in my contacts, and calls him for me. She has him on speaker, but I turn that off as soon as he says hello. She scoots closer to me on her bed.

His "hello" is curious, surprised, maybe even a little defensive. Like maybe he was replaying our argument in his head just before I called.

"Hey. Great show. You asked some really good questions." I try to sound upbeat, but I stumble through the compliments. Aubrey frowns at me, then with her hand encourages me to keep going. "You made me smile a lot."

"Thanks?" He's still curious and surprised, but the defensiveness is gone. "Why does your voice sound like that?"

I clear my throat. "Like what?"

"Shaky."

"I don't know why. It *shouldn't* be. You're a very easy person to talk to." I smack my forehead with my palm and roll my eyes at myself. That was the corniest thing I could've said.

He doesn't laugh or tease, though, he just says, "Yeah?"

"Yes," I answer quickly.

It goes quiet then. Completely silent except for the faint sound of Aubrey's parents downstairs in the kitchen.

My heart starts to beat fast enough and hard enough that I actually feel it in my chest. "I don't like being in a fight with you."

He lets out a shaky, kind of relieved breath. "Me either."

"I'm sorry. I know I have a lot to explain, but can we be made up now?"

"Yes. Please. Let's be made up." He swallows. "But I don't need an explanation. That's what I was trying to say yesterday. I'm good. I know everything. You know everything. And that's just how it is, you know."

I look at Aubrey as I talk, getting all my fearlessness from her encouraging nod. "You don't know everything."

"But I don't—"

"You want to come over? Or I can come over there? Just for a little while. I really need to talk to you."

The silence from his end is filled by Aubrey mouthing *yes* and pantomiming clapping. My heart is beating even faster now but I still manage to smile at her.

"You can come over. Nobody's here so you don't have to worry about anyone eavesdropping."

"It doesn't matter. You're going to tell Jake everything I say anyway."

He laughs. "At least I ask first."

The last time I was at Winston's house was the night of the interview. This is a way different kind of night. Thankfully I'm not sweaty and gross.

He opens the back door a little less excitedly than he did that day. The only things that are remotely the same are his bracelets. But I guess they're different too, now that I know he knows what's written on them. I wonder if he wishes he still had the ones he gave me. I happen to be wearing them.

He has on the same plain black tee from his show earlier and sweat shorts that, based on their rough hem, are just sweatpants that weren't long enough anymore. Even though I know he's expecting me, he looks surprised. Like maybe he's trying to figure out what I'm going to say before I say it.

I smile. I am genuinely happy to see him. I want him to know this isn't going to be like yesterday or any other day where I'm in denial about my feelings. "Hey, Winston."

He doesn't smile back. He just opens the door wide enough for me to come in. He stays a few paces behind me.

I point toward the family room. "In there?"

He exhales a humorless laugh. "You called this meeting. You run it."

I go in and sit on the couch. The seats are really deep, so my feet don't touch the ground when I sit all the way back.

Winston notices a pair of socks on the seat next to me. He rolls them into a ball and tosses them toward the steps. He sits down facing me, leaving a whole seat between us. I don't know what to make of that. I'm hoping it's because he doesn't know what I want, not because he doesn't want to be close to me.

"Oh. Aubrey told me to tell you to tell Jake hi." I scrunch my face. "I don't know why she doesn't just text him or something."

He locks his hands behind his head and stretches. "She *did* text him. Just before you got here he texted me to let me know that he knew you were coming over. I think they talk about us behind our backs. They've gotten kind of close."

I laugh a little, not sure if I understand. "Uh-uh."

He chuckles. Finally I see a glimpse of *my* Winston. "I think it's a thing. At least on his part."

I let out an *oooooh* like I'm in third grade. "You can tell him she thinks he's cute, but that's all I know."

Winston takes out his phone.

"You're telling him right now?"

He nods. "He told me to see what I could find out. I didn't even have to work that hard."

"Not after I hear they've been gossiping about us. I'm telling everything I know."

His eyebrows go up as he puts his phone back in his pocket. "Right. They deserve it."

"What...what are they saying about us?" I try to keep it playful, but I feel my smile fading. My face is going hot. "They can't be giving away too much. There's a lot she didn't know until today."

He lets out a nervous breath. "That's good to know. Once he started smiling when her name came up I figured she knew every thought I ever had in my head."

We sit there. It's quiet enough that the hum of the refrigerator seems loud. The silence makes me feel like I'm running out of time. Any minute now he's going to tell me he's late for something or his parents are going to pull into the driveway, and we won't have any more privacy.

I have to start talking. I have so much to say, but I can't get my words together in my head.

I sit up in my seat. "Have you decided what your topic's going to be for your presentation at the camp?"

"Nope." He scratches the side of his face and then rubs his palm over it. "I have so many ideas. They all sound good until I sit down and actually start to put them together."

"I don't know if I'd be any help, but if you want somebody to talk through the ideas with, I'd like to hear them."

He shakes his head. "I can talk it through with Jorda."

Before I can stop myself, I slouch, completely deflated from what feels like rejection. I know it isn't, though. Of course he wants to talk his ideas through with Jorda. I try to straighten up, but I can tell by the way his face softens that I'm too late.

"But guess what," he says, as if what he's about to tell me is just as good as one of his ideas.

I perk up at the excitement on his face. "What? Tell me."

"They added me to the group chat for the Chicago seminar."

"Oh." I huff out a laugh. "It's a *seminar* now."

He puts his palms over his eyes and lets his head fall back onto the couch. "I'm just calling it what the organizers call it."

"And what? You have little *seminar* friends now?" I tease.

He sits back up, straight-faced like he's too sophisticated to be embarrassed. "Why, yes. I have friends who are going to the seminar."

We both laugh, but the silence takes over again.

I run my hands through my hair and stare down at the bracelets he gave me. It's time for me to talk. "Can I ask you a question?"

Every remnant of laughter is gone now. There's a pause like he's actually contemplating telling me no. "Yeah."

"Okay." I glance up at him and back down. "Why did you sit so far away from me?"

He's quiet for a while. Just sitting there tapping his pointer finger on his thigh. It's hard to be patient waiting for an answer, but the longer it takes, the less I want to hear it. If there's something good to say, I don't think it would take this long.

His pointer finger stops moving. "How was Everyway?"

My head shoots up. "We didn't go out. I canceled. Me and Kai are just friends. I only *want* to be friends with him."

Maybe I should've led with that.

"Oh. I don't want to be all up on somebody's girl, that's all, and"—he looks up at the ceiling and squeezes his eyes shut—"when I'm close to you, it puts this extra spin on everything you say. I start seeing things that aren't there, making things the way I want them to be. I don't want to do that."

I sigh, trying to get rid of this knot in my chest, and look back at my lap. I expected that any real conversation between us, regardless of what we talked about, would be hard, but I didn't expect to feel winded before we even got started. I didn't expect Winston to be listening to me while bracing himself. I'm mad at myself for that, but I'm frustrated with him too.

"Winston." I swallow hard. "I didn't know I could hurt you. You never even tried telling me it was possible until I'd already done it."

He's still looking up at the ceiling. He's either processing what I've said or choosing his words carefully. "I assumed you wouldn't be able to hurt me because you had started to have feelings for me, but it seemed pretty easy for you. A couple days after I kissed you, you had plans with somebody else."

He looks at me. When our eyes meet, I try hard to hold his gaze. I do, but not for as long as I want. He finds something to focus on across the room. I don't let my eyes drift. I want him to hear me and know I'm serious about what I'm saying.

"I can admit I was wrong for saying I'd go on a date with one person when I was thinking about another, but—"

"You were thinking about me?"

I sit on my hands. "I was. I think about you a lot."

He sits up straight on the couch again. I don't have a ruler or anything, but I would swear he's inched closer. "I didn't know that, Dru."

"I never got a chance to tell you. When you said kissing was basically part of the critique, I started to think the way I felt was based on this relationship between these pretend people, and you were able to keep it straight when I wasn't." I take a long breath and shake my head at myself. "I thought all I had to do was go out with Kai and everything would fall back into its usual position because that's what you told me to do. But things just got more confusing, and you were mad at me. You kept saying 'friend' and it was pissing me off."

"I should've been honest about the kiss. I wanted to kiss you. I thought you wanted to kiss me, but you looked shocked after." He shifts on the couch again. Now I'm sure he's closer. I can smell his soap. "But once I got in the car, I was like, *Hell no. She liked it. She knows I liked it. She's just surprised at how we are together. Once she thinks about it, she's going to call me. Finally, she's going to see it. I'm just going to be chill and wait.*

"But that's not how it happened. At school it was back to everything as usual. Then you showed up at that restaurant nervous about *him*, wanting to make sure you looked good to go out with *him*. I was embarrassed for being the bitter dude, but you caught me off guard. On top of that you looked beautiful. I felt like you could be with him if that's what you wanted, but without being in my face about it."

After all that, *I* find it hard to look at *him*. "'Finally'?"

He stretches his legs out in front of him and slouches down on the couch. "Yes, finally. I've been thinking about you for a very long time."

"How—"

"Don't even ask. I'm never telling you that."

Winston's feelings not being new is a surprise to me. At no point, except maybe when he kissed me, did I think he felt anything more for me than friendship until he got all weird about my date with Kai. But I didn't let myself really think it until then. I thought he just wanted to be a great friend. And he is.

He's also a boy I want to kiss and talk to before I go to sleep and tell that he is fine, and watch the best cartoons with and have *just-me-and-you time* with.

The fact that he's a great friend makes everything even better. I'm glad he tried to make me see... Wait.

I tilt my head in thought as all the ways that Winston tried to show me his feelings over the last few weeks become clear. "Is that why you said no at first?"

"It seemed like the worst idea you've ever had. Then the more you started talking about it, the more I was like, hold on, I get to pretend to be her boyfriend. Nothing bad can come from you seeing me like that." He shakes his head as if he's still disappointed in himself. "Even if the whole idea was because of how you felt about somebody else, I shouldn't have even thought twice about it. And once I heard you and Michael, I had to do something."

He reaches over and runs his hand over my braid. His touch is hesitant, like he's waiting for, maybe even expecting, an objection. I just watch until he gets to the frayed end, which he skims with his fingertips.

I have no idea what anybody else has gone through to get my attention or how it compares. All I know is that the idea of me being on Winston's mind that much, of him putting even a second's thought into how he could get me to give us a chance at being something more than friends, makes my palms sweat and my clothes stick to me. The melting is everything but figurative. At the same time, the tension between us is immobilizing me. I'm scared.

But he's so close he's pretty much in my lap. It makes me giggle. He starts tapping his finger on my thigh instead of his own. "Are you sure about this, Dru?"

"About you? Yeah, I'm sure. Are you?"

"Yep." He leans back on the couch, taking me with him until he's stretched out and my head is on his shoulder.

I listen to his heartbeat. It's steady but loud against my ear. It's wild to think that this sound is because of me.

"I ended up asking Jayden where he thought things changed between us."

He hums his understanding. "That was brave."

"I had to." I play with the hem of his T-shirt. "Long story short, your first theory was probably right. Nobody wants a boyfriend answer."

He hums again.

I prop myself up on an elbow to see his face. "And I've been thinking and thinking about it, and I wanted to be with him, but not enough to be me all the way. I didn't want him or anyone else to see *me* and decide that it wasn't what they were expecting or that I wasn't worthy."

He runs his hand along my forearm. "Why do you automatically assume that people are going to decide that?"

"How me and my sisters are with each other, mainly. I think. I don't know." I clear my throat. I'm not sure if I do it because of how hard it is for me to admit the reason or because I don't really want to accept it yet. "And, yeah, I realize that not being open makes people give up on me. It still hurts but it feels easier to deal with than somebody knowing me and deciding."

"Those are a lot of hard things to say. I'm glad you're saying them anyway." He gives me a sad smile that says he appreciates me confiding in him, and also that he gets it.

I'm about to rest my head on his chest again, but the crease that forms between his eyebrows stops me. He looks at some place right past my ear but not directly at me.

"That makes me wonder."

He's quiet for so long, I'm not sure he's going to continue with that train of thought. But eventually he does.

"I think you're easy to know. So, I'm just trying to figure out if you only hide from people you really care about or if their opinion matters more?" He says this quietly. It feels like a wonder he'd be happier keeping to himself.

His whole thought process makes me sad and angry at myself. I force past anything that gets in the way of making sure Winston fully understands what I feel.

"If you don't think you're somebody I really care about or whose opinion really matters to me, then you don't know me like either of us thinks you do." He switches his gaze to the ceiling. I keep talking before whatever thought he's having goes too far again. "Except when I wanted to avoid accidentally telling you I like you as more than a friend, I never think about whether it's okay to be myself with you. I've never thought it would bother you if I wasn't what you expected. Sometimes I think you like getting something other than what you expect."

He looks at me then, keeping his lips pressed together over a full smile. "You don't have to call me out like that."

I two-finger push his shoulder. "That's actually a compliment. Like, not even one time during this conversation have I thought about not telling you anything. Only how to tell you everything. I'm scared that if other things start happening between us, then I could lose that part."

He lowers his eyebrows and dips his head. "All I can say about that is, my feelings aren't new, and you haven't lost anything yet. Nothing changed for you at all. You never even noticed."

That's true. Winston is nothing if not consistent. In the best way.

"And if you need any more proof about how sure I am, I can show you the group chat my team made about me breaking the pact *with you*. It has pictures and everything."

He raises an eyebrow. "And they're okay with it?"

"No," I shout. "They are pissed."

"Aw. I'm sorry, Dru. I know how much you want their respect."

"I do. I want to respect myself too. And I want you to feel like you're important to me." I take a deep breath. "I'm going to talk to everyone before people start finding out about"—I wave my hand between us—"this. And let them be mad at me. Try to earn trust back if I can."

"That's going to be hard too."

"It will." I take slow breaths to keep myself from going tongue-tied. "Now what?"

Winston's answer is his hand in my braids, pulling my face close and putting his lips on mine. I am the same, pulling him closer by the hem of his shirt, making him shiver a little when my fingers graze the bare skin underneath.

We are both searching for purchase against each other. He's stronger, and the pressure of his kiss and the way it makes me pliable everywhere lands me on my back with him above me. There's a continuous cycle of little kisses that I'm afraid might be the unfortunate end of this moment, and then long, deep ones that I know are just the beginning again.

Basically, I forget I'm on Winston's couch until I hear a car door close outside. If I'm honest, I don't think anyone in either of our families would be surprised about us ending up here. But us getting caught in this position on a couch would change the house rules significantly.

I don't want that.

We're both slow to part. I don't know his excuse, but I'm a little dizzy and I feel a lot interrupted.

He pulls in his bottom lip, making me want to kiss it free. That's what I'm looking at when he starts talking. "Can you do me a favor?"

I nod. This would be a perfect time to ask for a kidney. I'd be all for it.

He looks at me seriously. "Don't forget how this feels. When you wake up tomorrow, still be right here with me. We've got a lot of kisses to go."

I laugh but it also makes me kind of sad. This reminds me that he's been looking forward to this longer than I have. It doesn't mean that I want it any less or that it means any less to me. But, somehow, even with us lying here together and me just as unwilling to separate as he is, he has no clue. I want to make sure he does. I want him to just know. Like I do.

I guess I'll have to work on that.

"Yes. I promise."

DAY 7 OF COUNTING UP

The Championship

I wake up on the day of the girls' state high school soccer final as a spectator. The only thing that surprises me more, but in a good way, is being with Winston.

Good in my heart at least, but not on my conscience. I have a lot of explaining to do and I need to do it as soon as possible. I don't want Winston to think he's some kind of secret or he's not worth me owning up to and accepting whatever I get for it.

It's already been a few days since we worked everything out. It's been so hard to keep my distance at school.

Last year when we didn't make it to the final, a lot of us showed up at the championship game, hoping to learn something from being there. Just in case, I put it in the team group chat to get as many people there as I can.

Eighteen of my teammates say they're going to come. With twenty-one on the roster, that's not bad. I ride with Capri. I haven't admitted anything to her yet, so she's still talking to me. It is so packed we end up parking at an elementary around the corner from where the game actually is.

By the time we get inside the stadium it's already started, and we can't find a seat. That's not an altogether bad thing, seeing as how the whole team is split into three different groups around the bleachers. Making a choice between them seems like a bad idea.

Charlotte sees us and texts Capri that they can make room if we hurry up and get to them. We go as fast as we can, and I realize I just got a seat because of who I'm with. Capri has built some good alliances and relationships. If I get to be co-captain with her next year, I think it'll be good.

I promise I'm not bitter, but the Lakers made it somehow and their strategy is the same. Keep the other team away from the net even if it means they never get close either. It makes for a very slow and methodical game, not one I would take someone to if they were just learning about soccer. They'd never watch again.

It's good for me as a player, though. I need to see examples of this strategy being cracked and points being put on the board. It doesn't look like it's going to happen until they're thirty minutes into the second half. In fifteen minutes, the Lakers have three goals put up on them. Once the other team gets them on their heels with pure athleticism, the Lakers can never get right-footed again. Being fast and in attack mode is the only way to beat them.

Could we have beat the other team if we'd made it here? I'm not sure. Watching them celebrate makes me sad all over again. It reminds me of how much I want that feeling. I want the ultimate win at every level I get to play.

When I asked everyone to show up, I suggested we meet behind the goal on the north side of the field if no team was there after the game was over. I get lucky, as the champion players are in the center of the field getting their medals and trophy. The Lakers are on the way to their bus, choosing not to watch.

As we stand at the back post, the tension is high. Everybody, even the seniors who have no real reason to have stayed for this, is staring at me. I can read on their faces that some of them are only here because they assume I'll be captain again next year and that means I'll have some sway with Coach.

I won't. Coach expects my teammates to listen to me. He is his own entity.

I scratch my head, trying to figure out how to start. I want to keep it simple. "I just want to apologize to everybody. I came up with the pact originally because I needed an excuse not to go out with somebody."

"Okay, Miss I Love My Team," someone says.

I nod at the sarcasm because I deserve it. "I was dedicated to it. It wasn't fake. It wasn't to make somebody look bad. It was for me first and the team second. I really did think it would be good for us.

"Meanwhile, I started doing this dating experiment. With Winston Portis. And when a lot of you guys saw me and took pictures, that's all it was. We weren't having lunchtime make-outs." A nervous laugh escapes. "We've never had a lunchtime make-out, hookup, or anything like that. But eventually we did kiss. I didn't feel like I was breaking the pact at the time because I didn't think it was real."

"You were in denial, you mean," Capri says next to me.

I nod nervously. "Exactly. When I found out about the group chat, I told Capri that I could prove I didn't break the pact because I would not end up with Winston."

Some of my teammates start laughing, and not in a nice way.

"But you have ended up with Winston," Riley says.

"I have, and I know that makes a lot of you mad and it looks like I lied or wasn't true to the team." I swallow. "I just want to say sorry. Next year, I want to be here with a medal. I want to be laughing and joking with you guys at practice. So, I thought I'd put everything out there now so next year we can start off in a good spot."

As usual, there's mumbling in the group. Nobody actually committing to anything, not even Capri. That's probably because she at least believed me a little when I told her Winston and I would never be together. Her trust will be the hardest to earn back.

Eventually everyone starts to go their separate ways and I realize I have something else to say. "Hold on. One more thing.

"I want to apologize for not standing up for you or myself when things were going too far and it was pulling the team apart. It was my job as co-captain to say something, and I didn't because I was too afraid."

Those words produce a few eye rolls and violin sounds, but not the majority. Maybe that's the best I can expect. Not everyone will forgive me all in one sitting.

"And," I say loudly, and look directly at Meegan, "I should've offered to talk to Meegan myself. If we were having issues, I should've been the person to at least try to fix things. No one should have to find out their team is talking about them behind their backs.

"I'll be afraid again," I say, because I know it's true, "but I'll try harder, and if I have to come back and fix something after the fact, I will."

Capri pushes me in the shoulder so hard I have to brace myself so I don't bang my head on the post. "I don't know about them, but that's what *I* wanted to hear. Dru with a backbone."

That gets a few laughs, but there are still skeptical faces.

"I want to apologize too." Heads turn seemingly all at once in Meegan's direction. It's not the shock of her speaking; it's the shock of what she just said. "I was only hard on you guys because I thought that was the way to win. I thought if we won we'd all be okay anyway. I guess we'll never know if I was wrong about that, but I don't want to graduate and feel like I can't look my teammates in the eye because they think I'm mean."

I know from my own experience how hard that was for Meegan to speak up, so I'm the first to tell her that we're okay. Surprisingly, many of my other teammates follow my lead and accept her apology.

Before I know it someone has a ball from the nearby bushes, and we're divided up for a half-field game. Even some of the seniors. We stay until we're the way we know and like one another best—tired, and sweaty, and stinky, and having left it all on the field.

DAY 14 OF COUNTING UP

When your sister decides her shower should be outside the neighborhood clubhouse instead of inside because it's such an "unexpectedly beautiful day," there are going to be problems. But instead of telling her no, your father will remember he can get a really nice tent with the tables and chairs from the university. We'll just need to transport and assemble everything ourselves. And your mom will go on and on about the sunset and the way string lights will help to create a really romantic atmosphere as opposed to canned overhead lighting.

What no one will consider before we're all committed, whether we like it or not, is that the chairs and tables, as pretty as they are, will have to be cleaned by hand one by one and not hosed down because they may not dry in time. Or that the chair legs will seep so deep into the soft ground, trapping anyone who dares to sit.

Winston and Jake are lugging the last of the batch from the sidewalk in front of the clubhouse around to the back where I am. The area that is somehow going to turn festive and romantic as opposed to groggily waking up from winter in a matter of hours.

I try to stay focused on scrubbing a spot on a chair leg that I'm not sure is dirt or a paint smudge. If something doesn't turn out right, it will be on me. I am trying so hard to stay focused.

But every time Winston comes into my space with more chairs my eyes are drawn to him. And his to me. And every single time our eyes meet I get these pangs in my chest. They're not pleasant either. They're electric, breath-stealing annoyances. And he smiles at me like seeing me is the best thing that's happened to him all day. Or maybe I'm projecting.

It hasn't even been twelve hours since I've seen him, and only an hour since we last talked.

"I'm going to go back with Dad for the tables." Jake looks down at all the filthy chairs piled on the ground and frowns. "I know you want to stay back and help with this."

Winston smiles big at his brother. "Of course I want to stay, but don't make it sound like it's for me. I know you want to be at Aubrey's house as soon as she gets out of the test. You can just say that."

Winston and I give each other a look.

Jake waves us both away but doesn't disagree. As soon as Jake disappears around to the front of the building, I watch Winston eye the chair from different angles before sticking his hand in the rectangle space between the back and the seat, and letting it dangle like the bracelets we're both wearing.

"Do you think I can wrist hula-hoop with this?"

I chuckle. "Very painfully."

This is a very Winston question. And I don't know why, but every time Winston starts Winstoning everywhere, he gets cuter to me. I just stare at him.

He notices me staring and sets the chair down on all four legs and heads toward my makeshift workstation with two clean and dirty water buckets and a towel. "I'm trying to be good."

I go back to scrubbing a spot. "I'm not stopping you."

He stops in front of me and squats down. "Yeah, okay."

He's laughing when I stretch up to kiss him.

"Hello," a female someone sings from the pathway. We break apart.

It could be because just the millisecond of a kiss has thrown me off balance, but I don't recognize the voice.

Maybe it's a delivery. I pull myself up and dust myself off as best I can. We're only two hours into these unexpected preparations and I already need a bath.

When a woman looking like a slightly older, thinner version of Ms. Teddy comes into view, she makes a beeline for Winston.

He blinks. "Auntie?"

She pulls him into a hug. "You're going to have to stop getting so handsome. It's too much."

Over the top of her head, he stares at me in confusion. I put both palms up. Auntie smells and looks too good to be helping with the setup. And there's a gift bag dangling from her arm.

She's a guest. She's a guest?

I have no idea what to say. Are we expecting her, and someone forgot to tell us? I pull my phone from my pocket. Who can I text who will keep a level head and not blame me even though it's obvious I'm blameless?

Winston turns her toward me. "This is Moriah's younger sister, Dru."

"I see it," Auntie says, but her eyes are making a study of my face searching for any resemblance. It doesn't take her long to get back to business, though. "Where are the guests of honor? They should be here. I know I'm a little early, but I've been reading about these open-house showers. I'm not sure if I like it, but it was clever to give it some structure with brunch, dinner, and after-dark meal."

Me and Winston exchange a look. That's all this is. A simple mix-up. We can just explain that the time listed on the invite first is the time that she was buying a gift for. If she would've read to the end of the invite, she would've found the time she was actually supposed to show up and give that gift. Then we could just tell her where Ms. Teddy is or something.

Winston smiles. "Auntie, I think you made—"

For the second time in less than five minutes, Winston is interrupted by a greeting. It's the former owner of the dance studio and her husband. After she chides me about ending my dance career, as she does every time I see her, I leave it to Winston to make introductions and I call Dad first and then add LeArra. I need someone who can manage her before she wastes time going in on me.

There's silence for more beats than we can afford after I tell them that people are coming early. If I had to guess, Dad is problem solving quietly while LeArra is stunned into speechlessness about something she planned not turning out perfectly.

Because this impacts other people even more than LeArra, I try not to find any joy in her silence.

Dad is the first to speak as four more brunch guests arrive. "I'm going to handle your mom and Moriah. Get them there. LeArra, go to the clubhouse."

"Dad," LeArra shrieks. "And do what?"

Just then, Winston shouts, "We're making mimosas and Bloody Marys."

There are nods and sounds of approval and anticipation from the growing group. Not one person questions this coming from the mouth of a seventeen-year-old.

"But first we have to watch something very special."

The mimosa and Bloody Mary ingredients, along with plastic champagne flutes and highball glasses, are the party favors for the "morning" guests. Attached to each package is the special recipe, along with the URL for a short documentary explaining both drinks.

"That's a great idea," Dad and LeArra say in unison on the other end of the phone. Except LeArra adds a really surprised "actually." It's kind of like the shower-related texts she's sent since family Monopoly night. It sounds like she's giving a compliment but then she adds one word or some punctuation and you're like *nah*.

I smile at Winston appreciatively. It *is* a good idea. Really the only idea that makes sense at this point. He just shrugs.

"At the end of that video, they even talk about different variations of both drinks. That'll give us about thirty minutes." LeArra pauses. "I'm at the beauty supply getting some type of heel cream because Mom decided to wear sandals. I'll go to the gourmet grocery store and get pastries, sliced fruit, eggs, and good bread for French toast."

I nod, but we all know it's going to take more than thirty minutes to get all of that going. "I'll get bacon delivered from the Coney up the street," I say. "Then I'll run home and get the griddle. I'm pretty sure we have some pancake mix, blueberries, and syrup. I can make those really small and stretch it until you get here."

"If everyone thinks that they're supposed to show up at the time of their theme," Dad says, "we can expect the dinner crowd which we're ready for, and an 'after dark' crowd. Me and Rashid Sr. will get on that."

I laugh. "Great. Looking forward to bourbon and glow golf."

Without a goodbye we all hang up. I edge around the back of Winston's group of attentive partygoers, trying not to be seen. But before I make it to my car he texts me.

> **Winston:** Are you leaving me? Don't leave me.

> **Dru:** These people love you. I'm just going to get stuff for brunch from my house. If I'm not back in 15 minutes you're allowed to quit.

> **Winston:** You know I'll do it.

> **Dru:** You know I'll be back.

I wait a second I don't have but he doesn't send anything back. Instead, his loud booming laughter comes around from the back of the building and I know he's got everything under control. But before I start the car, my phone vibrates again.

Winston: Kiss Kiss

Dru: Kiss Kiss

When I get back to the clubhouse, Mr. Portis and Jake are in back working on the tent. Jake stops to help me carry everything in. By the time the video is over and Winston brings everyone into the kitchen area, I've got syrup and blueberries in Mom's best dinnerware, and small pancakes on their way to being plated. I keep the bacon in the microwave.

I hug the guests I know, but when someone asks me where Moriah is, I pretend to be pulled away by pancakes. Winston does his best to keep everyone, all twenty of them now, focused on the drinks.

When LeArra comes tumbling through the back door with everything she promised, I know we got this. We have food, drinks, and a party host with the most. Speaking of the party host, every time I look up, he's looking at me. I stare right back even though somehow one of my best friends makes me nervous.

By the time everything is served, I almost forget that Moriah and Rashid are still MIA. When Dad slides open the glass door and yells *surprise*, my own plate of French toast and bacon goes flying. All our guests laugh and burst into their own "Surprise!" as Moriah, Rashid, Mom, and Ms. Teddy stare back, stunned.

If their faces aren't enough to signify that Dad got them all here without a clue what was happening, my mom, sister and Ms. Teddy all have on beat-up T-shirts and sweatpants. Not a way they would show up for any wedding shower, especially not one this special.

But when I think about it, Dad's way of dealing with them was genius. He'd still be stuck explaining had he not said whatever he said to get them over here immediately and as is.

There's some time between brunch and the actual catered shower we planned, and we all use it to rest and dress for the occasion. The remaining RSVPs who were supposed to bring the morning gifts show up on time while some of the dinner guests show up at "after dark."

Dad and Mr. Portis are ready with their smoked old-fashioneds and the best chocolate they could find in driving distance. When it's all said and done, no one is the wiser. Most importantly Moriah and Rashid are both smiling from ear to ear. She's finally in the dress she intended to wear.

LeArra is in the back of the tent with all the invites set out in front of her. She seems to be reading them over and over and over again, trying to figure out where she went wrong. I'm ashamed of all the joy her little defeat brings me. She's still my sister.

It's not rainy or hot. There's no reason to be covered. I figure she's just keeping out of sight for some reason. I understand that instinct. Her head snaps up when she hears me.

"If it helps, I don't understand how so many people misread the invites. It seems clear to me."

She shakes her head as she blinks. "Maybe it's because we know what was intended, because clearly we are in the minority. I can't see the issue."

Me and LeArra in the minority together is a concept I'm not familiar with. I doubt she feels the significance, but it sort of makes me want to take a seat. I don't, though. LeArra and I aren't confidants or even sisters that bicker and then hug it out. There's a chance we never will be.

And even if a relationship like that is going to happen between us, she's going to have to be the one to start it.

"You and Winston did an amazing job making sure everything went okay. It could've been a disaster, but you both thought on your feet and stuck to tasks." She shakes her head in obvious disbelief. "You were great."

I cross my arms over my chest. I want to feel all those warm fuzzies I do when somebody appreciates me, but I don't. The surprise in her voice makes her words feel like the opposite of a compliment.

She bites her bottom lip and lets out a puff of air. "I don't know you. You were right about that."

That subject change is unexpected. I swallow hard and look around for the most logical excuse to leave. "Okaaay."

"I was ten when you were born. You were almost the same age when I went away to school." She stacks the invites and places them away from her, as if just their proximity is frustrating. "That's a reason, not an excuse for the way things always erupt between us."

I nod. I get what she means, but it doesn't completely make sense. Not knowing me doesn't cover everything.

"I get what you're saying, but I don't know you either and I respect you and accept you. I even admire some things about you." I shrug. "Right now, I just feel like the only reason you're talking to me is because I helped make today okay for Moriah. I don't want to feel like I have to do something in order for my sister to be nice to me for a few seconds. For all the things you've had to endure because of me, you've never had to deal with that."

She licks her lips and lets out a long sigh. "You're right. I haven't. I have no idea what that's like."

I give a half-hearted smile. "Lucky you."

She can't meet my eyes after that. "Why don't you and Winston go find something fun to do?"

That's something she never would've said before the last few weeks. Maybe there is hope for a real sisterhood or at least civility between us.

I look back over my shoulder and find Winston at the dessert table, filling a plastic champagne flute with chocolate.

I turn back to her. "He earned his name today?"

She jerks her head back. "I wouldn't say all that. They just don't look that much alike."

I can't help but laugh.

EPILOGUE

Day 102—The Wedding

Mom and Ms. Teddy are crying by the time Winston and I make it down the aisle as the second-to-last couple. Jake and LeArra are up after us.

After the comic relief of the flower girl from Rashid's side of the family dropping her whole basket of flowers on her head as soon as she comes in, Winston winks at me from across the aisle and nods his approval. I almost laugh out loud, but LeArra turns on me like she caught the wink too.

It isn't LeArra who sobers me, though. It's Moriah. She's beautiful in her dress. The very first one she chose. Square necked and lacy with cap sleeves and a train so long she needs ushers to make sure it doesn't get shut in the doors leading outside to the ceremony, before she reaches Rashid. My opinion was irrelevant after the Bridal Magnifique disaster, but I think she chose correctly. But the way Rashid is looking at her, I believe what he said in response to the poll. He would marry her in absolutely anything.

Dad smiles bigger than I've ever seen, and Mr. Portis does a lot of thoughtful sighing.

They wrote their own vows. They are so sweet, and somehow, even though they kept them a secret from each other, they both talked about all their near misses and how they almost never ended up together at all. Their words made most people either smile or cry. I did both.

Winston and Jake do their speech together with one of them pretending to be the other at one point, and it actually confuses people. As soon as everyone thinks they have it figured out, they switch. In the end I am more than confused by the guests' giggling and surprised reactions to who's who. They don't look that much alike, and I stand by it. When I can take my eyes off Winston, they go to Aubrey sitting at a table near the back. She plays it way cooler than me when she's into guys, but it didn't take long for Jake to win her over and I can see how she feels about him on her face all the time.

LeArra and I aren't anywhere near as creative as Winston and Jake. But we are able to stand at the microphone together. She talks about all the best memories of Moriah, while I focus on Moriah and Rashid and how nice it is to see how happy they make each other.

Whenever we're together, I can tell she's making an effort to hold her tongue. At the same time, I'm making an even bigger effort not to care if she doesn't.

The wedding party dance is the highlight of the reception. After two more practices, Winston and I got super comfortable on the dance floor. His granddad was hyping his grandson up from a table near the front. At one point, when we were front and center,

Winston deviated from the routine. I was able to follow well, but still a little worried about what Monique might say until I remembered that she couldn't say anything once it was over.

And even if she did, she would be the only one with a complaint. After we left the dance floor and it opened up to the rest of the guests, Winston was the most sought-after dance partner. I would prefer to be dancing with him, but I can let the people have him for a little while. Plus, he comes and gets me for every slow song and that makes me very happy.

I'm shaking my head as he makes his way over for the third time of the night after detangling himself from three grown women.

He puts his hand out to me, and I take it. "You like watching me dance."

I side-eye him playfully. "Who said that?"

"Your face said that. Your smile." He flashes his own as he leads me to the dance floor. "And the way you've been watching the dance floor the whole night."

I shrug. "It's okay, I guess."

He laughs and pulls me close. My face is against his rented shirt. The jacket had to go about ten minutes after the floor opened. "Is that when you started liking me? At the first dance rehearsal?"

I expected Winston to ask me that question a long time ago, especially with how many times I've asked him when he started to like me. But I've still never gotten an answer, which is probably why he never brings it up. He doesn't want to have to give an answer to get one. I don't mind telling him, though.

"That's the first time I thought maybe my heart beating fast or my getting warm when you were around had something to do with you."

He pulls his head back. For the first time tonight, we're swaying more than dancing. "Your heart beat fast or you got warm when I was around before that?"

I laugh. "When you did something sweet for me, yeah. But I thought it was about the sweet thing you were doing for Girlfriend Dru, not because you were doing something for me." I pull us close again. "Not that it only happened when you did things for me. Sometimes when you would smile at me for any reason, or when you walked in at the cake tasting and I was in shambles."

He pushes me out for a random turn. When I come back to him he's smiling. "The cake tasting. The greatest day of our lore."

I push him out for a turn, and he laughs as he ducks under my arm. "The cake tasting was better than our first date to you?"

"Oh. What?" He jerks his head back. "One hundred percent. On the first date, you were all wishy-washy and I was pretending nothing mattered to me, even kissing you.

"But at the cake tasting you were all in. You told me I would make a perfect boyfriend. That changed everything. That's when I started thinking I had a chance."

I look up at him seriously. "That day wasn't good for me. That's when I realized I was launching you. I thought in a few weeks you'd be walking down the hall smiling and holding hands with somebody."

He bites his bottom lip, making his dimples pop. "I was."

I don't know why but we both look away and then we both smile. And then we just stare at each other.

"I'm glad to have finally made my last launch. I gave up way too much time to the community."

Winston shakes his head at me. "You still don't get it, do you?"

"Get what?"

He leans down to me and whispers in my ear. "You didn't launch me, Dru. I launched you."

Acknowledgments

Not to be redundant, but my *people* remain the same. (And I am so thankful for that.) Damon. Foster. Elle. Mom and Dad. All the kiss kisses in the world wouldn't be enough to show how much you all mean to me. Thank you all so much for your continued love and support.

Thanks to my agent, Natalie Lakosil, for pushing me. My editor, Ruqayyah Daud, for helping me bring another Black main character into the world. And a special thank-you to Lily Choi for *getting* this manuscript.

Thank you to everyone at Little, Brown Books for Young Readers. I appreciate you all so much for seeing me through to the point where I get to write this final page again.

Last but not least, thank you, readers. I know time is precious and your willingness to spend any of yours reading my words is so appreciated. I hope I've brought you some joy in return.

Malaika Hilson

RAECHELL GARRETT

has written everything from marketing plans to health insurance benefit schedules, but she much prefers writing novels about the ups and downs of carefree girls finding their way in the world. She lives in Michigan, where she's likely to be found trying a new recipe, talking sports with her husband, or philosophizing about life with her two teenagers. RaeChell is the author of *Promposal* and *The Boyfriend Launcher*. She invites you to visit her at raechellgarrett.com.

CELEBRATING 100 YEARS OF PUBLISHING

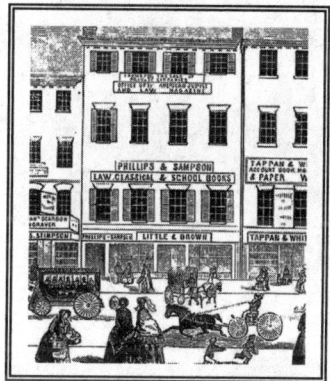

Dear Reader,

You may have noticed the words "Little, Brown and Company" on the title page of this book and wondered what they mean. Well, Charles C. Little and James Brown were the founders of this publishing house, and the "and Company" is all the editors, designers, marketers, publicists, salespeople, and more who help produce each book and bring it to readers like you. Little, Brown was founded in Boston, Massachusetts, in 1837, and some of its early publications included *The Writings of George Washington* and *The Works of Benjamin Franklin*. The catalog grew to feature works by Emily Dickinson and Louisa May Alcott, among many other notable authors. In 1926, recognizing that the literature we read when we are young has a deep and lasting influence and requires expert curation, the company appointed an editor to lead a dedicated children's department.

In 2026, Little, Brown Books for Young Readers celebrates one hundred years of excellence in publishing. Today, we are a division of Hachette Livre, the third-largest publisher in the world, and we are based in New York City. Our staff has grown from a team of two to more than one hundred people. And with the changes in technology, our books are read by more readers, in more ways, and in more countries than ever before. However, one thing has not changed: our commitment to providing a supportive home for all creators and superb stories for all readers. Thank you for being one of them.

Megan Tingley

Megan Tingley
President and Publisher

LITTLE, BROWN AND COMPANY
BOOKS FOR YOUNG READERS

To learn more about Little, Brown's history, authors, and books, please visit LBYR.com.

MORE SWOON-WORTHY STORIES FROM
RAECHELL GARRETT